I0819666

I,
SPY

I, SPY

L. M. KEMP

MINOTAUR BOOKS
NEW YORK

This is a work of fiction. All of the names, characters, organizations, places, and events portrayed in this work are either products of the author's imagination or used fictitiously.

First published in the United States by Minotaur Books, an imprint of St. Martin's Publishing Group

EU Representative: Macmillan Publishers Ireland Ltd, 1st Floor, The Liffey Trust Centre, 117–126 Sheriff Street Upper, Dublin 1, D01 YC43

For information, address St. Martin's Publishing Group, 120 Broadway, New York, NY 10271.

www.minotaurbooks.com

The Library of Congress Cataloging-in-Publication Data is available upon request.

ISBN 978-1-250-42036-7 (hardcover)

ISBN 978-1-250-42037-4 (ebook)

First Edition: 2026

10 9 8 7 6 5 4 3 2 1

FOR THE J'S, ALWAYS

I,
SPY

PROLOGUE

In a small, white, windowless room beneath London's most secure secret service offices, a man sat in a chair surrounded by archaic PC computers. He wore a cheap blue suit and patterned socks. His feet were resting on the desk and his mind was firmly on his phone. He scowled at a sports result. Then, one of the screens under his command came to life. Spinning on the chair and groaning as his feet swung to the ground, he entered his password and leaned in for a closer look. On the screen were a name, coordinates, and a rough image captured from CCTV. The information and a variety of codes known only to those above his pay grade were headlined with two words that made the man's face flush white. He muttered, "Well, well, look who it isn't," and stared keenly at the image, trying to establish its accuracy. He was looking at the blurry face of a target who was "high value," in more ways than one. His brow furrowed as he picked up the phone and relayed the words to a man who answered with a smooth, deep voice and no time to waste. "Got an alert on your cargo. Looks legit." He listened for a few seconds and smiled. He packaged the image and sent an email. Then he resumed his post, picked up his phone, and continued to scroll. His team had lost, but he had just made a fortune.

1

Kendal Carter sat on a bench in a suburban playground in Dübendorf, a nondescript neighborhood on the outskirts of Zurich, Switzerland. She watched as her four-year-old daughter, Rosie, pushed a toy unicorn on a swing. The park was flanked by low residential blocks, beige buildings huddled among highways and spindly forests. It was about as innocuous as a place could be. Kendal thought of it as a residential strip mall; the houses generic, and the residents miscellaneous European jetsam. In five years of living here, Rosie and Kendal had made exactly two friends: Mrs. O from the DRC, who had appointed herself the spokesperson for the community and ran an unofficial day care for the working families of Dübendorf, and Lula from next door.

The summer's day was bright and crisp. It was Kendal's favorite time of day. Older kids were still in school and the little ones were content, not yet needing a meal or a nap. From a grassy knoll, a father of twins played Mr. Wolf (Signor Lupo) with admirable vigor, sending kids tottering keenly across the tarmac. Rosie watched the game with a detached interest. Not jealous, just curious. She preferred isolation and rarely interacted with children her own age. Kendal didn't know if it was a language barrier or a deep mistrust carried in her genes.

Rosie stood before Kendal, her arms raised. "I'm the queen!"

Kendal gave a British salute. "Your Majesty."

"Can you play with me?" Rosie peered at Kendal like a cartoon puppy.

They did a lap of the apparatus, Rosie designing a world for them. "The sandpit is where the unicorns live, the king lives over there. The babies live in the bin."

"The bin?"

Rosie stopped mid-stride, as if Kendal was way off base.

"Kids live in the bin," she explained more slowly.

Out of the corner of her eye, Kendal watched as a black Mercedes with tinted windows and diplomatic plates pulled up and parked by the entrance to their block.

"Oh fudge." Some ancient instinct made her move around the climbing frame out of sight. She placed Rosie inside the house at the top of the slide.

"This should be our palace," Kendal said quietly, watching as two average-everything men in suits got out and looked around.

Kendal scanned the area. The apartment that faced into theirs was a corporate rental. It should have been unoccupied, but its window was open. Rosie sensed a change in Kendal's disposition and tapped her face. "You're not being the queen."

Kendal seamlessly adjusted her focus back to her daughter. "So sorry, where were we?"

"Oh no! The unicorns are dead!" Rosie squeaked joyfully.

"Jeez, Ro, that's bleak."

In case it was this that was causing the thin veneer of sweat on Kendal's face, Rosie whispered wetly in her ear, "It's not real." She tried to land this fact with a reassuring wink that involved her whole face.

Kendal watched the two suits glance around the neighborhood and toward the park. They were the men of security companies the world over. They went into the foyer of her building.

The world shrank to nothing but possible hostile vantage points.

She kept Rosie out of direct line of sight and watched. The playground was in the center of a flat green with at least three hundred feet of open space in every direction. At four years old, Rosie was forty pounds with a maximum speed of three miles per hour. The thinly wooded area in the opposite direction from the block would provide minimal cover; with Rosie in her arms she could get there in ninety seconds. She had a tactical pen in her pocket but was otherwise unarmed. Everything she needed in order to evacuate was in their apartment, on the second floor of the block directly behind the Mercedes.

"Down." Rosie held her arms up to be lifted back to the ground, but instead, Kendal turned and pulled herself up into the playhouse. Rosie was thrilled. Kendal had never got in with her before, their knees squidged together and they stayed low. Safely ensconced, they played a version of Rock Paper Scissors that made no sense. Twelve minutes later, the two men reappeared, took another glance around, got back in their car, and left.

Kendal took a few deep breaths. There were many reasons diplomats might visit the area: it was near the airport; there were business suites in the block. She allowed herself the possibility that there was nothing to worry about.

On the third floor of the block to the west of the play area, a yellowed curtain fluttered. Inside the unfurnished, unloved, and technically unoccupied apartment, a pair of binoculars slammed onto a sill.

"*Merde*."

A phone was tapped to life, and a deep voice spoke into it. "*Il est ici.* Ortez."

The phone went dead. The binoculars and phone went into a black bag, the area was wiped clean. The door slammed.

2

Cautiously, Kendal returned to the apartment. When they got there, their next-door neighbor, Lula, was outside her front door smoking a cheap cigarette that made Rosie screw her face up in protest. Lula just smiled at her. She was a wiry woman. She wore a dusty-pink tracksuit and had bare feet, her toenails a vivid pink. She had blond streaks in darker blond hair and, despite her twenty-five years, looked tired to the bone.

"You saw the suits?" she asked Kendal, her Lithuanian accent so strong it sounded fake.

Kendal nodded. "Did you speak to them?"

"They were looking for someone who lives here." She gestured to her own front door. "Kara something."

Kendal kept her face neutral as she unlocked the door and opened it a fraction. "What did you say?"

"I told them she moved to Buenos Aires." She grinned at her deception.

"Did they say who they were?"

"Who cares? They're all the same. I never helped a cop in my life. *Skūras*," she spat.

Kendal pushed her door open fully and scanned the hall for any signs things had changed.

"They had a photograph," Lula said, staring at a plane passing overhead. Kendal froze. Rosie snuck under her arm and disappeared into the apartment.

"You got a good-looking sister?" Lula asked quietly.

"Something like that."

"Better tell her to watch her ass, no?" They shared a look. Lula was curious but not concerned. Kendal was grateful. She knew Lula would be discreet, maybe even fight for her. Like many women who had suffered at the hands of men they had trusted, Lula would have her back without question. She was a rare example of someone Kendal could rely on.

Inside, Kendal's rental unit was 450 square feet of Swiss indifference. White walls, hints of mustard, a small hallway where their shoes waited, a pair of size-12 men's brogues alongside their own smaller pairs, to give the impression of a big male occupant. Technically a two-bed, with a galley kitchen and a tiny lounge where their lives had played out in full color. Light poured into the space through thin glass doors that led onto a small balcony. It wasn't much, but it was enough to call home. Kendal equated luxury with danger; the more opulent a home, in her experience, the more likely the owner was to be a target.

"Muuuuuuumma." The call went unheeded except for a brief sigh.

"Mum. Mumma. Mum. Mummy. MUMMY." The escalation to staccato coming from the bedroom was more sudden than usual.

"What?" Kendal replied from the sofa, just a few feet away. She was looking at a laptop, a clunky machine she used for the internet and nothing else. The screen was open on a map of Europe.

The shouting stopped abruptly and the silence that followed was a ferocious battle of wills, invisible to the human eye. Kendal stopped scrolling and waited. She liked Rosie's silent challenge, it required more restraint than screaming and tugged at a different strand of her nervous system. Suspicion: more powerful than irritation and infinitely more interesting.

She glanced at her watch and timed the pause, forty-five seconds, a new record. Whisper-quiet and smiling, she stood and moved toward the bedroom. At the door she dropped to her knees and with her loudest "BOO!" she sprang into the room. Rosie screamed with delight and rolled off the bed into a crouch in the corner. She stayed statue-still with her eyes closed, as if invisibility and blindness were the same thing.

"Muuuuum?" She looked up with a puppy-dog smile, patting Kendal's arm with pudgy digits.

"Rooooosieee?"

"Can I watch TV?"

"After dinner, which is ready right now."

Rosie was on her second fish finger and holding a green bean like a cigarette.

"I'm Lula," she giggled happily, wafting the bean around and blowing out dramatically. "Dragon!"

"Don't smoke the veg, Ro," she murmured, watching the windows. She was jumpy. She had checked their go bag, had packed passports and currency, but had not made the decision to go. When Rosie was born, Kendal had made an oath to normalcy—Rosie's childhood would be the opposite of her own. It would be static and unremarkable. The oath was being tested and she was loath to break it for a couple of suits in a shiny car. Rosie sensed the tension and was subdued. The apartment was too small for a bath, and Rosie wouldn't shower (too splashy). So instead she sat in a massive yellow bucket that she was too big for, staring at Kendal like a dejected toad. She was in her pajamas and tending to her favorite toys when the estate-wide fire alarm went off. It was a familiar sound; there were monthly tests and at least three times a year the teenagers got bored enough to burn a bike or kick in one of the manual call points. Kendal swaddled a drowsy but curious Rosie in a black hoodie, tugged socks and shoes onto them both, and picked her up. She unlocked and opened the door an inch, glancing quickly into the corridor. Their neighbors were loitering along the concrete passageway or making their way down to the green. There was a definite smell of smoke. Kendal mimed but did not say a swear word. Under Rosie's watchful eye she changed her expression to mumsy concern and threw open the door. "Is it real?" she asked a kid who was hanging dangerously over the edge of the walkway.

"*Oui, c'est les poubelles.*" He nodded over to the basement doors of the adjacent block where the communal dumpsters were on fire.

"*Ça pue putain,*" he added unnecessarily. *Fucking stinks.*

Lula appeared in her doorway. "Is it real?" She looked like she very much could not be bothered to deal with the building being ablaze.

"I'll go and have a look," Kendal said.

Lula nodded toward Rosie. "You want me to watch her?"

Kendal considered it, but Rosie clutched her tighter, so she shook her head. "I'll text you if it's serious." Lula shrugged and went back inside.

Rosie hung around Kendal's neck, delighted by the action at bedtime. The last of the sun dipped below the horizon and the world changed color.

The dumpsters were indeed on fire. Rosie and Kendal approached the residents gathered on the green, their faces aglow. If it wasn't for the smell, it would have been quite pleasant. Mrs. O beckoned her over gleefully and blamed the government. Rumor circulated that the fire was set by local kids expending pent-up aggression. There was a sense of bonhomie in the tutting and worry for the young. Kendal felt Rosie start to droop with exhaustion. A fire engine pulled up and nonchalant fire-people unfurled a hose. Kendal had turned to go home when a shout broke out from an apartment on the ground floor. Someone had been broken into. No, everyone had been broken into. They'd gone house to house, robbing anyone who was naïve enough to leave their door on the latch while they took a peek at the fire. Could it be kids? She heard her mother's voice, echoing through time. "*Nature abhors a vacuum; intelligence abhors a coincidence.*"

"Oh shit," Kendal muttered. *Is it an op?*

"You said the S-word," Rosie murmured from the edge of sleep.

A cold flush tickled down Kendal's spine. She backed out of the crowd, who were dispersing urgently to check their homes. She moved toward the stairway eyes tuned for anyone out of place, but everyone was behaving unnaturally, dressed strangely, or totally foreign to her. Could Kendal simply turn around and walk away? No, Rosie was too heavy. Feeling the world closing in, she went toward the apartment. They would have to hit harder than this. She wanted to scream it into the evening air but realized that wouldn't be very discreet.

Up the stairs her arms started to strain under Rosie's weight; she was dozing off and it made her heavier. Kendal's walkway was empty and poorly lit; one of the bulbs had been knocked out. There was no sign of her neighbors. Instead of going to her place, she knocked on Lula's door and as soon as it opened, she pushed in and handed Rosie to Lula, who didn't protest; instead she sang softly to Rosie and took her through to the bedroom to lay her on the bed, where she went immediately to sleep.

Lula stopped in the doorway of the bedroom watching Kendal check the windows and the back door. They were locked, but the locks were standard issue and could be breached in seconds. Kendal took up a spot by the front door and turned to Lula. She adopted a tone of whimsy, but her smile was crooked and her eyes were bright with fear.

"Silly question, but I don't suppose you've got a gun I could borrow?"

Lula's eyes widened and she shook her head.

"Okay, lol. No worries, probably overkill anyway. I'll just wait here to make sure no one's coming and then we'll go, okay?"

"Someone tried the door, but I told them *Va te faire foutre*," Lula said in a proud whisper.

"Did you see who it was?"

Lula shook her head. She was pale but defiant. "Just kids, I think."

"Could be," Kendal said. "Probably."

They stayed like that, not moving or talking, ears straining for clues.

"Can you text Mrs. O and see if anything's happening?"

Lula pulled her phone from her pocket and her attention disappeared into its light.

"She says stay inside. The police are looking around. Everyone has gone home." She looked at Kendal for further instruction but Kendal just murmured, "Okay." Without a weapon she felt the situation was untenable and made a decision.

"Okay, I'm gonna take Rosie home. Come to mine just in case?"

Lula put her hand on Kendal's shoulder reassuringly. "It's just kids. Don't worry. They'll be gone by now."

"Yeah, I know, scary though." Kendal gave a goofy smile, readied her keys, and put Rosie over her shoulder. Rosie barely stirred.

Staying as low as she could, Kendal slipped out of Lula's apartment and into her own.

Inside, she left the lights off, put a sleeping Rosie on the bed, and tiptoed along the edge of the bed frame, reaching up to a secure metal case that she long ago tapped high up into the bricks, where Rosie could never reach. She pulled a cold, dusty Glock quietly from the box and checked the magazine. She heard the word in Rosie's voice, "mazagin," and felt nauseous about how close a deadly weapon was to her baby. The biscuit scent of Rosie's body combining with the cold smell of gun metal in her hand.

Kendal pulled a black holdall from the drawer under the bed. It contained passports and currency, first aid supplies and food bars. But it had nothing that covered Rosie. Five years in hiding had left Kendal with limited kit, dangerously out of touch. She perched on the edge of the bed, clicked the safety on, and thought about how she would get into the flat if it was her. If it was an op against her, it wasn't over. She couldn't think of a reason the attacks so far had been so indiscriminate. If they knew where she was, why go door-to-door? Maybe it was just kids after all.

As her heartbeat returned to normal, she dispelled the adrenaline that harked back to a different life. How many times had she sat in the dark with a gun? In none of them had she been the prey.

Eventually, she left the bedroom and sat on the sofa, back straight, lights off, the gun comfortably in her hand. In the darkness she listened to the reassuring familiarity of Lula's routine through the plasterboard walls. Their shared pipes would clank and hiss with the news that she was getting ready for bed. But where those sounds should have been, Kendal heard a short, tight yelp. She stood smoothly, clicked the safety off the gun, and moved silently across the room. She pressed her ear against the wall. There was no movement, then suddenly, two distinctive pops followed by a heavy thud. It was an unmistakable set of sounds. Kendal's scream was a silent, airless gasp.

She kept the gun trained on the wall and scrabbled in the drawer for a phone. It was a dusty burner that had one bar of battery. She fumbled the passcode on the first try and flinched when it unlocked with a beep that sounded loud as a siren in the silence of the flat. It had one number in the contacts list. She pressed it. It rang once before Rico Ortez answered, as if there had been zero years between this call, and the last.

"Go ahead, 96."

Kendal spoke in an urgent whisper. "I'm pinging coordinates. I've got multiple masks. Minimum two. They're armed. They're next door, apartment 8. One civ but I think she's down." She swallowed a panicked sob. At the other end of the line, Rico paused. He recognized the voice of course, but he'd never in his life heard fear in it. Kendal pressed Send on the coordinates of the house.

"Exfil in seven or armed response in . . ." He paused. She could hear keys being tapped. "Closest pro is twenty-eight minutes away."

"I can't hold that long, Ricky, I'm trapped in here with a kid."

"Armed?"

"I've got a nine millimeter but it's a piece of shit."

"So dash. Wheels in six."

She hung up and swore. She'd been warned already. Why the almighty fuck was she still in the building? It was a rookie mistake and she knew it.

Kendal stood completely still against the wall, weighing her options.

She wanted desperately to go to Rosie, but Rosie was safer where she was. She could hear the vague sounds of people looking around in Lula's flat and speaking a language she didn't know. A Baltic twang to it maybe. She checked the time on the phone. Would it take them six minutes to realize they had the wrong apartment? Probably not. She moved silently back to the cables drawer, took out the spare key to Lula's flat, and slipped it into her pocket.

She could carry Ro like a backpack, lower herself between the balconies and drop away in the darkness. It was a move she had practiced when Rosie was a baby. Even at two she might have managed, but now? Rosie wouldn't stay quiet; she couldn't make her understand. In that moment Kendal realized that for all her experience, she might as well be a civilian, she might as well call the police.

She lowered herself to the floor, listening against the wall, with a cabinet to her left. She heard the balcony door of Lula's flat slide open and tucked her legs in close to her body. She watched as a shadow from Lula's side rose up and stepped from Lula's balcony to hers. They were outside. She held the gun close to her, ready to train it in his direction; she would have the element of surprise. It was a big guy with a shaved head wearing a face mask. He shined his light into the house and tapped gently on the glass. The torch swung around the room, missing her feet by inches. The beam paused on Patch, a maniacal battery-powered bear that had musical ears and a relentless soundtrack of nursery rhymes. Kendal half expected him to start singing under the spotlight. She'd happily shoot Patch herself. She stopped breathing, frozen in time and space, her fear that Rosie would emerge so intense she felt sick, but nothing inside the apartment moved. The man on the balcony tapped harder on the glass and then he tried the handle. If he was more than what . . . six feet tall? . . . he might be able to see the top of her head behind the cabinet. She wanted to lower herself farther, but any movement might catch his eye. He rattled the handle more aggressively and then started tinkering with the lock, a basic standard-issue catch buried into the door handle on the inside. She risked the slightest move of her head, and his movement stopped. Then she realized that for all her lovely secret-service standard security, she had left the window unlocked. He started to pluck at the window. Another minute and there would be backup. If not, if he got his arm in, she'd break it and shoot. Instead, the man paused and leaned back toward Lula's balcony, calling to his partner. Kendal took the distraction and dashed into the bedroom, picking Rosie tenderly up off the bed. She folded her limbs around Kendal and stayed in something close to sleep. She opened one eye, seemed to understand that she was better off out of it, and muttered, "Take Barry."

Kendal glanced around the room for the bear. She picked him up and shoved him in the crook of her elbow behind Rosie. She was out of time. She ran past the living room door and paused by her front door, throwing the go bag over her other shoulder. She could hear both men on her balcony. Clumsily because she had only one hand spare, she closed then double-locked her door, leaving the key hanging from the lock on the outside. Then did the same to Lula's. Not so easy to pick a lock that still has the key in. Not easy to kick down a door that opens inward. She had bought enough time to make it down the stairs. They were both inside her flat now, she could hear them smashing it up. She spared a thought for Patch. Taking one for the team.

She ran for the stairwell at the far end of the walkway. She couldn't believe how slowly she had to take the stairs with Rosie, who was now wide awake but shocked into silence.

At the bottom of the stairs she nearly screamed when she recognized the Mercedes from the playground. The passenger door of the car hung open, and the driver lowered the window as Kendal scrabbled backward for an escape.

"96. You need a lift?"

Her fear changed instantly to relief as she realized he was not a hostile. She slid gracefully inside with Rosie's head protected.

The door slammed and silence fell as the car drove away into the night. Only now did Rosie whimper. She looked terrified. And cold in her cartoon pajamas. The driver noticed too and turned up the heat. Kendal flicked the safety on the gun, released the magazine, and dropped them into the pocket in the door. She held Rosie tight and shushed gently as they pulled onto the motorway and took off to the north.

"Where are we going?" Rosie whimpered.

"Somewhere safe, don't worry," Kendal said softly, but that made Rosie's lip quiver, because what was safer than being at home in bed?

Kendal looked out the window as her heart rate started to normalize. The city faded and became the blurred lights of the motorway. Rosie curled up into her lap and miraculously went back to sleep.

"Where to?" she asked.

"Airport."

"Is my neighbor dead?"

"Yes. I'm sorry." He sounded Scandinavian.

"It's my fault. I used her address; I thought it was safer."

There was a long pause.

"To be fair, ma'am, it *was* safer."

"Not for her."

Kendal stared out the window, trying to think what she should have done differently. She was horrified and hurt for Lula. Her neighbor had never been anything other than a good friend. The danger Rosie had been in felt like a band around her throat, suffocating and heavy as concrete shoes. She looked at Rosie's sleeping features, her soft baby hair and her chubby, relaxed fingers. She wanted to scream that it wasn't fair to make something so precious so vulnerable. What if Kendal herself had been killed tonight? Did Rosie even know her mother's name beyond Mummy? Who would have got her? Where would she have ended up? And somehow, the worst of these thoughts, would she have been better off? Safer in the Swiss social system than she was now, in a random car with this mum of many names, running away as she had vowed never to do. Kendal wasn't a crier, had been taught to conceal emotions from an early age. She felt tears gathering behind her eyes and sent them back where they came from, staring out of the window with no discernible feeling at all. On this journey she made a new vow, that Rosie would have a network. She would have other people to rely on and trust. People who knew the truth about Kendal and who would die to protect Rosie if they had to. Rico was a weak start, but at least it was something, someone. She pressed her finger against Rosie's outstretched palm, and Rosie instinctively closed her grip around it. Maybe Lula's mother was going to get a call that would ruin her life forever. She shook the image away. She hoped Lula's mother was dead.

3

As if it were perfectly normal to be awake and flying at thirty thousand feet over the north of France, Rosie Carter sat on a beige leather seat on board a six-seater Cirrus Vision Jet happily pressing buttons. Every few minutes she placed a hand reverentially on the window and whispered, "Cloud."

Their car had been waved through a hangar and onto an airfield without interacting with a single official, dropping them at the base of an aircraft where the pilot stood vaping at the bottom of the stairs. He saw them approach, pocketed his vape, saluted by way of greeting, and then took his seat next to his copilot in the cockpit without formal introductions.

Kendal had traveled by private jet enough times to have used the acronym PJ. But that had been in other lives, with other names, and not in the company of a four-year-old, who had discovered a minibar attached to her seat and was gleefully unloading it. Kendal looked around to identify whose PJ she was currently riding, which of his assets Rico might have purloined it from and under what guise.

Despite being just a few feet away, the captain used the intercom to announce that she had a call.

A screen lowered from the top of the plane, flashing with the word "Accept." She tapped it and Rico appeared. He was older, and gray flecked the edges of his black hair, but otherwise unchanged, ethnically ambiguous and undeniably handsome. They took each other in.

"Kara Corelli," he said, not disguising his pleasure at seeing her. "Goddamn, it's good to see you."

"Kara is dead." She kept her voice somber but felt relieved. If she was dead to Rico, it was official, Kara Corelli was truly gone, and with it an identity and life that Kendal had been haunted by for too long.

"Well, RIP, she will be missed. Kendal Carter, should I say. It's good to see you too. Glad you've dropped that ridiculous accent."

Rosie had figured out the seatbelt mechanism and released herself from the seat next to Kendal's in a bid to see the screen.

"WASSAT," she shouted into the camera.

"And who is this lovely duckling?" Rico cooed at the camera in a voice Kendal had never heard before.

"This is Rosie."

Rosie clambered up onto Kendal. Her face filled the screen and she glared at Rico, swiping at the camera.

"Hello, Rosie. I'm Rico."

Rosie stared into the screen, wiping a film of snot from her face while she considered him.

"No you're not," she decided eventually. And went back to her buttons.

"Smart kid." Rico chuckled. "You sly dog. And there I thought you were in some Taliban torture hole. You should have told me. I would've knitted a hat."

Kendal changed the subject, acutely uncomfortable with the idea of Rico and Rosie being in the same space. For the first time in their long history, she had more to lose, and she didn't like it on this side of the power balance. She maneuvered Rosie out of frame. "Still clinging to the British schtick, I see."

He laughed heartily. "And you? California by way of north London, is it?"

"Something like that."

They were both smiling, the meeting reminiscent of some absolutely wild times they'd shared. Rico was the first person Kendal had spoken to in nearly five years who actually knew who she was.

"Well, mazel tov, anyway."

"Thanks. She's four."

"I guess time flies even when you're not having fun."

"Speaking of which. Where do we land?"

"Officially?"

"In real life."

"I've got you a spot at Blackbushe. But if anyone asks, you're a thoroughbred colt."

Kendal looked skeptical. "Why the UK?"

"Keep you close, make things right. I've got a little job I thought you might like."

"I'm not seeking employment right now, I was just looking for an evac."

"Sure, but I think you'll like this one because it comes with a safe house and lots and lots of money."

Kendal glanced around the interior luxury of the plane. She was forced to admit both of those sounded pretty good.

"This is all very high grade. I was expecting some meatheads in a transit van."

"No way, Bon Temps is booming, babe, we didn't twiddle our thumbs while you took a five-year parental leave like some Swedish dad."

The pilot interrupted to tell them to belt up for landing. Rico paused, then smiled at her. "I've got you an overnight and a quick change. Hope you haven't forgotten your counter-surveillance game. I'll meet you at your new home. Welcome back, Kendal Carter."

He hung up before she could think of anything clever to say.

The first time Kendal met Rico was in 2005, when Bon Temps was not much more than a blue door on the Hammersmith roundabout, a scrappy slip of paper next to one of twenty silver buttons, stuffed between an orthodontist and solicitor's. Ostensibly a staffing agency, Bon Temps provided temp staff—caterers, drivers, and all manner of zero-hours contract crews—to companies, events, and conferences from around the world. The back door, however, opened for a different class of client. Rico split them into categories according to where they came from and how much he could charge them.

C-class contracts: cleaning up after the British government and her affiliated agencies. Chronically underpaid and usually dirty—wet work, patsies, cover-ups, and anything to avoid nice English hands on messy smoking guns.

B-roll meant work for foreign governments who didn't want their presence felt. Blue-collar projects for decent money—surveillance or undercover cleaners, waiters, drivers, delivery guys—good proper temp work that Rico used as training grounds for his Wahlbergs (New Kids). Not particularly dangerous but with a higher-than-average chance of getting done for treason if caught.

And the A-list. In espionage, as in life, the Bon Temps big bucks came from corporate cases. The IDs varied but always required well-trained agents with ironed shirts, long hours, close contact with client assets, and full immersion into an organization.

The day Kendal pushed the button on the blue door, she joined a sprawling team of freelance agents, heavies, and ex-intelligence officers, most of whom she would never meet. In twenty years, she and Rico had saved each other's lives countless times. Rico saved her literally, and she had saved him professionally. Theirs was a bond forged in fights and fires, and she wondered if the lifetime of trust they had placed in each other was strong enough to hold Rosie too.

They disembarked the plane into quintessentially British weather; a fine, flimsy rain, not falling so much as skirmishing around them. Rosie scrunched her nose in disdain. Four identical cars were waiting on the runway surrounded by people Kendal's height and wearing the same clothes. They put up black umbrellas and walked forward to meet them. Kendal picked up Rosie, and one of the team draped a hoodie over her. The group did a deliberately obfuscating dance from the plane to the car, guiding Kendal between them, switching umbrellas and changing direction. It was a counter-surveillance, like a card trick. Anyone watching would have to try and keep tabs on which of the baseball-cap-wearing white women was Kendal. She was impressed—if nothing else it proved the manpower at Rico's disposal. They drove to a hotel drop-off to rest, change their clothes, and further confuse any surveillance. Rico had brought out the big guns for this trip, and she went to sleep trying to figure out why.

4

The next morning another Mercedes pulled up to take them to London. As fields gave way to suburban sprawl, Kendal felt the pull of her old life. She reviewed her memory of the city. She had contacts here, including Fini Meridian, her first and maybe only friend. It was a city she had spent lots of time in, but always under an alias and never for longer than a few months. Good for raising a child? How could she possibly know when she'd only ever traveled alone, with bottomless expenses and no anchors? She was still reeling over how hard it was to be stealthy with a child. English was Rosie's first language and her accent was neutral. She knew Rico had many hidden hands in the city and he would put them at her disposal. At the back of her mind there were bigger questions. Memories fought to surface, and she tried to drown them.

Khalil Masoumi had died here; her coming back wouldn't change that fact. She let the memory of him, and the grief it came wrapped in, wash over her. He had never completely left her, because Rosie had his eyes, but being back in London brought him, and his death, closer than he had been in years. It didn't matter where she and Rosie ended up, Khalil was dead the world over.

As the car crept through the city, the ops of her past flickered into view . . . Slipping through Mayfair, her movements smooth and untraceable, dancing with oligarchs, whispering to politicians in bathroom stalls. The excitement of it all briefly flooded her system. She didn't miss the job exactly, but the woman she had been. There was grief, she noticed, for that person she had lost. She glanced at Rosie, for whom time was an ocean. It was bizarre, Kendal thought, that her primary occupation now was handling this little person, and it was the hardest, most dangerous job she'd ever had. They drove past an apartment block that she'd lived in at various intervals across a decade of assignments. Its surfaces had been sleek and shiny. She had never particularly considered the logistics but somehow the fridge had always been well stocked, and if she ever brought an asset back, it would look like she had a life, and friends, and connection, although she'd had none. As she let the memories slide by, she examined them for people who might be seeking her out. Why was she a target? Who would come for her? Rosie leaned across the seat and pressed her sticky paw in Kendal's, watching the biggest city she'd ever seen swooshing past.

Kendal put thoughts of rogue agents aside to point out landmarks she recognized to Rosie, who quietly absorbed it all.

Was it her hometown? Not really, but it was at least somewhere her plan to build a network for her daughter might succeed.

Eventually, they pulled up outside an imposing three-story house on a tree-lined street near Highbury Corner in north London. Rico stood in the driveway and greeted them with a cheerful wave. He was tall and slim, but the sinews in his neck gave him away as deliberately strong. He had cold, clever brown eyes that he tried to hide behind a dopey smile and black hair that he tousled to look like bed head. He wore a visibly expensive suit, a starched collar with no tie, and double-monk-strapped shoes that were surprisingly soundless against the slate-tiled driveway. Kendal had forgotten how attractive he was, and it irritated her that she wished she was wearing a smarter outfit.

"Well, look at you, 96, in full bloom." Kendal sensed a punch line, but he didn't add it. They smiled at each other, revising old files, updating their databases, filling in the blanks. He ignored Rosie and embraced Kendal in a strong hug. She breathed him in. He wore Grey Vetiver by Tom Ford, and the scent transferred her to their distant, glamorous past. She had missed him.

They stood and took stock of the house. It had a dark gray door that oozed security. Kendal could see two cameras in plain sight, and another one buried in a brick on the edge of the building. Despite these measures, it was a friendly facade. There were sunflower stickers in one of the windows, trees and blossoming shrubs up the stairs to the door. Kendal did a 360. The road was quiet, the door protected by the gate and a cement blockade. The ground-floor windows were frosted, with the wooden shutters closed. Kendal thought, *There's hiding in plain sight, and then there's just showing off.* She checked the time. Rosie was going to melt down if she didn't get a substantial snack in the next fifteen minutes. She picked her up and with an easy swing lifted her onto her shoulders. Rico noted the strength still stored in Kendal's arms. The muscles tensing, then disappearing back into the harmless flesh they'd been hiding inside.

"It's pretty," Rosie murmured, her chin resting painfully on Kendal's head. Rico addressed her directly. "It sure is, Rosie. And it's got two entrances but three exits, which is Mummy's favorite," he said, in a voice that made them all cringe. "It's got a playroom for you, and a safe room for Mummy, and it's hardwired against all the naughty boys and girls," he continued.

"Stop saying *Mummy*," Kendal warned. Rico barked out a laugh. "Shall we look inside?"

"YAY!" shouted Rosie, humping Kendal's neck as if she were steering a horse.

Kendal watched as Rico produced a pleasing set of keys. Two of the locks beeped, two turned, and finally, with a wink, he pressed a thumb against the top of the handle and it made the faintest buzz of a fingerprint reader. The security enthusiast in her grinned. "Not bad."

Inside, the door closed with a solid *thunk*, and there was a hydraulic swish as something autolocked. It was the sound of high-end security. Kendal relaxed by a fraction.

The house was beautiful, with a black-and-white tiled hallway that led through to the kitchen, and a mahogany staircase on the right-hand side of the hall. It smelled clean, and rich. Kendal hefted Rosie off her shoulders, and she went straight for the stairs, lumbering up them like she was bouldering. Kendal watched her go, lamenting both her lack of training and her unassailable love of stairs.

"Rosie!"

She stopped abruptly but didn't turn. "What?"

"Are you just running off? You don't even know whose house this is."

Rosie looked around for the correct answer, landing on Rico. "Him's?" she ventured.

Rico laughed. "Go nuts, kiddo. There's a playroom on the top floor." Rosie reached the top of the stairs and disappeared. They heard her gasp, "SWIMMING POOL!"

They followed her up and found her in a bathroom at the top of the stairs, eyes wide and mouth theatrically agape.

"That's a bath, Ro. You've seen a bath before," Kendal scolded, then tried to think if she actually had. It was big, to be fair.

Rico grinned at Kendal's expression. "She's very cute, Ken. How did you manage that?"

"I have no idea."

He walked her into the main bedroom, and they heard Rosie plod up more stairs, throw open a door, and go "whoa." Then slam the door.

Rico saw Kendal's face. "It's just toys . . . Kids' toys," he added quickly, because in their past life "toys" meant things that were not cuddly at all.

"The whole place is protocoled to fuck, there are shutters embedded behind every door. The security in this building is better than Number 10."

Every room was more beautiful than the last. Their steps made the deep, rich echo of high ceilings and real wood floors. The doors closed with a satisfying clunk. It was fully furnished to the point of bedding, a full wardrobe, and high-end toiletries.

They followed Rosie up another flight of stairs that led to a study and the playroom, where they found her. It was a converted attic, with eaves creating a space both cozy and cavernous. Light poured through a skylight onto more toys than Rosie had ever seen in her life. She was teaching a group of them an incorrect approximation of the alphabet. She looked up as they entered. “Donkey can’t count,” she said sadly, pointing at a giraffe.

“That’s a giraffe.” Rico couldn’t help himself.

“No, *you’re* a giraffe,” Rosie countered.

Rico shrugged cheerfully. “I’ve been called worse.”

In that moment, Kendal realized Rico was a father. She saw a look in him that she recognized, a nostalgia for a bygone age. She wondered how old Rico’s kids were, and where he was hiding them.

Downstairs, the main living space was wide and open plan. Floor-to-ceiling French doors opened onto a wide wooden deck with stairs down to the garden. The kitchen was marked out by white tiles around a breakfast island and covered in counters that were dark gray with silver fittings and dark wood surfaces. The sofa looked like one of the most comfortable pieces of furniture she’d ever seen. Rosie took one look around and threw herself onto a giant beanbag in the corner, where she lay whispering into its beans.

Kendal sat on a barstool at the marble island and watched Rico produce coffee, juice, biscuits, and fruit from various cupboards. He opened the fully stocked fridge to reveal four different kinds of milk and spoke with his back to her. “Nice place, right? It’s a brand-new addition to the arsenal. Yours for as long as you like.”

“What’s the catch?”

Rico closed the fridge and turned to face her with a wry smile. “The catch is a Canadian called Joel.”

From the floor, Rosie smacked herself in the forehead and rolled her eyes. Rico laughed. “Do you want a cookie?” Kendal knew a distraction when she heard one.

"Yes, mister, I do." Rosie hopped up from the beanbag and came to join them. Rico didn't notice, but Rosie had just accepted him into her tiny circle of trust. "He's just arrived, he lives in the granny annex downstairs. I need a pro to show him the ropes. He's an HVT, but he's had zero training."

HVT stood for high-value target. "High value" could mean many things to many people. For Rico it almost exclusively meant money.

Kendal glanced around the room. "There's a downstairs? Where?" She hopped off the barstool and followed the walls around the room. In the corner there was a light switch, a dimmer switch, and a bookcase. Rico grinned.

She clicked the dimmer, and a light in the kitchen turned on. Rico chuckled. "Cold." Rosie squealed and hopped up and down; she could sense a game from a mile away. Rico lifted her onto the island. She was absolutely delighted. Seeing them together gave Kendal a short-lived fuzzy feeling.

She went to the other light switch and flicked it. The hallway light turned on.

"COLDER!" shouted Rosie, Rico openly laughed. "It's not *The Addams Family*."

She rounded the corner, where one panel of the white wall was unusually inset. Next to it was a control box that a normal person would assume was an AC control.

"Is this a door?" Kendal asked incredulously, pushing against the wall and finding the panel very slightly loose.

"My best agent, everybody," Rico said, clapping slowly. Rosie joined in the applause.

"There's a code. Want to crack it or have we not got all week?"

Kendal looked at the box. The cover panel flipped down to reveal a keypad. She couldn't help but smile. Rico and his gadgets had had a serious upgrade. She examined the keypad for signs that any of the numbers had been used, but the entire rig was so new there might as well have been protective plastic on it. If Rico had set it for her, it would be 9614, her extended code name. But Rico only ever thought of himself. She typed his name in, 7426. The box beeped a quiet but firm rejection. From across the room Rico smirked, and Rosie shook her head *nuh-uh.*

Kendal realized she was overthinking it, something Rico could rarely be accused of. She pressed 1234. He laughed out loud at her withering look as the door audibly unlocked. She pushed it open to reveal the top step of a glossy, white-tiled staircase. Much like the rest of the house, it smelled of fresh paint, newness, and plastic. Rico popped Rosie onto the floor and they all stood at the top of the stairs, peering down.

"Shall we have a peep at his den?" Rico said cheerfully.

The stairs led down into a small, clean apartment. It had a bedroom, bathroom, tiny lounge, and kitchenette, all decked out in gray and beige with Japanese styling. Low, clean surfaces and minimal clutter. Light came in through two massive windows facing out into the garden that Rosie immediately put greasy fingers and her whole face against.

"Don't lick the glass, Ro."

The occupant had a gamer's chair and a multiscreen setup on a clean white desk looking out into the garden. There were no accoutrements, no pictures or papers around the room. Nothing to give away a personality of any kind.

"Tech bro?" Kendal asked, and Rico nodded. "Full-on nerd."

Kendal looked out into the garden. It was completely private, with strong, high fences and no hiding places, entry points, or overlooking houses. She could tell whoever had chosen and designed the house had understood security.

"It's got its own entrance. He need never interact with the rest of the house, but it's an emergency exit if one is ever needed. And look! Safe room!"

He grinned as he pressed a button that made a section of wall slide open to reveal a white padded room that looked more like a cell than a safe room. Rosie took Kendal's hand and looked into the room suspiciously.

"Grim," Kendal murmured.

"But safe," Rico bounced back unperturbed.

They returned upstairs. Rosie stayed close to Kendal; she seemed rattled by the basement flat, and Kendal respectfully thought her instincts were spot on.

In the living room Rosie was back on the beanbag having found an enormous remote control. She examined it carefully, and then used it to switch on the bazillion-inch screen on the far wall.

How is it that she can navigate a remote, but she's never seen a bath? Kendal thought guiltily.

Rico was still pitching. "Oh, this is cool, Ken, check it out."

He slid his hand along the underside of the breakfast bar, and a floorboard in the middle of the room mirrored the action, opening a space wide enough to drop through to the basement below. Rico grinned like a kid at Christmas. "Escape hatch!"

"That's insanely dangerous with Rosie in the house," she answered, secretly impressed. She looked around the beautiful room with its safety measures and ample space and considered their options.

"I don't love living with an asset," she said.

"It's not living together. It's just like having a next-door neighbor."

"Didn't work out too well for my last next-door neighbor."

"Maybe don't tell him that." He got a plate and made Rosie a sandwich—lightly buttered, thinly sliced salad, and cut into square quarters. He placed it next to her with a bow. Without taking her eyes off Mr. Tumble, she picked it up, and ate. Rico might never know the depth of appreciation Kendal felt for the simple act of someone else making lunch.

He came back to the kitchen and watched Rosie eating. Once he was satisfied that her attention was wholly taken he opened a smaller fridge and pulled two beers from it, popping the tops and handing one to her. "So, 96, bestie. Is it time you told me what the almighty fuck happened on Prom?"

Operation Prometheus. Khalil happened. He was a government employee; there were suspicions he'd been tapped by Iran. She was a high-grade agent commissioned to establish the facts; it should have been a simple assignment.

She held his stare. "It didn't go according to plan."

The look on Rico's face made the hairs on her arm stand up. "No shit." His eyes searched her face. "Is she his?" he asked quietly.

Kendal's voice was cold and calm. "She's mine."

Rico looked genuinely distressed. "She looks exactly like him."

They let the moment pass. Kendal didn't deny that Khalil was Rosie's father. It seemed pointless.

"What was the fallout?" she asked softly. Khalil's face appeared with crystal clarity in her mind. Dark curly hair, permanently tousled, rich brown eyes full of laughter and curiosity. He was, by any standard, a beautiful man. What was she hoping Rico would say? That he got away. That he'd been spotted in the field. That he was in some government cell and not at the bottom of the Thames.

"We sent a team to clean up . . ."

"You saw the body?" Her voice caught in her throat, and he was watching her closely for signs she was lying.

"The place had already been scrubbed."

She looked up sharply. "By whom?"

"To be honest, until about thirty seconds ago, I thought it was probably you."

"It wasn't. I barely made it out."

"So who were they?"

She shook her head. "A goon squad carrying M16s. I thought they were temps."

"And you ran?"

She bristled at the accusation in the question but kept her voice casual. "And you left me for dead."

He shrugged, as if these were everyday occurrences. To be fair, at Bon Temps they probably were. "Well, whatever happened back then, the holiday is properly over now."

"Parenting isn't a holiday."

He laughed at her knowingly.

"You've got kids?"

"Not that I know of," he lied. Rico pulled up one of the stools and sat down opposite her. "So what's the plan? You just gonna grow into those sweatpants in your European half-life?"

Kendal hadn't been insulted in years, and in spite of everything she laughed.

"I was hoping to. How did they find me?"

"Amazing though you are at hide-and-seek, your image has been splashed all over the dark net for days."

"Why?"

"We're looking into it. But in the meantime, stay here. Walk Joel through some basic tradecraft, make a shitload of cabbage."

She nodded, it made sense. "On one condition. Rosie is a civilian. She's not one of us. This doesn't touch her." There was a hint of pleading in her voice. She'd already exposed Rosie to violence and broken the promises she'd made at her birth. But, she reasoned, if danger was looking for them, it should at least find them in a house with evacuation protocols, a safe room, and a trapdoor.

Rosie hopped up from the beanbag, energized by her food. She looked around, decided she wanted to go outside, and ran full pelt into the glass doors. The collision with the window was face-first with a painful-sounding *donk.* She sat down as if to cry but then called out weakly, "I'm okay." She fluctuated between high-intellect and bloody idiot with incredible alacrity.

Kendal sighed, her decision made.

"She needs to go to school."

"I know. Don't worry, I've got you, Ken. I've got you both. I promise."

5

Across the road from the house was a black SUV with tinted windows. Inside the car, in the driver's seat, a white male in his late twenties sat holding the steering wheel tightly with both hands. His passenger hadn't spoken for nearly an hour and his stomach was starting to make embarrassing gurgles regarding the lunch that was sweating in the glove compartment. As if in answer, he finally heard a cold voice from the back seat.

"Is she in there, Taylor?"

His name was not, nor had it ever been, Taylor.

"She arrived by diplomatic vehicle this afternoon."

"Diplomatic from where?"

"Canada plates." He didn't know why this was funny.

"Any other eyes in place, cameras or bugs? Three children in an overcoat, for Christ's sake?"

He didn't answer, because he didn't know and didn't want to admit it.

"Take me to Mayfair. I need a drink."

6

They sat on green wrought iron chairs on the deck outside the kitchen. The table between them was increasingly laden: a tomato salad and fresh bread, glasses of white wine—the bottle in an ice bucket on the floor—an ashtray with Rico's cigarette butts accumulating as the day wore on. The garden was an expanse of grass with bushy flowering perimeter plants that Kendal could not identify. At the top of the garden, two mature alder trees reached for each other, creating a space beneath and blocking prying eyes from the houses opposite. Birds tweeted, planes flew overhead. Compared to their Swiss digs, this was solid. There had been a sort of safety in the many windows and small community of Dübendorf, but this was altogether preferable. Fewer eyes, less noise, and, so far, zero thugs with guns killing her neighbors . . . Kendal was reviewing the proposition internally. Placing her trust in Rico, living in London; it was a return to a past she thought she had walked away from. But this thought was swiftly followed by the sucker-punch realization that they had nowhere else to go. She kept quiet, working through the options while appearing to be listening to Rico. He was gleefully filling her in on five years of phenomenal success at Bon Temps.

"SIS had this big political prisoner exchange mapped out with Russia, but someone fucked up and it was about to blow. I heard about it and offered them Boris Getz for an obscene amount of cabbage, saved the day. Word got out. We got a bunch of contracts with the three letters, then the Mounties took note. Thanks to the absolute shit show at the Clown Factory, relations in the Burger are testy AF and yours truly is the middleman du jour."

He added a smug little *ch-ching* to the end of the sentence and drained his glass.

Kendal enjoyed listening while Rico spoke this coded language that only they could follow. "SIS" was the UK secret services, encapsulating everything from MI5 and GCHQ to dozens of departmental acronyms known only to insiders. The "Clown Factory" meant the British government. "Three letters" was trade-speak for the US agencies and their myriad departments, "Mounties" was Rico's chronically unoriginal nickname for the Canadian Secret Service. "The Burger" referred to the intelligence alliance between the US, Canada, UK, New Zealand, and Australia, more commonly known as the Five Eyes. Rico had tenuously extrapolated the nickname from a fast-food chain that rhymed, god bless him. She sucked her bottom lip and contemplated.

"Tell me about the rookie."

"He got headhunted by a firm called Glo-Tech."

"Why does that ring a bell?"

"They've had a few headlines. They're known as Bro-Tech because they have a rep for being incel fucks. But they have a couple of big government projects in the works and they are definitely becoming one of the major players on the Silicon Roundabout."

Kendal made a *blurgh* face.

"Glo-Tech recently made a change of management and no one has eyes on the inside. They're raking in data and dinero at a pretty compelling pace, but the new top tier are ghosts. They used to be all about Ferraris and followers, and all of a sudden they're being discreet."

"That's never good," Kendal agreed, weighing the merits of the case.

Rico continued. "The Mounties noticed when Joel got the job and asked me to tap him as an asset. They want us to run him *without interference.*" He waggled his eyebrows, gleeful about almost certainly committing treason. His favorite pastime.

Kendal couldn't help but smile. It was like hearing her native tongue after years abroad, and it was refreshing as a sea breeze.

"Since when is Canada running humint on foreign soil?"

"I know, right? They finally put their peckers in the poutine."

Kendal cringed at the expression and turned over the info. Humint—human intelligence. Last she heard, Canada didn't have assets overseas. It made her feel dangerously out of touch. Rico must have read the thought because he went on. "Officially he's GSRP, but I think Joel's an experiment. They handed him over to me like I'm day care."

Kendal sat with this info. GSRP was Canada's Global Security Report Program, historically toothless and solely focused on the interior.

Rico could sense Kendal's interest piquing and stayed quiet. Letting her curiosity come to him.

"So, what's he like?"

Rico made a *pffft* sound and smiled.

"Picture the least cool person you've ever seen."

Daddy Pig sprang to mind and she shook him away.

"He's absolute vanilla. I called it corporate espionage and he nearly peed his pants. I don't even think he's in it for the money, just wants a go at The Game. If he can keep his cool, he might be a natural. And if anyone can teach him to be cool, it's you."

Kendal accepted the compliment. They sat in a companionable silence and watched Rosie digging a hole. Kendal released a small sigh.

"I was hoping to keep her away from all this. Proper civvy street, you know?"

Rico nodded sympathetically. "I get it, Ken, I really do. But you're being watched."

"Nothing to see except a shitload of *Octonauts*."

"The perfect cover."

"It's not a cover, it's my life."

Rico tapped on the table. "Babe, life is one big cover story. You act all cranky about it, but you have to admit, we have the coolest job in the world."

"Motherhood is cool."

He gave a derisive smirk. "Is it fuck."

Rosie smacked the alder tree with a small stick. Rico turned to Kendal with a wicked glint in his eye. "However *cool* you think mumming is, you have to admit the paycheck is appalling."

He pulled a file from the bag at his feet. It was inches thick, probably more information than every other job they'd done together combined. "This is the file. And the house comes with a car, healthcare, therapists, gym membership."

"Sweet," Kendal acknowledged, skimming the file for the headlines.

"Rosie can go to the good school a ten-minute walk from here, they do fencing!"

"You've really thought about this."

"I'm excited to get the band back together. I was going to put someone else on him. Imagine my delight when you called. Remember how much fun we had? How much money we made?"

Kendal allowed herself a wry smile. She had missed the fun of it, and where else was Rosie going to do fencing and have a garden? She let the cold wine touch her lips and inwardly admitted that she felt more at home here with Rico than she had in years.

"You're sure he's clean?"

Rico gave her a withering look. "I'd like to think after thirty years in the business I can spot a player. He's a bar of soap in a sweater. Even worse, he's nice."

Kendal stared into the garden, where nobody was getting shot and nothing was on fire.

Rico closed out the pitch. "You're not a civilian. You're just in the cold with no cover and no backup. Get back in, the water is warm."

He didn't need to go on; she was in and they both knew it. They smiled at each other. It felt good to be home.

"How shall we play the meet with Joel?" Rico asked.

"Might as well get on with it."

Rico nodded in agreement and sent a text.

The sun was starting to dip behind the trees when Rosie froze. A cloud passed over the garden, throwing a cold shade over them and changing the atmosphere. Rico and Kendal braced, like foxes on a road.

"Mumma," Rosie said in a voice barely audible across the grass. "There's a man."

Kendal stood; she heard Rico whisper gleefully, "There she is." Then he reached out and touched her arm. "It's okay, it's just him."

Rosie took cover behind a tree and peeped out. The door to the downstairs apartment slid open.

"Oh, hey there!" a friendly Canadian accent said over the garden. "I'm Joel."

"MOTHER," Rosie yelled from her hiding place. Rico leaned over the balcony and yelled down. "Joel, we're up here. Come and say hello."

From under the overhang a strawberry-blond head of tight curly hair appeared, followed by a gray sweater over a starched white shirt and chinos with the creases ironed in.

He turned to face them, shielding his eyes from the sun with his arm. "Hello there!"

Rico beckoned him up, and Rosie, assessing the situation to be both safe and irrelevant, resumed her game of hitting trees.

As Joel came up the stairs to the deck, Rico sat down. "Joel, this is 96, you can call her Kendal. Try and make a good impression."

"Yes, sir."

He was so outwardly winsome that Kendal immediately mistrusted him. He had freckles, for god's sake. He pulled a third chair up to the table, facing into the house with his back to the garden. Before he sat down, he brushed at the seat. He looked like he would have put a napkin down but glanced at Kendal, incorrectly read her expression as disapproval, and sat gingerly on the edge.

"Good day?" Rico asked. Joel looked nervously from Rico to Kendal and back. "I went to the Tower of London!" He simultaneously beamed and blushed. "How was it for you guys?"

"Super-duper, Joel. Super-duper." Rico winked at Kendal, but Joel caught it, and for the briefest moment his face flushed. *Doesn't like being mocked,* Kendal noted, and Joel gave her a cautious smile as if he knew he'd slipped.

Joel pressed his palms together and tucked them between his knees, his shoulders curved forward in a protective hunch. "Is that your daughter?" he asked Kendal, turning to look at Rosie playing in the garden.

"Yeah. Rosie." She yelled across the garden, "Ro, come and say hello!"

"No," Rosie replied without looking up. Joel smiled. He had perfectly polished teeth, a light ginger beard, and bright, friendly eyes. Rico was right, Kendal thought, this guy was the epitome of *neutral.*

"She looks about five?" he proffered.

"Four and a bit."

"She's tall for her age, no?"

"Apparently so."

Joel acknowledged this with a small nod and seemed at a loss for what to say next. Kendal lamented the absence of "she looks just like you." An adage she never heard, because for all their similarities, their skin tones were different. She wondered if the thought had also occurred to Joel.

"I have twin nephews, they're a bit older than her but man, the energy of them. Kids bring such a magic to things, don't they?" he said shyly.

"Innocence," Kendal agreed. Joel looked grateful she'd picked up the thread and nodded happily. "Right? Innocence and curiosity. And love. They're so unafraid to just enjoy things. It's so nice to be around."

Kendal smiled. "It's true."

To interrupt what he clearly deemed too saccharine for his tastes, Rico cleared his throat. "Kendal is one of my most senior consultants. You could learn a lot from this woman, Joel, and not about parenting."

Rosie appeared at the top of the stairs.

"I'm hungry."

"Hi, Hungry, I'm Joel."

Rosie was so delighted by this she squeaked. She took her hand out of her mouth to accept the olive Kendal handed her. Joel stood up and brushed down the seat of his pants. "I guess I should leave you guys to your meeting. Great to see you, Kendal and Rosie."

Rosie said, "Ciao, Job." Which was her absolute best behavior. She watched him walk away and popped the olive into her mouth. He gave her a friendly wave as he went back downstairs, but Rosie had already forgotten him. Her face transformed into slow-motion horror, and she spat dramatically onto the balcony. "BAD GRAPE."

They heard Joel chuckle under the deck and the door close. Rico started gathering bits from the table. Rosie had put another olive in her mouth and was chewing it with disgusted fury.

"Come inside, I'll make spaghetti."

Rico had fogged the windows using the remote control, a privacy setting he must have known she would like. He had lowered the lighting and put on some music so it was warm and cozy in the kitchen. Rosie was grinding pepper onto the table and then licking it. She had also taken an indiscreet nibble off the corner of some butter. Sometimes it was like living with a family of mice.

"So, what do you reckon?" Rico had moved on to red wine and was borderline jolly. Kendal was enjoying the luxury of the room. She pondered the Joel question. She didn't altogether believe he couldn't hear them.

"I don't know if I'm buying his chipmunk schtick."

"He does give strong gopher," Rico answered.

"How far have you looked into his background?"

"All the way, babe, both Bon Temps and the Mounties. His file was immaculate."

"That's 'files' for you."

Rico raised his glass in acquiescence to the point. "Preach."

"Mumma, do we live here?" Rosie asked, butter smeared in a square-foot radius from her mouth. Rico reached over and put his hand on Kendal's.

"Two weeks in the field with the rookie so he doesn't get eaten alive, and then sit back and let the intel flow. No action, no drama."

"Please, Mumma," Rosie said.

"Yeah, please, Mumma," Rico added, sounding fully drunk.

Kendal considered the London she'd left behind, and pictured the rest of the world, how small it was, how much it shrank with every inch Rosie grew up. It felt right, the city and the house, even having a rookie to play with. A switch clicked somewhere inside her.

"Okay," was all she said. Rico held his hand up to Rosie for a high five and she smeared it with her buttered paw.

After dinner Rico left in a car that swooped by and picked him like he was the sultan of Brunei. Kendal checked all the locks, and then they got into the massive super-king bed in the main bedroom. It rustled with the calming luxury of duck-down bedding. It was the nicest place Rosie had ever slept, and she wasn't above rubbing her face along the silky cotton pillowcases with a happy purr. Kendal thought about what Joel had said about the joy children bring, and it made her smile.

"Tell me a make-up story," Rosie said, a cry for the ages. Kendal swallowed a groan.

"Which one?"

"The wife one."

Kendal smiled. It was a personal favorite. "Many moons ago, an old man lived, with his servants and his horse, in a high-up house with golden lights and crystal glasses. He was a nice old man, but he was lonely and lots of people were worried about what he might do without someone to look after him. And then one day, there was a knock at the door."

"Who was it, Mumma?"

"It was a delivery. A huge box. And inside that box was a wife."

For a reason that Kendal could never quite fathom, Rosie found this incredibly funny. She giggled and rolled around clutching her tummy. "A box of wife! Like shopping!"

"Sure," Kendal went on, "just like shopping."

"Say about the settings, Mumma." Kendal was relieved that Rosie was pushing for the abridged version this evening. She glanced at the clock; it was nearly 9:00 PM. She made a note to ask the internet what a normal bedtime was.

"Well, they took the wife out of the box and she was covered in buttons. And each button was a different setting."

"Do the frog bit!"

"And on one of her buttons, it said 'Frog.'"

Rosie was in bits at this long-familiar story. "What happens when you press it, Mumma?"

"The wife goes 'ribbit.'"

Rosie went into a glazed trance of appreciation. She released a little coo and rolled into her pre-sleep fetal position. "What are the other buttons, Mumma?"

Kendal dimmed the lamp by the bed so the room was bathed in mellow light. She couldn't hear an AC unit but the temperature in the room was perfect. A tiny shred of stress released from her shoulders. Rosie had two fingers in her mouth, which was starting to slacken. This exact moment was Kendal's favorite, watching Rosie drift into another realm. It seemed miraculous. Speaking more slowly and deeply, she went on, knowing if she stopped too soon, Rosie's eye would peel open and she'd wake herself up to demand the ending.

"She had a cat setting for when she wanted to slink about at night. She had a peacock setting for looking very beautiful. She had a flamingo setting, for standing on one leg."

Rosie laughed a filthy little giggle at this new setting. "Tell the end."

"The wife went through many years on many different settings. People always wanted her to change into something new. Then one day, the wife met a little girl. She had big brown eyes and dark shiny hair, and she was the loveliest little girl the wife had ever seen. The girl asked the wife, 'What happens when you're not on a setting at all?' The wife thought about it, but it had been so long that she wasn't sure. So the little girl unplugged the wife and turned off all her settings, so she wasn't a cat or a frog or a flamingo. She wasn't even a wife anymore. She was free. The girl asked her, 'Who are you now?' But the woman shook her head sadly, because she didn't know. So the little girl took her hand, and said, 'Let's find out.' And they set off on the world's most glorious adventure." Kendal reached over and stroked Rosie's lovely hair, soothing her as she closed her eyes.

"And then what happened, Mumma?"

"They're still on it."

"Was it us?"

"Yes."

This was also a well-practiced routine.

"How do I know?"

"Because only you know where my frog button is."

Rosie reached over and pressed Kendal on the face.

"Ribbit."

Rosie laughed again, a new, cheeky smirk she was developing. Kendal listened to Rosie's breathing and wondered if her own mother had ever loved her like she loved Rosie. It didn't seem likely.

7

From age twenty-one up until her pregnancy, Kendal had been Russian. As a child, it was her favorite character to play. Her mother called it *The Matryoshka*.

"If you ever want the M's to pay attention . . ."

(Kendal was six when she found out this meant MI5 and MI6, the two main branches of UK secret services.)

". . . Just give them a whiff of Moscow."

Her mother made declarations like these, wafting a paintbrush, or a cigarette, wearing a suit or a lab coat or the garb of a small-town teacher, depending on who she was pretending to be. And little Kendal, who was in thrall to her, would collect careful mental notes, squirreled away for the day they might make sense.

They moved constantly, and in each location they had new IDs, identities that included names, interests, and a set of idiosyncrasies. Kendal's initials were always KC, her mother's first name always began with J. Each time they landed somewhere new they would play a game called Meet and Greet to establish and memorize their new IDs, and decide which special interest their new personas would have: languages, martial arts, cookery, ballet, chess . . .

Her mother was not someone who had ever been described as "playful," so little Kendal was delighted by these games. For Kendal, the game I Spy had been an exercise in sleight of hand. "Something beginning with A," her mother would whisper, and Kendal would have to find and deliver an item that would glean maximum approval. Her mother called the stolen goods "souvenirs," and it was in this way that young Kendal learned the endless hypocrisy of parents. Of all their games, her favorite was Play Dead. Any time her mother said, shouted, whispered, even signed the words "play dead," Kendal had to stop and drop. She was rewarded according to how seriously strangers took it, so if she giggled or moved, she would get nothing. The longer she stayed down and the further up the healthcare chain she went, the bigger the prize. Once, on the Paris Metro, she got so close to a defibrillator that her mother bought her a trampoline.

The first time she fully grasped the abnormality of her childhood was at a slumber party in the early '90s. Her name was Kallie Campbell and she was with a group of preteens, watching *Pretty Woman* and talking about boys. Kallie (like all of young Kendal's personalities) was a quiet child who listened well, and she noticed something she absolutely could not relate to: they had history. Personal and collective pasts. They knew all about the lives of each other, their classmates, even their teachers. Their community was a collaboration, and they liked it like that. They had boundaries to bounce off and limits to push and a wide safety net to fall into. Kallie Campbell had no borders, no network, no footprint. These kids were trapped in one ID, they had tunnel vision. Kallie thought about her mother, who had taught her sign language, self-defense, card dealing, stunt driving, and CPR. Whose smile was only for her, partners in crime. And at that tender age she thought that one tether was enough. One and strong. She briefly believed that bond would last forever. She thought their shared experience made them inseparable. She was wrong.

The splitting of their family atom had come when she was eighteen.

Kendal finally rebelled against The Game. Fed up with anonymity, she wanted piercings and heels and distinguishing features that her mother was appalled by. She wanted boyfriends and a friendship group and to be recognized and remembered. She wanted to officially exist. She enrolled to study history, politics, and economics and moved into student halls. Her mother declared her a liability and "shut down the op," and in this case The Op was parenting.

Before she vanished, she left Kendal a coded location for a dead drop, and every six months Kendal would find it full of cash. The drop stayed active until Kendal was twenty-one, at which point she found it was under surveillance and never went back.

By the time she graduated, Kendal was disillusioned with life outside The Game. Her university education had too frequently run counter to the values she'd been raised on. Being part of an establishment felt claustrophobic, and she resented the pro-colonial stance that all history seemed to take. She found the boyfriends boring and the friendship groups near impossible to maintain. She felt sure the government had eyes on her, either as a target or a potential recruit, so she changed her name again, built a Russian ID just to piss off her mother, and went to work for Rico Ortez at the Bon Temps agency.

8

She arranged to meet Joel on Hampstead Heath and packed a lunch for Rosie. It was day one, and already work and parenting had overlapped. She chose the heath because she suspected he'd read many London spy thrillers and he'd enjoy the cliché of it. She liked traveling overground, and she had an errand she'd been putting off.

On the train she sat, tense, amazed at the number of people completely absorbed in their phones. Rosie kneeled on the seat next to her, face pressed against the window, watching the terraced gardens zipping past. Her curiosity was interminable, as was her disregard for hygiene. Kendal gently tried to explain. "Ro, literally thousands of people have touched these surfaces, so try not to put your mouth on them." She might as well have been giving her a recipe for borscht.

Rosie was too old for a stroller, and her pace was languid at best, but still it was with plenty of time to spare that they arrived at the eastern entrance of the heath. Kendal took Rosie through woods and up and over the hill, showing her the wild, rugged expanse of land before they had to go to the more sterile, managed area where the playground was.

In an area known as Boadicea's Grave, there was a large mound protected by iron railings and covered in tall Scotch pine and oak trees. It was probably a Bronze Age burial ground, and the mound was thought to be a bell barrow or funereal monument. It was officially known as the Tumulus. These were details Kendal only knew because Khalil loved London's history. She headed for a spot to the east of the mound, *their* bench. Khalil had talked about Boadicea's, sitting on this bench while gazing across green hills, a view that seemed insane in central London. How had the city managed to cling on to this glorious wilderness even as it sprawled ruthlessly in every other direction? Kendal held Rosie's hand and guided her along the pathways that her father had walked. Kendal and Khalil had visited the heath often, in summer to sprawl on the grass, privacy granted by the vastness of the space, and in winter, wrapped in big coats, huddled together, greeting the dog walkers and giggling at the amazing names they gave their dogs.

Sitting on the bench with Rosie tootling happily nearby made Kendal miss him to the point of physical pain. He was the first man who had ever made her feel safe. She was tall, but he was taller; she was strong, but he was stronger. His voice was deep and silken, like good coffee. A voice that she could somehow hear across a noisy room, his frequency a perfect match for hers. His arms; she couldn't pretend the way she felt about his arms was anything more poetic than plain old lust. He worked out, his arms were hot as all fuck.

She allowed herself a small, sad smile, sitting on their bench.

Why was she here? *Just in case.*

It was a phrase he used a lot. So much so that she could anticipate it and say it along with him. She needed to say goodbye, but in the age-old injustice of their craft, there were no goodbyes, no fanfare or medals. No trumpets, flag-wrapped caskets, or releasing of doves. Spies die a quiet death, and, especially if they were good at it, their remembrances will never include their greatest achievements.

Kendal wanted to visit a grave, and Boadicea's would have to do.

Their relationship had been conducted in two stages. Kendal thought of them as *before* and *after*. *Before* had been the big pretense. She was an insurance broker, he a civil servant. In the way of all intense relationships, they had unpicked each other, delved deeply under the skin, and held hands in public. *After*, when he knew too much and she should have left him, disappeared into a different persona. Instead, she stayed, she spoke in codes, they watched each other's backs, they tried to hold on to the joy and innocence of *before*, but it wasn't possible, and still they held hands in public. As if nothing could stop them, as if old rules didn't apply. Love had made them willfully naïve.

Rosie hauled herself up to sit next to Kendal, placing her hand softly into Kendal's pocket. She was so sensitive, Kendal thought, a mind reader.

"You hungry, Peanut?"

Rosie ignored her, lost in her own train of thought.

"You hungry, Ro?"

"Can we go to the park?"

Kendal wanted to tell her, *This was your dad's favorite part of London. This is where we used to sit. If he was alive he would be here with us, and he would know what kinds of trees these are and what happened here long ago.*

Instead, she cracked the lid of a Tupperware box and handed it over.

With Rosie distracted by carrots, Kendal ran her hand discreetly along the underside of the bench. Chewing gum and splintered wood. Her breath caught when her fingertips brushed a cold, curved button, but it was just the rivet. There was nothing to find. From the inside pocket of her coat, she found a tiny black disk, no bigger than a penny, and peeled off an adhesive strip. She attached the disk to the underside of the bench. It contained a single, grainy image, the only one they had taken together—Christmas Day on a deserted English beach. It wasn't a particularly fitting memorial, but it was all she had.

Rosie was looking at her with wide eyes, and Kendal smiled, aiming for neutrally reassuring. She must have missed, because Rosie folded her mouth downward like a sad clown and frowned. "What's wrong?"

"Nothing, my love. Let's go and meet Joel, shall we?"

"Who?"

Kendal chuckled; he *was* utterly forgettable, which might be a useful quality in an asset. "Joel, from downstairs."

"Why?"

"Because he's new here and we can help him make friends."

"But we're new too," Rosie noted.

"That's a good point. I used to live here though, before you were born."

"Here?" Rosie tapped the bench.

"Not literally on this bench." Rosie cackled at the thought.

"But my house wasn't far." Kendal wondered if this was it, if the questions would come, and she would answer. It was apt that it would be here, where she felt close to Khalil for the first time in ages. But Rosie's attention was commandeered by a squirrel, and she took off down the hill.

Joel was standing near an ice cream van in light blue jeans, a dark blue polo shirt, and walking boots; tech bro takes on the outdoors. He wore tortoiseshell-rimmed glasses and a chunky watch, and it was these alone that looked expensive. The glasses suited him, he had good posture, he was a nice-looking guy.

He spotted them approaching and waved happily, then a flicker of concern crossed his face, and he lowered his arm. He walked toward them, his eyes on Kendal. "Are you okay?" he asked as soon as they were within earshot. Rosie looked up at Kendal, as if trying to find the source of Joel's concern.

"Yeah, I'm fine," Kendal answered, surprised. She felt sad, but she wasn't wearing it. Joel stuttered, "Oh, good. You just looked so glum for a second there." He looked like he was going to hug her, and then thought better of it.

She was begrudgingly impressed. "No, I'm all right. Thank you."

"Should I buy us all an ice cream?" He aimed this at Rosie, who nodded *yes, you should.*

They walked toward the ice cream van parked at the edge of the playground. Rosie got a soft serve and Joel picked a Twister, a neon-green-and-yellow swizzle on a stick.

"Interesting choice," Kendal chuckled, watching him work through it.

"It's my first." He held it at arm's length and examined it. "Also my last."

Rosie took off at her version of a sprint, head bobbing like a penguin, and followed a group of kids into the play area. Kendal and Joel sat on a bench next to the slides. The playground was expansive, well-funded, and properly maintained.

"You excited to get started at Glo-Tech?" Kendal asked, never taking her eyes off Rosie.

"Heck yes. I don't know how much more tourist stuff I have in me. I didn't really enjoy M&M's World." He gave her a look. "It's just a really big shop."

Kendal wondered if his childishness would serve him well or be his undoing.

"Rico said you'll be assigned to an app called Cadu. It will be tightly controlled because the government is invested, so don't make any moves until you're completely up to speed with the situation."

"Copy that," he said gleefully, stopping short of a salute. She allowed him the fun of it.

"You'll have a couple of weeks where it won't seem out of place to be curious about people. Ask questions. Find out as much as you can about who everyone is in and outside of work. Notice the cliques, notice the tensions. Gather everything you can about anyone and everyone. Your first impression will set the tone, so make sure it's one that you can maintain, not a complete departure from your personality. The leadership is your priority but you never know who has the ear of the king, so don't rule anyone out. There are some big black holes at the top of the org chart that it would be good to color in, so be aware of big players, new names, anyone commanding a lot of fear or respect. That sort of thing."

Joel nodded and looked genuinely excited. "Absolutely. Makes sense."

"I feel like this will come naturally to you, but accept all the invites, sign up for after-work drinks, join the clubs, get in the gang, be present as much as you can. Be a yes guy."

"Okey doke."

"Stay receptive. Be who people need. You can read a room, right?"

"I think so."

They sat in silence and watched Rosie trying to befriend a pair of kids who were not interested in her. She seemed unperturbed.

Kendal worried she was giving him too much information and not enough context. She paused to let him play scenarios and ask questions.

"Why does Rico call you 96?"

She was surprised but she smiled. "I'm not sure. It's been a long time. He's given me many explanations—it's the atomic number of curium. He's also said it's because I'm the same upside down."

She shrugged. "I turned up to Bon Temps a long time ago, I suspect it was just my file number."

None of these was true, but it was better to give a boring answer than to let his imagination take the wheel.

"Can I have a code name?" he asked, blushing.

"Sure, why not. What would you like it to be?"

Joel's eyes scanned the park for ideas. "Something cool, I guess."

"Twister?" Kendal pitched.

"What about Red Sparrow?"

"I think that's literally a film about a Russian spy. Jennifer Lawrence. What about Red Panda?"

"Because I'm ginger?"

"Because you're so cute." *And endangered*, Kendal thought, but didn't say.

"What about Dragonfly?"

"Dragonflies are the world's most successful hunters. Or did you know that?" Kendal asked with a sideways glance.

"I didn't, but that's cool."

"They have a ninety-seven percent success rate. Probably a good omen."

Joel's phone buzzed in his pocket and he took it out and unlocked it, scrolling through messages in an app Kendal didn't recognize. Kendal noticed he had four-tier identification, and instead of a smart phone he was using a blank handset, no apps, limited connectivity. Impressive. Bon Temps' kit had got a lot better since the '90s.

"One of the main things, when you're in the field, is situational awareness."

Joel tucked the phone back into his pocket. "Sorry."

"You don't have to apologize, but just know. Phones absorb attention more than people realize. Also always worth noting that anyone on a phone probably isn't paying you any attention. When you're in action, stay awake, be aware of the baseline for normal. Be alert to anything that feels out of place."

"Like that guy?" Joel nodded over to a white man in his thirties, bald and wearing sunglasses, a black puffer jacket, and heavy boots. He was sitting on a bench on the far side of the park, between the toilets and the sandpit.

"Yeah, actually, exactly like him," Kendal agreed, surprised she hadn't clocked him herself and realizing it was because she'd been absorbed in their conversation and keeping eyes on Rosie.

"He doesn't have a kid in here."

Kendal stared at the guy. "You sure?"

Joel nodded. "His attention isn't on a particular kid, he doesn't have any stuff, and no one has talked to him. Plus, he's giving me the creeps."

At that moment, the guy seemed to sense them looking. Kendal lifted her hand and waved, followed by a gesture that said *what gives?*

He immediately stood up and walked toward the exit.

"Good call. Rico said you'd be a natural."

Joel beamed. "Why did he just leave, that's a dead giveaway, isn't it?"

"He knew he'd been spotted. A good way to defuse a problem is to confront it head-on."

"That's a fact," said Joel happily, as they watched the dude disappear around the corner.

"How's your short-term memory?" Kendal asked. "It's going to be useful to notice and remember details without taking notes. Observation and retention. Practice them so they become habit."

"I think I'm pretty good at that."

"Oh yeah? What did creepy guy have on his feet?"

"Incredibly ugly boots," Joel answered correctly.

"And the ice cream man, what was he wearing?"

"Hmmm, that's harder. An apron, I think, and a black T-shirt. Maybe a paper hat."

"He didn't have a hat or an apron. You've put them on him in your mind because it fits your image of an ice cream seller. Brains are amazing at invention."

Rosie approached them, kicking a bottle cap across the tarmac. "Will you play with me?"

"What do you want to play?" Kendal asked.

Rosie shrugged and looked bored.

"You wanna play tag?" Joel asked, perching on the edge of the bench.

"Yeah?" Rosie said, uncertain. Joel leaped from the bench, tagged Rosie gently on the arm, and whooped off across the park. "You're it!" he yelled.

Rosie looked at Kendal with a furrowed brow. "What's his problem?"

Kendal laughed. "He's not it."

9

It was a couple of days until school started. The summer was dying out and it created a kind of tension in the house. Kendal was staring at the fridge, which had been emitting a low tone for almost two hours. Rosie was sitting at the breakfast island coloring, openly enjoying the spectacle of Kendal versus fridge.

"Just turn it off," she advised.

Kendal clenched her jaw. "I'm trying! I pressed all the buttons. What does it want?"

Rico had repeatedly referred to it as a "smart house." She'd asked him to disconnect the kitchen from the internet, but he'd just replied, "Okay boomer." From the corner of her eye she saw Joel watering the garden. She slid open the door, and he looked up with a beatific smile. "Lovely day."

"Yeah. Do you know anything about fridges?" she yelled across the lawn.

"Probably an average amount," he answered.

"It won't stop beeping. We're going nuts, could you take a look?"

"For sure, I love a mystery beep."

Joel came up and stood staring at the fridge. It had a series of settings that Kendal had already pressed. He opened and shut the door.

"Do you have a house app on your phone?"

"I have a phone that Rico loaded and I have never used." She plucked the phone from the fruit bowl, unlocked it with her fingerprint, and handed it to Joel, who took a seat at the island next to Rosie. For want of something to do, Kendal offered him a coffee. "Do you have green tea?" he asked politely, and Kendal put the kettle on. After a minute, the beeping stopped.

"Oh thank god for that," Kendal said, enjoying the absence of the sound. Rosie let out a disappointed "aww" without looking up from her project. "I liked it."

"It was trying to warn you to order milk. It's actually amazing. It changes the temperature according to what's in it, it scans the barcodes and tells you when things are about to expire. It can email you recipe suggestions based on what you've got."

"Can we disconnect it?"

He laughed and then looked up and saw she was serious. He widened his eyes conspiratorially and tapped the side of his nose.

"Oh right, yeah, smart. I can turn off the reminders at least."

Kendal noted that he didn't immediately hop up and leave. Lonely, she figured.

Joel placed the phone on the counter and looked around, seemingly for something to say. "Oh, I signed up for an organic veg delivery box. Do you want to go halves on that?"

"Sounds good. Do you cook?"

"I sure do, my mom raised me to help her all around the house. How about you?"

"Not at all, I come from a long line of women that do not belong in the kitchen."

Joel beamed at this response as if a lightbulb had gone off. "Awesome!

A skills swap, then? You teach me . . ."—he glanced at Rosie and managed to bite back whatever he was going to say—"and I'll help in the kitchen?"

"Can you make cake?" Rosie asked suddenly.

"I can make the best Victoria sponge you've ever had."

"For real life?"

"Absolutelydutely."

The pair of them beamed at Kendal from the breakfast bar.

"What?" she asked, pouring the tea.

"Cake day," Rosie answered, as if stating the obvious. Joel was looking at her phone again. "Says here you've got everything we need."

Kendal sighed and ran her hand through her hair. "I'm going to take a hammer to that phone. But yeah, fine. Go nuts."

"Donuts!" Rosie shouted, ecstatic, as Joel hopped off the barstool and rubbed his hands together gleefully. "Cake day!"

Two and a half hours later, Rosie triumphantly placed a piece of cake in front of Kendal. She took a bite and was genuinely surprised at both the flavor and the texture. "Mmmmmm," she lied, trying to scrape it from the roof of her mouth. "Best cake ever."

Rosie ran from the room. "My mumma says it's the best!" Joel popped his head around the door. "I forgot to add an egg. And then I think we overmixed it. And we used salted butter. Please don't report this to my mom."

"Copy that," Kendal replied, slugging coffee to get rid of the taste.

10

On Kentish Town Road there was a radio repair shop called Noisy Buttons, run by Kendal's oldest and arguably only friend, Fini Meridian, who spent most of her days behind the counter fixing kettles, fiddling with synths, and developing and dealing in spy toys.

Fini and Kendal first met, aged eleven, at an international summer camp in the French Alps, called Militante Di Montagna. The camp had been pitched to their respective mothers as an opportunity to develop useful life skills, try skiing, and live in the mountains with other kids. In fact, it had been a training academy for the surfeit children of military and government families. It was rumored to be a breeding ground for psychopaths and was shut down in its sixth year of operation by a UN decree. It had been a rough few weeks, but, to be fair, life skills were definitely developed.

Fini and Kendal stayed in contact through an online Scrabble game they'd been playing for nearly twenty years. Fini was winning 425 to 12.

Kendal had left Rosie for half a day at a "settling in" session at the school. She thought Rosie would fight when she stood up to leave, but for the first time in her life Rosie was surrounded by children her age, furniture her size, and people curious about who she was. When Kendal said goodbye, Rosie barely looked over, just gave a little wave of her arm and went to stand by a girl her own height. She glanced over at her shyly, and thc girl moved a tiny bit closer to Rosie. This was how they made friends, and it killed Kendal to see it. How could she make sure they were nice to each other? How could she protect Rosie from the errant behavior of other four-year-olds? She knew they were rhetorical questions but that didn't make any difference. Rosie looked blissed out. Kendal kept her feelings buried deep. She'd walked out of the school gates and straight to Kentish Town, hoping to find Fini as she'd left her: weird, well, and surrounded by cables.

To get into the shop, Kendal went to the café next door, ordered a coffee to go, and waited for it to arrive. She melted back into the queue and then doubled back to the women's bathroom. In the cubicle closest to the wall, she tugged the toilet roll holder and pushed against the wall to reveal a slim access point into the shop. The wall crunched open and released a cloud of antique-smelling dust. No one had been through for years; the other side was a mountain of junk.

"Shit, sorry!" Kendal heard Fini clambering through from the shop.

"Hang on, let me clear the way!" After a lot of dust and clutter, Fini stood back and saw Kendal emerge from the boxes. Hands on hips, she shook her head and beamed. "No way. Kevin Costner."

Kendal smiled knowingly and waited for her to get it out of her system.

"All the way from Washington, it's Kellyanne Conway!"

"Good one," Kendal chortled, brushing filth from her jeans.

"Welcome home, Kelly Clarkson." Fini paused her mocking to give Kendal a long, heartfelt hug. Fini was a foot shorter than Ken, her physical opposite. She was dark to Ken's pale, petite to Ken's lanky, and funny to Ken's severe. Her hair was a thick mop of curls that framed her face as if she was peeping through. She had a couple of smile lines around her eyes but Kendal couldn't detect any other signs she'd aged. She looked happy and well, and Kendal felt a wave of relief, finally acknowledging that she'd not just missed her friend, but worried about her too. Fini's features revealed none of the same emotions. Instead, in a seductive whisper, she added, "Karen Carpenter, alive and well. Amen." Then chuckled happily to herself. Finally, she released Kendal from her grip.

"You done?" Kendal asked.

"No, wait!" She strained for another one.

"Don't hurt yourself."

"Damn, you'd think I'd have more after all this time. So, who are we today, old lady?"

"Kendal . . . Kendal Carter."

Fini laughed loudly. "Sure, why not? Well, come on in, whatever your name is. Sorry about the mess, no one really does the secret door anymore, it's a bit passé."

"Oh sorry. What are the cool kids using?"

Fini shrugged. "Amazon."

The shop hadn't changed since the last time Kendal saw it; it was as if a hoarder had lived in a science museum since 1987. Boxes of household appliances stacked on shelves to the ceiling. Jewelry display cabinets on both sides of the room full of watches and cameras; anything battery operated, if it ticked, it was all there.

"Five years later . . ." Fini murmured, a lifelong habit of narrating her life as if it were being captioned.

Their friendship was ancient, forged from the ashes of trauma. Despite the best efforts of their parents, they had endured. Fini looked Kendal up and down. "You reproduced?"

"Rude. How can you tell?"

"Dunno, it's a vibe. Your hips have changed. You don't look poised to murder someone . . . and there's a gummy bear on your jeans." Fini plucked it off and looked like she might eat it

"Don't eat that," Kendal said automatically.

"Okay, Mum." Fini smirked, turned back to the shop, and popped it in her mouth.

"And you?" Kendal asked.

Fini picked up a cup from the shelf next to her and gestured for Kendal to follow her into the front of the shop. "No offspring, but my miscreant mother put a lovely house in my name before they shipped her out. So that's nice." She walked around the counter and took a seat. Kendal followed suit on the customer side.

"Shipped her where?"

"I can't tell. She's either in a gulag doing hard time or she's on a cruise in the Med. I only know she's alive because I stuck her with some tech in '94."

"You did what now?"

Fini cradled her coffee and flashed her most mischievous grin.

"I made a microscopic heart monitor that runs off energy from the pulse, and I wanted to test it on a human so I injected it in her while she was asleep."

Kendal was mildly horrified. "Are you serious?"

"Yep, and it still works . . . Not that you can trust something just cos it whistles."

Kendal stared at the walls of electronics and muttered, "Isn't that incredibly dangerous?"

"Oh yeah, I definitely should have told her about it. But I was a teenager and she was one of the most frightening women on the planet."

It wasn't hyperbole. Kendal raised her cardboard cup in a low-key toast. "Mrs. Meridian."

Fini knocked her cup against Kendal's. "To Edith. Wherever she beeps."

"Any gossip on my mother?" Kendal asked quietly.

Fini glanced over her shoulder, flicking a switch under the counter.

"Not a sausage. If anything, she's gone suspiciously quiet. Last I heard she was back in town, but that was years ago."

"I thought I could feel a chill in the air." Kendal laughed but it was hollow. The safest place for her mother to be was far away. The UK suddenly felt like a very small island, indeed.

"You think she's still in The Game?" Kendal asked.

"Hard to say. She never struck me as the type to retire. *Never give up, never let go, that's how the bastards get you.*"

Fini's impression was eerily accurate.

"Keep an ear out for her. Let me know if she surfaces. I'd like to maintain a healthy distance. Ideally an ocean or two."

Fini nodded, understanding. "I'll send some feelers to the boomers. There's probably a fax machine in here somewhere. Or a carrier pigeon." They shared a dirty chuckle from the old days.

"Tread carefully though, you know what she's like."

"Like a seagull on a Saturday," Fini agreed. She produced a packet of cookies from behind the glass counter and tore them open. They reveled in one another's company; the friendship hadn't missed a beat.

The counter they were leaning on was full of historic tech. Pagers, novelty landline phones, and the original Nokia 3310, which Kendal pointed at nostalgically. "That was my first phone. I had it in purple."

"Such classics. You can't beat the burners, they're like a pair of proper boots."

They looked closely at each other. Fini hadn't lost the air of someone who knew who they were and why they were here. She had always been this way. She thought that Kendal looked tired, and uncharacteristically anxious.

"So what brings you back to this haunted crevice of the universe?" she asked gently, leaning forward as if she wanted to reach out and touch her friend, but knowing that affection might repel her.

Kendal smiled, but there was no joy in it. "Rico Ortez, in a nutshell."

Fini nodded and it was clear that she wasn't surprised. "I noticed Bon Temps was doing well. How is Rico? Still hot?"

"Older, richer, none the wiser."

"Sounds about right." They touched cups again. It was like time travel—for a second they were adults, and preteens, and every age in between.

"So how can we kit you up against that slimy bastard?"

Kendal pulled the phone Rico had given her from her back pocket and put it on the counter. “Have a peep inside this and see what he’s up to? Also, what’s your reach like in Switzerland?”

Fini’s face lit up. “Surprisingly, I have a Swiss lover and they are tooled up to the eyeballs.”

“Why do I feel like that’s true of many destinations?”

Fini sighed contentedly and stared out of the window as if in a wistful dream. “I know, my international quest for passion continued in your absence. A paramour in every port. Beloved beyond borders.”

“How many do you see in real life?”

Fini frowned and tsked at her. “Don’t be so provincial, Kendal Carter. All the best love stories happen in here.” She tapped the side of her head. “What do you need in Switzerland, and I’ll see if they can help.”

Kendal gave as many details about Lula’s killing as she could without revealing too much about her own time in Zurich. “I couldn’t see anything in the media,” she explained, “but I might have accidentally become a dinosaur in the tech department. I need an update on what’s happened while I was thinking I could just use a VPN and be covered.”

Fini nodded. She didn’t condescend; instead, she picked up Kendal’s phone, took it over to the console behind the counter, and plugged it in.

“It’s hard to stay on top of it. Every time there’s a security development there’s some hacker who can crack it. It’s like a Road Runner cartoon, all just chasing each other toward a demise that never quite comes.”

“Meep meep,” they said in unison.

Fini kept her eyes on the screens. “So you’re out of retirement?”

“Not really, just taking a hiatus from the cold.”

“What’s Rico got you doing?”

“Babysitting a nerd. I think he’s clean, but it’s the house. It’s all connected. The management app is on the phone. Rico calls it smart, but I just want a sense check.”

Fini shook her head. “Why do people buy this stuff? Does it require military-grade common sense to know that it can all be hacked?”

"I can't tell if they don't know, or if they don't care," Kendal agreed. "Literally every appliance knows my birthday and my mother's maiden name."

Fini feigned outrage. "But that is redacted!"

Kendal chuckled. "Rico says the house is one of the good guys, but who knows anymore."

"Them versus them."

This was an adage handed down from the previous generation.

"Amen."

Fini clacked green varnished nails thoughtfully against the glass. "The appliances will be benign, the app itself is the real problem, so I'd delete that to start with. But while you're here, let's get you some kit." She turned around and pressed a button to slide a cabinet of harmless gadgets down into the counter. It should have been a cool move, but instead, it jammed on a Pringles lid and Fini had to ram it to unstick. "Sorry, not very James Bond, is it, having everything covered in shite." The original display case lowered to reveal a bunch of much more exciting gear. Fini gazed at the cabinet. "I'll give you some trackers for the kid and you can use a burner to keep tabs if you need to."

She handed Kendal an unmarked white box that rattled. "Just stick them in her clothes, jacket, bag, et cetera. Mind the glue though, I got one stuck on a finger once and it took the bloody print off. Ooh, you'll like this." She pulled out a metal cylinder that looked a bit like a lipstick.

"It's a banger. Press the button on the bottom and it'll kill everything you can see for three hundred feet. It'll blow all your fuses, fry your Wi-Fi, pop any civilian laptops, and phones . . . Not much use for day-to-day but fun to have in reserve."

She handed it over to Kendal, who admired the design. "Nice." She popped it in her bag. Fini went on, "It's also good if you've got a tail driving anything made after 2015. Super annoying for any Teslas nearby but still, fun for us."

She pulled what looked like a Glade PlugIn from a shelf. "This is quite good. It's a temporary fix for if you want a bit of privacy and you think there might be ears in the room. Just flip this little switch, and when the charge light is green it's creating interference, so your phone and Wi-Fi signals and any cameras and bugs will scramble. Then when you're done telling secrets you can just turn it off, and they'll think their systems glitched."

"Sounds good. What do I do about my phone?"

"I think rather than fight it you just give them something to look at. I can create a clone if you want, redirect everything that's connected through an alt-account, so you basically get a bot running interference. It'll let them see anything harmless, your Spotify and Amazon, chats to your mum friends, and your pedometer or whatever, and I'll add an incognito screen. It's just a smoke screen, but it means they've got something to track so you can send them on a mess-around if you need to."

"Sounds good."

"I'll clean this up and put the clone on it, and I'll beef up the security. Everything that's proper private will be on your second screen." She held the phone up to show Kendal how to navigate it.

"It needs to stay operational, in case the school calls."

Fini gave Kendal a long look as if recalibrating the person she was looking at. "I'll give you a burner backup as well, so you have one that's completely clean."

"Thanks, buddy. It's so good to see you. You must come over for spaghetti hoops some time, meet the fridge."

Fini turned away and sat on a tall spinning chair in front of three computer monitors. She turned them on, put on goggles, and connected Kendal's phone, visibly melting into her mental work zone. Kendal watched, entranced.

After a few minutes, Fini murmured, "It's pretty clean, but spyware is so easy to install now they can just put it in and take it out willy-nilly." She was bouncing from screen to screen, and then looked at Kendal with a frown.

"You into games and stuff? Have you installed any apps?"

"No."

"KC, be honest now. Are you the kind of person who's like 'allow cookies' because you can't be arsed to manage settings?"

"I'm not that bad, no."

"There's weird things running in the background. Have you connected the camera to anything? Been on work calls or something? There's some glitchy code, but it could just be detritus from Candy Crush or something. Rico recycling his handsets."

She continued to tinker at her computer.

"So tell me about your pet nerd, what's he like?"

"Yeah, Joel, he seems harmless."

"Kendal and Joel? Sounds like a reality show."

"We're not a couple," Kendal snapped back, more aggressively than intended.

Fini went back into the zone and tinkered away, then suddenly she stopped and shouted, "Kurt Cobain! Oh my god, how was that not top of my list?" They both chuckled, and Fini looked rueful and shook her head. "Kendal Carter, you're such a knob."

When Kendal was ready to go, Fini gave her two phones and a lighter with Noisy Buttons branding. Kendal took it, but she didn't approve. "Who smokes anymore?"

Fini tutted. "I know, but I've got to do some marketing and I thought merch was the way to go. It's also a thumb drive, if it helps. Speaking of cash money, can I invoice Rico incognito?"

"Always."

"And maybe send him here to shop? Sounds like he doesn't buy his toys out the back of a van these days."

"Will do." Kendal put her bag over her shoulder and was about to walk to the back of the shop, but Fini shook her head.

"You can leave out the door like a normal person, all the cameras on this road will catch is a blur."

"You're a genius, Fini Meridian."

"Welcome back, friendo." She held up her cup and blew Kendal a kiss. Kendal turned her coat inside out and pulled on a baseball cap to leave the shop, enjoying Fini's patch of CCTV freedom. She headed for the train station, and on the platform she pulled out her nice, clean phone to play with and scrolled through the thread called "Reception Parents," where they discussed the upcoming year, school trips, PE kits, and lunch money. Kendal enjoyed it, so earnest and innocent. She was hoping for a life where school colors were her first priority.

11

For the first time in her adult life, Kendal had first-day nerves. Through all the parent-teacher intros, the school tours, the welcome sessions, and settling-in days, she'd been fine. Scouting for any sign of temps and making a note of the school's security, or lack thereof. She didn't love that anyone could just walk into the playground; there were no checkpoints or guards, bar an admittedly efficient administrator. She'd wanted to hack their tech, break into the teacher's lounge and search it. She wanted to do active shooter drills and give Rosie a run-through the school for the best hiding places and exit strategies. Obviously, there was a possibility that she was being overprotective.

The background tension that agents and asset runners carried at all times had taken up a familiar position across her shoulders, and Kendal sat on the edge of the bed, taking deep breaths to settle her mind. In four and a half years, she hadn't let Rosie out of her sight for more than a couple of hours. Playgroup with Mrs. O in Switzerland was the extent of their time apart; Kendal had been a few hundred feet away and Mrs. O was a fierce guardian. Kendal had trusted her implicitly. This was something new.

The teachers would have hundreds of kids to supervise; the form teacher, Ella Baines, seemed soft and tired. The other children would have personalities and politics and some of them might be assholes. But worst of all, if Rosie needed her, she couldn't just call out. For the first time in her life, she'd be on her own. It felt excruciatingly unnatural to Kendal, and she was a woman who lived by her instincts. She shook it off and stood up to get ready. She'd put trackers in Rosie's bag, coat, and shoes, and if she ran at full tilt she could be at the school in six minutes and thirty-eight seconds. It was fine.

Her enormous wardrobe had been filled by Joe & Pete on the Bon Temps data desk. Joe & Pete were men in their twenties. They were posh and cocky. They had googled "mum clothes" and pressed Select All. After a lifetime of black jeans, black tee, she was now looking at an incredible array of oatmeal, fleece, and florals. All the shoes were variations on a theme—military chic? She pulled arbitrary items off hangers and put them on. They were designer labels, and the good cuts and expensive stitching helped her get into character—a wealthy, working, well-organized mum. Every day, she practiced walking down the stairs silently, but they were old mahogany wood and they creaked. She was getting better at them though.

In the kitchen, Rosie and Joel were debating the nutritional content of Coco Pops. She walked into the room, and they both stopped to admire her. "Who's this fancy boy?" Rosie asked, quoting god knows what.

Joel smiled benignly. "You look nice."

She gave him a look that made it clear his opinion on her appearance was not required.

"Her royal Rosiness and I are making breakfast. Can I get you some coffee?" Rosie squeaked with delight at this nickname, and Kendal was momentarily gutted that she wasn't a more playful mother. Gratefully, she accepted a coffee. Joel wasn't supposed to be upstairs, but Rosie enjoyed him. She habitually went out on the balcony and summoned him up to play. Kendal could admit their relationship was sweet and Joel was a good influence. The house, the man, the whole setup echoed around Kendal uncomfortably, but these guys, they barely registered a shift. Rosie might have been living here, with Joel, her whole life.

"We have to leave in twenty minutes, Ro."

"I'm going with Joel."

An alliance had formed. If Kendal's feelings were hurt it didn't show. Joel cleared his throat and slipped away through his door.

"Let's go and get dressed," she said as her phone buzzed.

"No."

The text was from school. "Please remember to pack a snack for your child. ONLY fruit or veg. And remember to bring in your pound coins for the Year 6 Welcome Cake Stall!" The text from school was immediately duplicated on the Reception Mums WhatsApp, and again in an email.

"Pick a lane," she mumbled, throwing an apple from the bowl and a fiver from her pocket into Rosie's unicorn backpack, and picking her up off the stool. "NO!" Rosie yelled directly into Kendal's ear, simultaneously wrapping her arms and legs around her in direct contradiction to this.

Rosie's uniform was blue and white and came with a hat. Kendal loved and hated it in equal measure. It was unbelievably cute, but it immediately identified Rosie's school, which she hated. It did make them indistinguishable from each other once they were inside the school, which she liked, but it stopped her having any unique or identifying outfits, which she both loved and hated.

The ten-minute walk took closer to twenty because Rosie was a child born with absolutely no sense of urgency.

"Mumma, when's my birthday?"

"March."

"Is that soon?"

"No."

"Is it after your birthday?"

"Sort of. My birthday's just gone."

"Did you have a cake?"

"No."

"Did you get presents?"

"No."

"Aww. Why not?"

Kendal allowed a brief flashback of her childhood birthdays to montage across her thoughts. It didn't take long. "Because birthdays are for kids."

And that's how they'll find you, registering your birthday on every website in town. She heard her mother scolding through time, because she had got a card from a classmate. It hadn't even been her birthday; she'd made it up to see how it felt to have one. Kendal felt bad. "Next year you can make me a card and we'll bake a cake if you like." But Rosie had lost interest in the topic. They walked past a woman dragging a dog down the hill.

"Mumma, can we have a puppy?"

"No."

"Can we have a rabbit?"

"No."

"If a bird flew into our house could we let it live there?"

"We could let it live with Joel."

"Is Joel my daddy?"

Kendal stopped abruptly. Rosie had never asked about her father before. Naïvely, Kendal had thought she might never. She squatted so they were at eye level and spoke gently. "No, honey. He's our neighbor. He's our friend." *Your daddy is dead.* She couldn't bring herself to say it, had never said it to Rosie. She had spent many hours wondering when the question would come and what she would do when it did. She braced for Rosie to interrogate further, but she had gone quiet.

Rico had suggested a relationship with Joel as part of the cover, but the pitch had been halfhearted and he nearly got killed selling it in. "It plays, Ken, women your age love a nice guy with cash and no kids. Trust me." It was a hard pass.

The school came into view, and Rosie slowed even further. They could hear the bell ring and the morning song start up. Year 6 had weaponized "Bring It All Back to Me" by S Club 7, so it would be stuck permanently in the heads of everyone in a half-mile radius. It was the catchy air raid siren to let parents know they were almost late. Kendal's plan was to arrive every day exactly on the minute and avoid all contact with other parents. Rosie's ability to stay undercover was limited, Kendal's was not. In the half days and sessions, she'd noticed there was a nanny/parent divide and tried to make her own role ambiguous, exuding a professional disinterest. She would limit interactions to a polite smile, a jovial eye roll, but never ever volunteer to bake. Kendal believed that as long as Rosie stayed in the middle of the pack, she could do six years of quiet indifference and then bail. Inside the playground, Kendal knelt and buttoned Rosie's school-sanctioned cardigan. She felt like she was leaving her in a war zone.

"What's your assignment, Ro?"

"Stand strong, stay cool, trust my insects," Rosie parroted back, close enough. A nearby mum chuckled at them. Kendal watched as the kids disappeared into the classroom. Rosie walked off; she'd made a friend and disappeared without a backward glance. Kendal left in a daze, as if she'd lost a limb, a forty-pound limb that she couldn't live without.

She was walking behind a slim woman with jet-black shiny hair cut in a bob, clutching car keys and a phone. She was wearing a blue striped shirt, cropped capri trousers, and black loafers with no socks. Even from behind, Kendal thought she seemed what her mother would have called "well put together." But there was something off about her stride. She was upset. Ahead of them a black Mercedes was parked up and a bald dude was leaning against the driver's side scowling. When he saw the woman he shook his head.

"It's not funny, Sash, give me the keys."

Kendal was a solid thirty yards behind her but still heard him clearly. She couldn't hear the woman's reply but saw her jangle the keys angrily. When she got level with him, the bald guy grabbed her arm and held it tightly. Ken didn't love how tightly, but she was loath to get involved in a domestic on her first day of school. She watched as the guy leaned in, the woman's posture unchanged. She looked more weary than scared, and Kendal relaxed slightly, keeping her eyes on the guy, hoping he'd notice and back off a bit. He did notice, and instead of standing down and releasing her arm, he held her tighter and glared at Kendal.

"For Christ's sake, Alex, it's her first day. It's *normal* for both parents to wave her off."

Kendal was level with them now, and as she passed, she glanced back. "Excuse me, are you okay?" she asked the woman, who looked at her, surprised.

"Mind your own fucking business, yeah?" the guy said to Kendal with a sneer. The woman gave him an incredulous frown. "I'm fine, thanks." She shrugged out of his grip. "Don't mind him, he's just hungry."

Kendal laughed and carried on but heard the woman turn back to the guy and add, "And being a bit of a twat."

Kendal realized she'd misread the situation. He'd been holding her tightly because she'd leave if he didn't. Not so much a bully as a wannabe strong man. She walked on, the heaviness of Rosie's absence settled again, and she was staring down the hill when she noticed a woman had fallen into step with her.

"All right? I'm Sam's mum. Yours is Rosie, right?" She gestured with her head toward the school. "First day is rough but it gets easier. Suddenly we're free, and then you just go home and look at pics of them till pickup. You fancy a coffee?" She nodded over the road as if there was a café there, but it was just a line of houses.

"I can't. Work. Thanks, though."

"Another time, maybe? You might as well make some mum friends. It helps with the birthday parties. Take it from a seasoned pro."

"Another time, for sure."

"Okay, Rosie's mum. Should we even bother with our real names?"

"I'm Kendal."

"Natalie. You can call me Nat if we get on okay."

"Thanks, you can call me Ken either way."

She laughed at that.

"Sam's mum, formerly known as Nat. I'm like Prince!"

Kendal wondered if she was drunk. "Are you an artist?" Nat let out a laugh that was so loud it dragged attention from people across the road. Kendal pushed her sunglasses from her head to her face.

"Piss artist maybe," Nat muttered and then shook it off and said more brightly, "No, lawyer. How about you?"

"Publishing."

"Ooh. I had you pegged for a Pilates instructor or something."

Kendal smiled but remained impassive.

"No offense!"

They walked in silence for an awkward few seconds.

"What kind of lawyer?" Kendal asked, trying to sound more interested than she was.

"Corporate. Hence the perma-pajamas. Barely ever out the house anymore. My kingdom for a court date, you know?"

Kendal offered a wry smile, because, no, how could she possibly know?

"So is it Pilates?" Nat asked, as if it was a normal question at this point in their conversation.

"Is what Pilates?" Kendal replied, shaking off the segue.

"That keeps you in shape?"

"Oh. Yeah, sometimes. You?"

"Boxing, mostly. I joined a club, it's flippin' brilliant." She tensed one of her arms and Kendal saw real muscle. She lifted her glasses up and nodded, impressed.

"Two tickets to the gun show."

Nat laughed loudly again.

"Keeps me sane, to be honest, Rosie's mum."

Nat stopped to cross the road. "'Kay, well, see you around for more scintillating schoolyard small talk." She waved without turning back. Kendal watched her go with a bemused chuckle. She did look like she'd be a fair fight.

12

What's a 'portrait op'?" Joel asked, and Kendal had to smile. "Observation. Eyes open, mouth closed. It's a Rico-ism."

"He's used a lot of terms I don't get."

"Yeah, he likes to feel like the smartest guy in the room. If it helps, he's made most of them up."

Joel didn't answer. He seemed unwilling to be mean about people. It was a quality that Kendal liked, because it was a close neighbor of STFU.

"I've been studying tradecraft," he announced proudly. "He gave me a pamphlet."

She smiled at him like he was a toddler doing a trick. "A pamphlet?"

"Yeah, it's just like, undercover 101."

"Awesome. What did you learn?"

"The first rule is, you are always being watched."

"Crikey."

"You wanna know the other rules?"

"Let's go out in the field and see them in action."

"Yes, ma'am!" He hopped off his stool and went to get ready.

"Meet me out the front in T minus ten, Red Panda," Kendal shouted after him.

"Ah man, Red Panda," he said quietly, thinking she was out of earshot. She chuckled.

They were in a café near Regent's Park, a quiet, nondescript place serving English breakfasts and beans on toast. They ordered drinks and took a seat.

"Have a look around. Who would you peg as the biggest potential threat?"

Joel peered comedically around the café. "The big guy, by the door."

"Why him?"

"He could beat me in a fight."

"What if the thing we're worried about isn't physical violence though? What if we're trying to identify an undercover hostile?"

"Still him, he looks pretty hostile to me."

Kendal accepted this answer with a flicker of disdain.

"You don't agree?" Joel asked with an eyebrow raised.

"I would argue that he is one of the least likely to be dangerous in the room."

"Why?"

"He's got his back to the door, his headphones in, and his attention buried in his phone. He's taken his coat off and he ordered a toastie. So he's not in a hurry and he has no need to make a quick exit. He's not worried about the entrance . . . And not to be presumptuous, but I've never seen an active hostile order a tuna melt, you know?"

"Maybe that's how they trick you."

"Yeah, absolutely. That's a good point. And that's all useful for when you're flying under the radar. Be that guy, above suspicion."

"How do you even know what he ordered?"

"I listened. The second most useful sense."

"After smell?" he joked.

"I know it's dumb, and I'm not trying to patronize you. But there's a difference between looking and seeing. It does take practice."

Joel nodded as if impressed, although Kendal noted he was being polite and it didn't seem genuine.

"So who would you like for it?" he asked.

"The guy in the corner next to the counter."

"The guy with the puppy?" Joel scoffed.

"The best-trained puppy I've ever seen. That's a military-grade spaniel. He has black coffee in that cup. A boiling hot drink can be a weapon, in a pinch. He's looking at that paper, but hasn't turned the page since we got here. He could be doing the crossword, and that's what we're supposed to think, but that pen he's holding could be tactical."

Now Joel looked genuinely impressed. "Wow, okay, Sherlock."

"You need to habitually gather the information that is available to you and assess it on its own merit. You need to drop, or at least acknowledge, your bias and make sure it's not in charge. Why did you choose the kid by the door? Because he's big and brown?"

"No!" Joel looked affronted, but he blushed. "I'm not racist."

"Maybe you're not, but maybe you've been fed this profile of a bad guy your whole life, and it lives in you as unconscious bias. Your subconscious can be useful, but you have to know when it's leading you astray."

Joel nodded, considering this.

"Close your eyes."

Joel did as he was told.

"How many people are in the room right now?"

Joel barely hesitated. "Six."

"And what can you tell me about them?"

"There's Puppy and Toastie. There's a couple looking out the window that are maybe tourists, waiting for the coach to the airport or have just arrived after a long flight."

"Very good. Do you know what they're wearing?"

Joel tutted and shook his head. "She's in a dark wool coat, he's in North Face?" he ventured.

"Okay, who else?"

"There's a mother and her kid in the corner."

"Why isn't the kid in school?" Kendal challenged.

Joel furrowed his brow. "Too young?"

"Very good. That everyone?"

Joel nodded and opened his eyes, looking around.

"Did I get it right?"

"Not even close."

"Ah heck, how come?"

"You didn't count any of the people who work here. Why don't they count, Joel? Do you hate hospitality staff? Are they not worth your time?"

Joel looked stricken. "Ah shucks, you said *in the room*, I assumed you meant customers."

"When you're active, keep an eye out for *invisibles*, the cleaners and caterers, the drivers, delivery guys, anyone who has a remit to be in the room but no formal identity. That's who Rico sends into high-profile situations."

Joel looked demoralized. Kendal realized he responded better to positive reinforcement.

"Hey, don't be sad. It's early days. Let's head outside."

They walked across Regent's Park from east to west. Despite the gray skies, it was a festival of outdoor pursuits. Joggers versus strollers versus dogs versus cyclists.

"The woman who just walked past. What can you tell me about her?"

"Mid-thirties, burgundy vest, appalling shoes. Might be visiting friends in the area on an extended trip or is working on something in the UK but normally lives in the US."

It was Kendal's turn to be impressed.

"How did you get all that?"

"Her bag said T.J. Maxx, and in the UK it's TK, for some reason. All the other dogs around here are off the leash, but hers is still on even though he looks trained and docile, so maybe it's not her dog. She's looking around like a tourist, and she smiled at me, so almost certainly American." He looked unsure. "Unless that's unconscious bias?"

Kendal chuckled.

"No, I think that's fair."

They walked on. Kendal was feeling something she hadn't experienced for a long time. So long that it took a minute to name it. It was *fun*. She was enjoying herself for the first time in years. "What's next?" Joel said keenly. Kendal realized he was having fun too.

She handed him a box of matches. "I'm going to choose someone at random, and you need to plant this box on them. Find out their name and where they're from and at least one weird fact about them."

"Oh boy!" Joel replied eagerly, scanning the park for potential targets.

"Her." Kendal indicated a young woman on her phone sitting on a bench.

Joel branched off and Kendal walked on, paused by a fence, and leaned back to watch him at work. He approached her by talking to her dog, a French bulldog. He lowered to a squat and looked up to the woman with what Kendal thought he meant to be a seductive interest. The dog reacted badly and Joel hopped up to standing. From Kendal's vantage point it was clear the woman was giving one-word answers and was keen to get back to her phone. Joel took a seat on the bench near her, and she not very discreetly rolled her eyes and talked to him without looking up.

Kendal flinched at Joel's ramming of the brick wall. Eventually, with a savage flicker in her eyes, the woman told Joel in no uncertain terms to go away.

He hopped off the bench and walked back toward Kendal with bright red cheeks and a pained grimace.

"How did that go?"

"Don't think she wants to go to Disneyland with me."

"What's her name?"

"Gemma. She wouldn't give me her surname."

"Where is she from?"

"Fuckoffly. I think it's south of the river."

His goofy smile made Kendal all-the-way laugh. "Ah, never mind."

Joel kicked a rock balefully across the path. "Why was she so hostile?"

"By her age, most beautiful women have had enough of your bullshit."

Joel nodded with a sageness beyond his years. "Fair enough. Why should they give me their attention when there's Instagram?"

His pep returned in full force. He was not a man to be down for long, Kendal noted.

"I planted the matches though." He beamed.

"Oh really, I didn't even notice. How did you do it?"

"Stuck them down the dog's jumper."

Kendal glanced back and saw the dog squirming unhappily.

She rewarded Joel with a genuine grin and a clap on the back.

"Sneaky, I love it."

They walked through the park, admiring the late-summer roses. At a coffee stand Joel bought them drinks and they sat side by side on a bench watching middle-aged dads five-a-side teams be actively bad at soccer.

"Can I ask you a personal question?" Joel asked mildly.

"You can try," Kendal answered, registering a slight increase of tension in her gut.

"Is Rico Rosie's father?"

Kendal let loose a loud, unabashed laugh. "Good grief." She laughed again, it felt good. "What on god's green earth gave you that idea?"

"He described you as family."

"Yeah, like a fun uncle. Not lovers." There was a silence that Kendal broke first. "Her dad died before she was born. She's never asked me about him, but now she's started school, I think she's going to realize it's not normal."

"I don't think there's as much emphasis on *normal* anymore. And there will be others. I grew up without a dad . . ."

"I guess I thought the longer I waited, the more sophisticated her understanding would be. I'm not sure how to tell her."

Joel seemed to consider this. "Most of the guidebooks say just tell the truth."

Inwardly, Kendal bristled. She didn't like being advised by a twenty-six-year-old man-child, even if he was being kind. Luckily one of the dads hoofed the ball at the goal, missing by many miles and sending it pounding toward them. Joel leaped up, ever the Labrador, and punted it back at the game in a smooth arch. Bang on target. He tried not to look too pleased.

"That was well done," Kendal noted.

"Thanks. Felt like a lot of pressure."

He sat back down and scanned the park. After two sessions he seemed more aware of his surroundings, and for the first time Kendal thought he might do okay undercover.

"How much training did Rico give you? Apart from the pamphlet."

"He took me to the mall the first week I got here."

"Oh god, why?"

Joel chuckled. "He said it was the ideal training ground. We did a walk-through where he pointed out the cameras and stuff. He called me *Donnie* all day. I thought maybe he just wanted someone to go shopping with."

"He calls all the trainees Donnie or Marky."

"Why?"

"Because he's old and he thinks New Kids on the Block references are funny. What else did you do?"

"We played *Call of Duty*, and he said it was weapons training because a lot of those guns are fairly realistic, but he got super antsy because I beat him pretty bad. But I've been playing that game for twenty years. Anyway, then he told me not to do or say anything stupid and my training was finished. He said he'd send me a certificate, but so far he hasn't."

Kendal suppressed a chuckle.

"I'm just now realizing he was messing with me."

Kendal laughed openly at that. "Don't worry about it. He wears a nice suit, but he's a cheap bastard."

"He bought three shirts for twenty pounds," Joel added with a mischievous giggle.

"*Do* you have any weapons experience?"

"I grew up hunting, so I know rifles. And I went to ranges with my mom when I was a kid. It's been a while, but I know the basics."

Kendal nodded her approval, and Joel shifted in his seat with visible pleasure.

"The first time I experienced Rico, he was the keynote speaker at a tech conference in Ottawa."

Kendal nearly choked on her coffee. "What?"

"It was called 'Real-World Security in the Gaming Landscape.' Something like that. He kept calling us nerds. He wore sunglasses for most of his presentation, and then right at the end he took them off to prove that eye contact is the most effective way to communicate."

Kendal didn't hide her surprise. Joel, clearly enjoying the look on her face, went on. "He had a PowerPoint but it was mostly pictures of other people in sunglasses. One of the slides just had that green code from *The Matrix*."

"Why would he do that?"

"I guess he thought it was techy."

"No, why would he do a keynote? That's pretty high-vis for a man in his position."

"I think he was schmoozing for contracts. It seemed like his first time. Most of what he said didn't make any sense and he kept saying 'the way Bon Temps operates is non-creepy.' And, like, if you have to say it . . ." He giggled lightly, and Kendal thought he seemed incredibly young for his age.

"After the presentation he pulled me aside and said he liked the cut of my jib." Joel delivered the phrase in a hammy English accent.

"God, he's so ridiculous sometimes."

They got up to head home. When they reached the front door, Joel veered left to his entrance and Kendal paused. "You're going to be really good at Glo-Tech. You're ready."

Joel puffed with pride. "Thank you. That means a lot."

13

By the time the first term was halfway through, Rosie was absolutely done. When Kendal picked her up she looked like a child who had seen some terrible things. The teacher and TA stood by the door, waving the kids off and reporting any injuries or accidents to the parents. Rosie walked past Kendal toward the gate, dragging her oversized unicorn backpack along the floor. She hadn't even asked for a snack.

"You okay, Ro?"

"Do I have to go there every day?"

"Not every day. Tomorrow is Saturday and next week is a holiday."

That seemed to lift her spirits, and she handed Kendal her bag.

"Did you bring me a treat?"

"A banana."

"I want crisps."

"What did you have for lunch?"

Rosie looked as if she was thinking about it. "No idea." She stopped abruptly to shove her face into a jasmine bush, emerging after a few seconds with twigs and leaves in her hair.

"You good?"

"Smells nice."

Kendal handed her a half-peeled banana and she absent-mindedly took a bite. Kendal watched her, helpless to know what was happening in her young mind and with no way of finding out. Her terminal curiosity regarding Rosie's experience made her feel weak.

When they got back, Joel was in the kitchen staring at a recipe book. He had a tray of roasted vegetables and a blender.

"Jolly rice?" Rosie asked, her eyes wide and mouth hanging open. Another ritual had formed; Friday was jolly rice night. Rosie had told Joel about Mrs. O and her amazing (jollof) rice, and ever since, Joel had been trying to perfect the recipe. It was invariably bland but you had to give him credit, he persevered. "I'm giving it another go, Ro. This week I'm adding cayenne pepper!"

"Smells nice," Rosie said with encouragement. As she spoke she walked over to Joel and wrapped her arms around his legs. "Thank you."

Joel looked surprised and patted her on the head. "You're welcome. How was school?"

"I'm not going back."

"Oh no! Why not?" Joel and Kendal shared a concerned look. She was not herself this afternoon, and neither of them had the faintest idea how to broach it.

Rosie ignored him. She walked away and picked up the remote. She flipped on the TV and plunked herself onto the beanbag with a satisfied grunt. Sometimes she had the mannerisms of a forty-year-old middle manager.

"Is she allowed screen time before dinner?" Joel asked, pouring tinned tomatoes into the blender. In her mind's eye, Kendal ran across the room, leaped over the counter, and sucker punched him into next week. Luckily, Rosie answered for her.

"I HAVE AN HOUR A DAY AT A TIME OF MY CHOOSING WITHIN REASON," she shouted from the beanbag with the exact right amount of indignation in her voice. Kendal simply ignored the question.

That evening, once Rosie was finally asleep, having satisfied her curiosity regarding fish's ears, and the difference between a pen and a pencil, and with repeated readings of *Weasels*, Kendal sat in the kitchen alone. She stared at her laptop and drummed her nails on the table. She was looking for identification of the men who had murdered Lula but was repeatedly finding herself butting against brick walls. Her contacts within the Ministry of Defence and other government-affiliated organizations had gone to ground, her network conspicuously silent. She decided to relent to pressure from Rico and call Joe & Pete on the data desk. It was 9:30 PM, so she wasn't sure they'd be there.

The phone only rang once before a young, male voice answered.

"96, go for Joe."

"Hi, Joe. How are you?"

"Not bad, ma'am, how can I help?"

"Please call me Kendal or K."

"Okay—K," he faltered, but he caught on quick.

"Are you there all night, Joe?"

"During extended office hours you will generally connect to Pete and me together, at the data desk on site. Outside of those hours you will always be able to reach either myself or Pete with slightly reduced access unless there is an operational reason you might need full support in which case we will both be on board as long as is necessary to ensure your well-being and the smooth running of your project."

"Are you reading a script?"

"I have it memorized." There was a distinct pause where Joe clearly wanted to put "ma'am" at the end of his sentence, as if he had mimed it.

"I wanted to know if there was any more insight into the killing of Lula Ozolinaš."

She could hear Joe typing and pictured him trapped in Rico's dingy cave all night on his own, surrounded by tech and pizza boxes. She brushed the image away as clichéd and recast him in a sharp suit and glass office.

"We managed to find out a bit more about the dark net site where the job was posted. It's called BanJax. It's popular in Europe but not a major player internationally. It looks like the job went up following the release of an Interpol Red Notice. We couldn't get much on the source except it was likely UK based. The guys who picked up the job appear to be from an Albanian mob, but we can't confirm it had any mob affiliation beyond some heavies who might have been moonlighting. We couldn't find any link to you or to the victim, and we cross-checked against all prior Bon Temps assignments. Unless there are any other occasions where you might have angered Albania?"

"Rico would be best placed for that info."

"He was confident it was not linked to us."

"So I was flagged by Interpol and it prompted someone to order a hit? What's your take on it, Joe?"

"We're still digging. But in general BanJax jobs are pretty amateur—small-time drug dealers, jealous partners, that sort of level. We were interested in the price tag attached to your ticket. It was low, which suggests the hit was listed as civilian; an untrained, low-risk target. It was nowhere near what it should have been for someone with your . . . expertise."

"What was it, out of interest?"

"Ten thousand sterling. The UK average is around fifty K."

"Well, that's insulting."

"For a target like you it might normally reach into the millions."

"So maybe the job *wasn't* a hit?" She could hear the slight smile in his voice. Pleased they agreed.

"That's our thinking too. For that money it might have been what the dark net calls a redelivery."

"Kidnapping?"

"Not exactly."

"Pretend I'm a different generation and not up to speed with the lingo, Joe."

"For that sum of money we think they were either supposed to deliver a message, or they were supposed to bring you somewhere. We think when they realized they were in the wrong place and couldn't do the job they just . . ."

"Shot her for no reason?"

"Collateral damage."

"Pointless violence."

"It comes with the territory, I guess," he added quietly. *So, not completely jaded yet*, Kendal thought.

"Careful, Joe, you sound like Ortez."

"Yes, m . . . K. Please may I ask a favor?"

"Go for it."

"Please can I call you ma'am?"

"Okay, Joe. No worries. Ma'am, it is."

"Thank you, ma'am." He was audibly relieved.

She hung up the phone and dropped it on the table, considering the options. Someone trying to deliver a message or take her somewhere. Quite a broad remit. Not worth Lula dying for. Someone had paid cut-price for a simple job that had cost Lula's life. Whoever it was had Kendal's wrath in the post.

She was interrupted by a noise from inside the basement door. Joel was tapping on the fake panel; Kendal had to laugh. It was like having a cat.

"I've got a really nice Merlot if you'd like a glass?" he proffered in a loud whisper.

Kendal got up and pressed the lock release to let him in.

"Hey, boss! Thought I'd bring you some fresh intel. I finally met someone interesting!"

He seemed to function permanently on one level: upbeat. He had no night mode. Kendal got two big, beautiful wineglasses from a cabinet and sat back at the table, closing the laptop and flipping her phone onto its face. Then, after a moment's thought, she got up and switched on the bug scrambler. If Rico wanted reports, he'd get them secondhand.

"So."

Joel was practically wagging his tail. "I've been building up the org chart, like you said. Been chatting the ears off the receptionists and PAs. Been going for cigarettes with the cool kids and kept my headphones on silent so they think I can't hear, but I *can* hear." He did a comedically dramatic wink.

"So far, no tamales, right?"

"Right."

Kendal smiled to show she was excited for his news, then took a sip of wine.

"I've been working away on Cadu, which seems to be going quite well except that it's one of those super boring projects where the design keeps changing and it means we have to do everything again. Like standard government contracts, apparently. One of the other developers told me they'd basically been on a two-year-long sprint. Everyone is close to burn-out, but none of this is particularly unusual for a firm like Glo-Tech. I've been keeping an eye on the Slack channels to see if anyone from the board ever chimes in but they're not really in the day-to-day stuff."

This was all information Kendal already had, but she could tell he was giving a preamble to something big, so she let him do the build. She drank a little more wine.

"So I'm working on Cadu, testing the camera relay. It's complicated to explain, but ultimately the app has a 'live' function that will connect the kids to educators and places around the world. I'm making sure it's robust and can't be hacked or redirected. Cadu is for kids, right, so it has to be super secure, like airtight. Anyway, I was testing it and I found a glitch in the code."

His eyes widened, and he lowered his voice. "We have a bug-reporting system, so the first thing I have to do is log what I've found, then I can start fixing it. That's the process. So I'm getting on with it when this guy I've never met comes up to me. He's super friendly, almost too friendly, you know?"

She did not point out the irony but she did wonder how friendly was too friendly for Joel. "And he goes . . ."—here Joel broke into a roughly Cockney accent—"'Hey, pal, no need to flag that. We got it.' But they don't got it, do they, cos I just found it."

"Who is he?"

"That's the thing. He's called Alex Shapiro. He's the project lead. He's on the board!" Joel widened his eyes gleefully. "He dials in on Cadu calls sometimes, but he always has the camera off. I've not met him before."

"This is good work. Did you manage to talk to him?"

"Not really. I started to tell him about the glitch, but he just goes, 'Leave it alone.' And then he walked off. But if I leave it alone it's an insecure camera relay on an app that's for kids, so I think I should flag it."

"The name rings a bell, is he well-known?"

"No. The opposite. No one has ever heard of him."

"Why do I know the name?"

Joel shook his head. "No idea."

"Exciting though, your first intel. Did you keep your cool?"

"I think so. It was a little bit exhilarating," he admitted.

"So the next step is to find out if Alex has an assistant or any friends in the office, who does he play golf with, where does he go for coffee."

"Copy that, boss. Exciting, right? Do you think he's dangerous?"

On cue to make them both jump out of their skin, the kitchen door pushed open and Rosie appeared, hair tousled and eyes squinting against the light.

"I can't sleep, Mumma," she murmured.

"How are you getting down those stairs so quietly, Ro? You'll have to teach me." She scooped her up to take her to bed, and Rosie looked suspiciously at Joel over her shoulder. "Are you having fun without me?"

"Never."

"Night, Rosie," Joel called, picking up his glass and heading back to the basement.

Kendal tucked Rosie into the big bed and sat next to her in the dark.

"Tell me a make-up story, Mumma."

"Do you know the one about the wicked woman who always had a new name? She changed it every day until nobody, not even her family, knew who she was."

"I want the dancer one."

One of her earliest assignments. Kendal had been cocky and overt, she'd learned some harsh lessons, and all that remained was a short story.

"A long time ago there was a ballerina who knew too much. She was beautiful and popular and dangerous. On the other side of the world was a very plain girl who thought dancing looked easy. They became good friends, but one day . . ."

Rosie was already asleep, Kendal let the story fall away and instead she reviewed Joel's intel. Something was making her ears ring. *It's the name.* For some reason, the revelation came in her mother's voice. Shapiro. She'd seen it recently. Lily Shapiro was a kid in Rosie's class. In an ordinary world it could be a coincidence; with Rico Ortez in the mix, it was a problem.

14

Kendal checked the time and walked faster. The clamor of London traffic felt as if it came from within, a rushing, rising fury that swelled and subsided as she stomped toward her target. She had ninety-two minutes until pickup and this was a conversation she wanted to have in person. She arrived at Hammersmith roundabout forty-one minutes later and weaved dangerously between cars.

She reached the innocuous blue door of Bon Temps and found the same scruffy scrap of paper next to the same old button among many. A wave of nostalgia briefly interrupted her venom, as she saw herself, aged eighteen, alone and with the unfounded confidence of youth, pressing this very button, opening the door to the future she'd chosen. She snapped back to the present, where it wasn't possible to press it angrily, however hard she tried.

Eventually there was a crackle on the intercom, and the door buzzed open.

She pushed her way into a shabby carpeted stairway lined with menus and bills. At the top of the stairs she walked into a squalid little office, which she knew to be a front. A girl who was much too beautiful for the room looked at her calmly and spoke with an elegant French accent that amplified her good looks. "Hi, are you here for Mr. Ortez?"

"Obviously." She seethed.

"He will be just a few moments. Please take a seat."

"No."

She said it loudly, knowing that he'd be watching. She glanced at a clock on the wall; forty-eight minutes until pickup.

Sure enough, and with a smile that Kendal would have liked to physically wipe from his face, Rico appeared from behind a frosted-glass door.

"Thanks, hun. Good to see you, 96, who doesn't love an unannounced visitor in the middle of the day? Specially with an expression like you're wearing." He winked at "hun" and led Kendal into another office, past what would seem to be his desk, and through another door into what could only be described as a high-tech hub of activity.

"Wait, what?" Kendal gawped. The Bon Temps she'd known was cagey and poorly lit; this one was staffed, shiny, and alive. "It looks like an Apple Store."

Rico gave her a gleeful nod. "Welcome to Bon Temps 2.0. We've had a little facelift since your last visit. Come to my office and I can point out the team from a slightly more discreet distance."

Kendal's eyes swept the room for details as she followed Rico to a glass staircase that defied the architecture of the building. Bon Temps must occupy at least two of the facades on the roundabout. They entered an office, and the door swooshed shut behind them.

Rico struck a pose by a wall of windows that overlooked the floor below. Kendal looked from face to face, each peering into a screen she couldn't see, rapt in whatever work they were doing. So much had changed that she was disoriented. She had built and maintained a picture of Rico's world, and it wasn't this. She was deeply worried about what he had done to achieve it.

"We didn't just sit around waiting for you to stop breastfeeding. I told you we were doing good."

"You said business was booming. You didn't say you had become the crown prince of Hammersmith. How in the shady shit did you manage this?"

He just laughed, a corporate braying he didn't normally use. He clapped her on the shoulder and turned her slightly. "That's Joe and Pete." He pointed out two boys sitting side by side at a double desk. One was of Asian descent and the other was white, they both wore blue shirts with gray sweaters, they both had floppy hair—one black, one blond—and they had the exact same posture and the exact same expression on their faces: delighted with themselves, convinced of their coolness, happy to be there. Apart from their looks, they were identical. Kendal didn't know when she'd got old enough for them to look so impossibly young. "I'll introduce you if you want, they'd love to meet their leading lady. They don't get out much."

He was still grinning when he turned and gestured to a chair on the far side of a much, much nicer desk than she had ever seen him at before. Kendal took a seat, adjusted her entire mental assessment of Bon Temps, and allowed her anger to swell and subside so that she could concentrate.

"So, what brings you to Hammersmith on this fine day? Joel got something juicy for me?"

"What does 'safe' mean to you, Rico? Is it just a box where you keep your money?"

Rico picked up a pen and tapped it lightly on the desk. "Come again?"

She had thirty-nine minutes until pickup.

"You said you'd given me everything. You buried the headline. You said she was covered."

Rico frowned. "She is covered. What happened?"

He buzzed on an intercom. "Hey, Tommy, could you bring coffee." He released the button and clasped his hands together on the desk.

"You put her in school with Glo-Tech management."

Rico stopped, his pen midair. "Wait, what are we talking about now?"

"Alex Shapiro is the Cadu project lead and his kid is in Rosie's class.

Didn't notice that nugget in the file, Rico. So am I rusty or are you on a mess-around?"

"Who cares about Shapiro?"

"Joel said he's making Cadu creepy."

"Psh, Shapiro is a minnow. You're supposed to get Joel swimming with sharks."

"He may be a small fish, but he might have someone serious pulling his strings."

Rico seemed to be considering this. "Fine, check him out. But don't lose sight of the brief. Your project is handling Red Panda. Glo-Tech is full of moving pieces and we'd like to know who is doing what."

"I told you I didn't want Rosie involved. You couldn't respect that?"

"No one is asking Rosie to do anything."

Kendal wanted to punch him. She took a deep breath and watched the mechanics dancing behind Rico's eyes. She knew him well enough to know he was juggling information like a professional clown. He was a man who loved to make a mess.

"Have I ever told you about Katie Christmas?" Kendal asked.

"In two decades of working together I don't think you've once volunteered information. So, no."

Kendal decided to break the habit of a lifetime.

"For a brief spell back in the day, my name was Katie Christmas. It wasn't my op, I was a plus-one. But when it was over, they killed Katie in a car wreck. I found out by chance when I saw my face in her local paper. She was just . . ."—Kendal clicked her fingers—"dead."

"So what?" Rico shrugged. "Can't be the last time you killed an ID."

She looked into the distance. "I was eight."

Rico's pen stopped halfway to his mouth. "Jesus, Ken, how long have you been doing this?" It was the correct question, but she ignored it.

"The point is, The Game, the players, they don't care about kids. They don't care about anything or anyone. Imagine her classmates. Imagine the impact on that town? I was a child when I found out how flammable an ID is. And I don't want Rosie to ever know how that feels. I want her to have the same name for her whole life. I want her to grow up knowing who she is and where she came from and being allowed to tell people."

Rico was slotting an entire new dataset of Kendal intel into his mind. Eventually he said, quietly, "I'm so sorry that happened to you."

Kendal was about to speak, but at that moment Tommy entered and carefully placed tea and coffee on the desk.

"Thanks, Tom, you can go, I'll be mother."

Kendal grimaced at the phrase. She had thirty-three minutes until pickup, which meant she was out of time.

"No more games, Rico. Rosie is a hand tied behind my back. It's not like the old days, okay? No fun."

He nodded solemnly. "Absolutely zero fun."

"And you'll give me everything you've got about the senior Glo-Tech team?"

"You're welcome to everything we've got. It's the gaps we need to worry about. Put in a data request with the desk. It's not like the old days, all notes on matchbooks and whispering secrets on park benches. There's a procedure. But in the meantime, 96, listen . . ."

He leaned forward, his face serious, his finger pointed into the polished white desk. "You are in The Game, whether you like it or not. You always were. People like us do not retire, we only have one way out. You're supposed to be the best. I'm billing based on your capabilities, so I'd like some proof you still possess them."

Kendal stood up, tempted to do him some damage and remind him that her capabilities included extreme physical persuasion. That he was the admin and she was the action. But behind the laughter in his eyes there was something she hadn't seen before. Was it fear? Whatever it was, he'd changed, she thought, or maybe she had.

He held up his porcelain cup. "Welcome back."

She didn't give him the satisfaction of a response and left. At the bottom of the stairs she was flanked by Joe & Pete, who spoke over each other in a flurry.

"We've got you a packet of cool toys . . ."

"It's so great to meet you in real life!"

"Any time you need us . . ."

She smiled and thanked them but refused the bag. "Get me everything you can on Alex Shapiro and his immediate family. And send the kit to the house." They seemed even younger close up. She wondered where in Oxbridge Rico had found them. She slammed out of the new Bon Temps with twenty-nine minutes till pickup. She was going to get told off.

With a renewed sense of purpose she scrolled through the parents WhatsApp. Alex wasn't in the group, but Sasha Shapiro was. Kendal pulled up her picture and was surprised to find she was looking at the woman with the bully-boy husband. Somewhere inside this made her want to engage with them even more. She'd thought about that guy, the look on his face and his hand on Sasha's arm. Maybe this project would be fun after all. She sat on the Piccadilly Line, her ears ringing, feeling newly powerful. She wouldn't take any risks, but making a friend and dropping a bug were easy assignments. When she got to the school, she took it in as if for the first time. The playground would have been a brilliant place to train for black ops. The treehouse, courtyard, and central building had ample cover, the windows mostly blacked out by posters and paintings, civilian crowds at predictable times. The thought of all those tiny bodies providing cover made Kendal feel physically sick. She recalled herself on ops where she thought of people as shapes, as kit to be used, and she realized something fundamental was different in her now.

Rosie's class was on the ground floor, and, through the big windows, Kendal peeped her sitting alone at a desk looking at a book, while the teacher, Ella, was at an adult-sized desk on a laptop. She glanced up at the movement. Kendal propped open the door and waved.

Rosie picked up her bag. "Hello, Mother." She greeted her like a disgruntled businessman and walked past her into the playground.

"I'm so sorry, Ella, I got stuck at work."

"No, don't worry, these things happen. We had a nice little playdate."

Rosie dropped her bag on the concrete and folded her arms, tucking her face as far into her neck as it would go.

"I think I'm in the bad books now."

"And the late books!" Ella replied. Her voice was jovial, but Kendal couldn't tell if she was joking. Kendal scrabbled to keep it light.

"I was going to mention, if you still need people, I'd be happy to join on the school trip tomorrow?"

"Oh really? That would be amazing, one of the parents has literally just canceled! I'll put your name down."

"Fab. See you then." Kendal sighed, because she would have bet her life savings on which parent had dropped out.

Ella waved and turned back to her work. Rosie was looking at Kendal with a full-on glower.

"Come on, then, Ro-yo, let's get outta here."

Rosie screwed up her face.

"You were the last one."

"I'm really sorry, I had a meeting with Rico."

"Did you bring me a treat?"

"I haven't got anything on me but you can have a biscuit when we get in."

"Is Joel at home?"

"Probably."

They walked out of the gate and turned toward the house.

"Can I watch TV?"

"Do you ever play with a kid called Lily?"

Rosie made a yuck face. "Lily's rude."

"Figures," Kendal answered.

15

The coach had been in motion for less than five minutes before the first fart was launched. Kendal expected an uprising of outrage or mockery in response, but nobody acknowledged the appalling aroma that swept through the vehicle. Twelve minutes after that, a child called Johan vomited into his lunch box. Someone Kendal couldn't see was rolling a seemingly endless supply of Babybel cheeses down the center of the bus.

Rosie was in the window seat next to Kendal, who had been assigned a group of four children. Thankfully, Johan was not one of hers, but neither was Lily Shapiro. At four years old, these kids were already cliquey as teens.

The kid on the seat in front of Rosie was using his head to rhythmically batter the back of his chair and with each impact a puff of ancient bus dust was launched into Rosie's face. Rosie was oblivious; she gently kicked the back of his seat in return, happy in her own world. Her hand rested contentedly on Kendal's leg. The coach was driving to a theater in Angel to watch a puppet show about a flatulent tiger that might have been an allegory for sharing, or maybe difference, or maybe knowing your limits. It should have been a ten-minute drive, but because it was a full-sized coach in a London one-way system, it would take closer to an hour. Lily Shapiro was at the other end of the bus, and Sasha Shapiro was the parent who canceled, because of course she was.

Watching the crocodile line of little bodies walk hand in hand through the school playground, along a main road, and onto the coach had given rise to an unusual sense of helplessness in Kendal. How could she protect so many of them? How could beings so vulnerable move safely through the world at all? She was profoundly affected not only by how damn cute they were, but how illogical. Her little squad spoke four languages, walked in circles, and had absolutely no concept of linear time. It was like herding lambs, but lambs from another planet who could speak French and liked balloons. When they finally arrived at the theater they disembarked like soldiers returning from the front line, except instead of blood and gore they were covered in crumbs and half suffocated by the windowless impact of thirty kids with no impulse control. They piled into the show, and the adults squeezed into pews at the back of a theater designed exclusively for small people. There was no more room to sit, and a puppeteer began a ditty about the tiger. Kendal was looking for a place to put herself, when Nat sidled up to her and whispered with a wink, "Shall we go outside and wait by the bathrooms in case someone needs a wee?" Kendal nodded gratefully.

Outside the theater they leaned against the walls and stared at their phones.

"Smart move," Kendal acknowledged. Nat laughed. "It's not my first rodeo." She eyeballed Kendal with an assessing expression. "How's life?"

"Can't complain. It would take too long," Kendal answered, repeating a line she'd overheard in the playground.

Nat remained stone-faced. She had no time for platitudes, and Kendal liked it. She adjusted her track.

"You have another kid in the school?"

"Jemma, in year 6. I've been doing this forever. I don't normally do volunteering but Sam begged me. It's his favorite book, *The Tiger's First*

Fart. He loves anything puerile. I dunno where he gets it." She waggled her eyebrows, and then her phone rang. "Can you cover me while I take this? I haven't told the office I'm not at my desk."

"Go for it."

Kendal listened as Nat answered her phone in an entirely different voice and then began a serious conversation about confidentiality clauses. The door of the theater creaked open and Lily Shapiro appeared. She was taller than Rosie, with straight blond hair. She was wearing a waistcoat over her uniform, denim-effect leggings, and she had black boots with cartoon dolls embroidered into the tongues. Her whole outfit was clean and new. Kendal wondered if she dressed herself or had a fashion-conscious parent.

"I need a wee," she whispered quietly.

"Okay. I can come with you."

Lily looked her up and down and must have approved because she nodded and headed for the toilet.

"Do you need help in the cubicle?"

"No, thank you."

Kendal stood outside the door and waited.

"My mummy was supposed to come today."

"Oh, that's a shame, what happened?"

Lily didn't answer. "Whose mummy are you?"

"Rosie's." There was a pause and the lid slammed down. Then a flush, but Lily didn't emerge.

"Rosie's bossy," she said from inside the stall.

Kendal laughed. "I know, right? She likes to be the leader."

Lily threw open the cubicle door and eyeballed Kendal. "And she doesn't have a daddy." Lily said this as if it were a degrading fact, and Kendal felt a unique combination of sadness, anger, shame, and guilt surge through her core. Funny, how much you could hate a kid.

"Yes, she does." She answered with a calm kindness she didn't feel.

Lily was at the sink but couldn't press the tap hard enough to get it going. Kendal reached over and pushed it for her.

Lily caught her eye in the mirror. "I've got a mummy and a daddy and a Patty."

"That's nice. What's a 'Patty'?"

"For in the day."

"How lovely for you."

Lily struck a pose that seemed much too old for her years, then looked at the hand dryer nervously.

"You want to dry your hands on my jeans? That's what Rosie does. She hates the dryers. We call them the toilet monster."

Lily giggled and wiped her hands gleefully on Kendal's knees. "Rosie has nice hair," Lily said, as if to repay the favor.

"That's a kind thing to say. And you're both named after flowers. Maybe you two will be friends one day."

Lily nodded but didn't look very confident. "My birthday is in August."

"Ah, fair enough." Six months. An insurmountable age gap. "I'll tell you a secret about Rosie though." Lily's eyes widened with glee. "She thinks you're the coolest kid in class." Lily looked thoroughly pleased with that secret and went back to the show. Kendal had never been a treacherous asshole before, and she did not like how it felt.

That afternoon, with nothing but a headache and a chocolate-covered shirt to show for her efforts, Kendal sat down to read the report on Sasha compiled by Joe & Pete. It was scant, so she called them up, not knowing which one of them she'd catch. Then she realized it was only 4:15 PM, so very much within a normal working day.

Joe & Pete were in full swing. Joe kicked things off. "Sasha Shapiro née Ebner. She's thirty-six, born in the UK to an Austrian father and Swedish mother. The parents met at Oxford, nothing particularly newsworthy about them. She was raised in Belgium until her teens, then they moved to Norwich. Went to art school in London. Nothing in her background to suggest any dark spots. Her resume tracks."

Pete picked up the thread. "She had an early career as a digital artist but has pivoted her work and now identifies as a multimedia sculptor. Her current practice is informed by body and modernity . . . She wrestles with bouts of insecurity that are intense to the point of mania." Pete was the cerebral one, evidently. Joe reined him in. "She's been married to Alex Shapiro for nine years. Lily is their only child, conceived through IVF with a Portland Place company. We haven't probed their files, but we can refer it to the breakers if you're interested."

The breakers were the hacking team at Bon Temps; they were ruthless.

"No. Let's keep her reproductive health confidential for now," Kendal instructed.

"She struggled with her identity as an artist after the birth, but used the experience to inform her new work." Pete sounded almost whimsical and Kendal was enjoying their routine. They were considerably more useful than she had given them credit for based on their enthusiasm and youth. She could hear Joe typing and reading. "She's got her first solo show next September at the Rayburn Gallery, New Bond Street."

"Oh wow, she must be so excited," Pete mused.

"You like to color it in, don't you, Pete?"

"Yes, ma'am."

"Thanks, boys."

Kendal hung up the phone and continued to clean the kitchen. Sasha Ebner was easier to find online. She appeared on various gallery socials with works that Kendal found intriguing and funny. She wasn't sure if she was supposed to find them funny and that made her like them more. There were muscular bronze figures locked in dramatic battle with inanimate objects, like a toaster and a set of keys, and weird close-ups of hands in impossible positions. Kendal thought they were good, but that was the extent of her critique. Once she had unveiled Sasha's artist identity she found a rich seam of info. Sasha was part of various art groups. She raised money for refugees and went to marches. Lily was markedly absent from her online presence. As Sasha's profile began to take shape, Kendal tried to find a natural way in. She had been tagged on Facebook in a group called Walk 'N' Talk, at the park close to Kendal's house. She clicked to join the group, billed as "a brief, weekly respite from life. For women, mothers, and nature lovers, to spend time among the trees and each other's spirits."

Kendal spared a thought for her former life, where she'd been glamorous and cool, and then clicked to join.

16

Sasha Shapiro left her house in sunglasses, a white cotton shirt, tight jeans, and a pair of polished black brogues. She stood outside the gate of the property peering at her phone, and then up and down the street. A black cab rounded the corner, and Sasha stepped in.

Twenty yards farther down the road, Kendal hopped onto an electric bike and followed. As they approached Soho, Kendal dropped the bike and followed on foot, the traffic meant that the cab moved no faster than she could walk. Eventually Sasha hopped out at the Ritz on Piccadilly and headed west. She crossed the road and stopped on the corner of Green Park station to rummage in her bag for some money. She handed a twenty-pound note to a homeless guy, squatting to pet his dog; they seemed to know each other. Kendal stood at the bus stop opposite and looked at her phone.

Sasha took the next right, on Bolton Street. About halfway down she let herself into a Georgian town house that had been converted from an upper-class abode to a series of studios and offices. Kendal took up a spot opposite and waited.

At lunchtime, Sasha reemerged and headed west. Kendal left her perch and jogged over the road as someone else exited the building, and they gallantly held the door for her.

The buttons on the elevator were unmarked. She took the stairs. At the first floor the door was locked, but through a small, meshed window she could see a messy office, a map of London on the wall, and a maquette of the south London riverbank. An architect's firm, maybe, or something around real estate. She continued up the stairs and turned a corner to find a young woman staring at her phone and puffing on a small, pink vape. She let out a little yelp when Kendal turned the corner. "Sorry, you scared me!" she giggled.

"I was looking for Sasha, is she around?"

The girl turned back to her phone with a shrug. "I think she's gone out, but she usually leaves the door open. Top floor." She signaled up with a nod. "Cheers," Kendal said quietly and went up the stairs. At the end of the stairs she found a door propped open with a large, gold ceramic pot. She pulled on a pair of leather gloves and walked into the space.

"Holy shit" was the best she could think of. The studio was vast; two floors had been merged and the double-height room was flooded with light from tall sash windows and a skylight. The floors were solid hardwood, the walls exposed brick. At the back of the space a mezzanine platform was accessed by an iron spiral staircase, and leaning against the wall, wedged between an old oak workbench and a rolling ladder, was a gigantic bronze arm holding a modern car key. Kendal rummaged in her bag for an audio bug and stuck it underneath an old leather armchair that was in the corner, surrounded by dirty cups and notebooks. Her mission accomplished, she stood and took in the beautiful mayhem of the room. She wasn't particularly into art, but even she could appreciate the incredible, fascinating drama of the sculptures. Every surface was strewn, and in the center of the room a heavy oak table was daubed in paint. Pots overflowing, dirty plates, wine bottles, and ashtrays. It was truly bohemian. The walls were covered in sketches, and there was a bar next to Kendal with fridges full of champagne. The bar itself was covered in textiles, bric-a-brac, and glasses. Kendal spotted a head of broccoli, a stuffed raccoon, and an animal skull. She didn't want to move, was utterly in awe. The main door of the building slammed her out of her reverie, and she pressed the button for the elevator. She pulled her cap low over her hair and put oversized shades on. As she descended in the tiny, gated elevator, she checked her career history for her knowledge of art. She cursed her lack of creativity; hers was a left-sided brain. It would take too long to access Sasha through the art world, and if she was as brilliant as she seemed to be, it would take even longer. The connect would have to be made through the kids.

17

Kendal approached the park with an indulgent, if wary, smile. A group of women in various states of athleisure wear had gathered at the gates with reusable coffee cups, colorful water bottles, and sensible shoes. She waved at Nat and Sasha, in a huddle by themselves a little way from the group. Nat gave her a searching look as she approached. "All right, Rosie's mum? Didn't have you for a chat-and-rambler."

"Need some air. And some friends, I didn't know it was a school thing."

"It's not, just us and Louis from year 6. Have you met Lily's mum?" Nat pointed inelegantly at Sasha. "Sasha, Kendal, and vice versa."

"Hello, Kendal. Welcome." Sasha shook hands with a firm, confident shake; if she recognized Kendal from their interaction at school, she didn't reveal it. She had Lily's perfectly straight hair, but it was dark, almost black. She was average height and slim. She seemed like someone who watched what they ate but never deliberately exercised. It was her eyes that Kendal was drawn to—they were alive, dark, and brooding. Her eyebrows were particularly striking, black and immaculately shaped. She was wearing rings on seven fingers and a heavy, drooping silver chain with a pendant shaped like a conch. She was carrying a bulky designer bag and had fashionable sneaks. She looked cool, Kendal realized, not something you could accuse many of the mums of. Kendal was surprised to find she instinctively liked her. She had expected her to be unappealing, given Lily's personality.

The group fluidly set off together without any announcement.

The park was not more than a square mile of trees, lawns, a swing set and slide, and a coffee hut on the other side and over a hill. Depending on the weather, the group did one to four laps of the park and then branched off to a coffee shop or back toward their respective lives. It reminded Kendal of the girl group with whom she had watched *Pretty Woman* as a preteen. They were deliberately entangling their lives, actively looking for ways to share more information and get closer together. Something about it made Kendal unbearably sad.

Sasha and Nat set the pace, marching ahead and leaving Kendal behind. She let them go for now. Louis from year 6 was the only dad. If he noticed that it was all women apart from him, he didn't seem put off by the fact. Within minutes of them setting off he had fallen into step with Kendal. "You new to the group?"

"First time," Kendal replied.

"First time?"

Kendal gave him a sideways glance; if he was using some learned chat-up technique, she was the wrong target.

"Yep. You?"

"I joined accidentally because I do this walk most days, but Tuesdays, the women come too."

Kendal chortled and took a better look at him. He was tall and broad and had the olive tones of eastern European lineage. He had a well-manicured beard and wore a flat cap and a good coat. He was probably bald under the hat and his smile was drenched in the confidence of a man who knows he's good-looking. He had just enough military about him for Kendal to immediately assume he'd been sent to watch her, probably by the government. They kept their people old school, and

Louis reeked of honey. She sped up, trying to get in step with Sasha. Louis kept pace.

"Are you new to the neighborhood?"

"No."

"Been here long?"

"Not really."

He rolled his eyes and muttered what sounded like "Jesus Christ" in what might have been Bulgarian. "Are you new to the concept of a chat?"

She glanced at him, but he qualified the remark with a likable smile.

"I'm not big on small talk."

"You're small on big talk."

"Fine." She sighed but she also kept it friendly. "Hi, I'm Kendal, I live nearby. I work in publishing. I like the color green. I'm allergic to peaches. I'm a Virgo."

She had an urgent and visceral flashback of her mother. *The best cocktails are two parts truth to one part fiction.*

"Hello, Kendal, I'm Louis."

"Is that it?"

"We've only just met."

Kendal pouted at him, and he winked at her. He was flirting, and she didn't hate it.

"What happens if you eat peaches?" he asked.

"My lips tingle," she answered, letting a blush surface briefly and failing to mention the itchy red rash and fat tongue that went with it.

"You married?" he asked with a nod at her left hand. She opened her mouth but found the answer escaped her. Not married, no, but not available either. She glanced briefly inward and was surprised to find that there was still nothing but a broken heart to look at. Romantic love was something she rarely considered. She'd found it once, and it had only led to pain and danger. She was about to reply, when Sasha screamed from the path twenty yards ahead of them. A small, stocky man wearing a gray tracksuit, a black baseball cap, and a face mask had barged into her, grabbing her bag and shoving her hard enough that she fell. Nat shouted after him, but didn't chase, leaning down to check Sasha was okay. He shoved the others in their party off the path as he ran. He was level with Kendal when she ducked and stuck her leg out to trip him. She grabbed his hood as he fell, spinning him so that he released the bag. He dropped it with an angry shout and barreled forward into Kendal, who caught him in the face with her elbow. He stumbled and twisted on the spot, abandoning the bag and running the other way. Louis tried to reach for him, but the guy shrugged him off.

Louis took off after him, giving up after a few yards. His shoes were too shiny and apparently he skipped cardio for abs day at the gym. The rest of them had regrouped around Sasha.

Kendal held out the bag. "I got it back, are you all right?"

Sasha grabbed Nat's hand to stand. She brushed her trousers down and checked her pockets.

"Thank you, you shouldn't have done that. It's dangerous. What if he had a knife?"

"I'm okay," Kendal said, looking back in the direction the guy had run. "I think it was just a kid."

"Karate Ken saves the day," Nat chimed in, already on her phone. "I'm gonna call the cops. Are you hurt, Sash?"

"I'm fine. Can we not with the police."

Nat opened her mouth to argue and then hung up the phone and put it in her back pocket. "As you wish, mate."

"Are you sure you're okay?" Kendal asked. Sasha looked on the edge of tears and took the bag from Kendal as if it were loaded.

"My husband is trying to convince me that the city isn't safe." She looked utterly miserable. "Maybe he's right." Her rich brown eyes implored the group. "We can't tell him about this. He'll move us to Hertford! I can't do suburbs, Nat. I won't survive!"

Someone on the edge of the cluster muttered that Hertford wasn't that bad, and Kendal laughed.

"I won't tell him, I promise," she offered. Nat put her arm across Sasha's shoulder. "No one's gonna make you move to Hertford, Sash. Not today." She looked around the park and then up at the sky, which was perfectly clear and blue. "All right, fuck this. Let's go and get a coffee." There was a general sense of dissatisfaction around this plan and Nat turned fierce. "All right, sorry, anyone who's just been attacked or isn't bothered about getting their bloody steps in and would rather get a coffee, come with me. Everyone else, see you next week, guys, take care, keep your eyes out, love you!"

The group turned to walk away. Nat, Kendal, and Sasha stayed behind. Louis seemed undecided. He almost chose Team Coffee, but apparently the welcome in their faces wasn't warm enough for him, and he turned and walked in a completely different direction from everyone.

"Damn," Nat lamented. "I could look at him all day."

"Outrage!" Sasha said. "Blasphemy!" Then she looked at Kendal to explain. "He's the only single dad in year 6. Nat says it's a cliché to fancy him and we're not allowed."

They were heading back toward the gate they had come in through less than twenty minutes earlier.

"I might make an exception for you though," Nat said to Kendal. "You'd make a fine couple."

They took squashed seats in a high street bakery, and Nat went to the counter, returning with a pot of tea "for the shock."

"Although to be fair you don't seem particularly bothered," she said appraisingly to Kendal.

Kendal shrugged. "I'm a city kid, not my first rodeo."

"Oh really, whereabouts?" Nat asked, but they were all distracted by a rockabilly mum at the table next to them as she chatted to a child in an unbearable singsong voice that made Kendal close her eyes against a wave of irritation. When the woman's cake arrived, she shoved her iPhone in the stroller, "The Wheels on the Bus" playing loud enough for the whole café to enjoy.

Sasha was still edgy, her cup jangling conspicuously against the saucer.

"Should I tell the police?" she asked quietly, distraught. "What if he does it to other people?"

"It's up to you, babe," Nat said calmly. "I can come to the station with you if you want."

Sasha looked pained. "I can't face it."

"And Karate Ken here might get done for assault."

The ladies on the bus go chat chat chat

Nat turned to rockabilly and snapped, "All right, Elvis, the kid's asleep, can you shut it down?" Kendal watched the woman shake from her reverie and murmur at her, then turn her attention back to the phone, cutting the noise and going into some other app.

Nat turned back to them. "Chat chat chat? Patriarchy much!" Then, with a mischievous grin, "Sorry, Kendal, you were saying. You're single?" Sasha tutted and muttered, *"Gossip,"* under her breath. It was clear these two had a well-established friendship, and it was fun to be around.

"I am."

"Rosie's dad out of the picture?" Nat pressed.

"Yeah." When Kendal didn't elaborate, Sasha broke the silence.

"Alex hasn't been home for a week. Lily keeps asking if we're getting divorced. She's absolutely obsessed with failed marriages at the moment."

"Sam won't shut up about tractors," Nat put in, but Sasha was on a roll. "I know we have a housekeeper and that's loads of the legwork. But it's not like I expect Patty to raise my kid. I don't believe in outsourcing love. Alex doesn't believe it's hard. He doesn't think these years matter. He keeps saying he'll make it up to her. But I've got a show to work on and I'm not allowed to just disappear. I'm back from the studio every day by dinnertime, even when work is going well. He hasn't been back before bedtime for literally months. As if some dumb app is more important than art. Or family." Kendal nodded, but Sasha wasn't finished.

"Do you ever just want to scream at them? 'It's fiction! It's a construct!' They invented this meaningless need for more. He never thinks to enjoy what he has. I don't understand his priorities anymore. He used to care about things other than money. I don't know how to get through to him that we have enough. His argument used to always be that it was tech that could change the world. Now it's all about how he has to pay the bills and *provide* for the family like it's our fault he never comes home. We live in a three-million-pound house, just eat spaghetti with your kid once in a while, you know?"

Nat gave Kendal a look that implied this was a familiar topic. "You've got to take the power back, Sash."

"I know. I tried to demand he be more present. Guess what he said?" Sasha laughed, but it was a dead sound. "Get a dog."

"Urgh," Nat said, fairly. "I hate the way we always end up talking about them."

"The kids or the men?" Sasha asked vaguely.

"Yeah," Nat answered. Her phone was buzzing on the table, and she picked it up with an aggrieved sigh. "Ah shit. Well, this has been fun, but if you're both okay, I've got to hit the road. Those team meetings won't mute themselves." They stood up to say awkward goodbyes in the tiny confines of the café.

"Actually, I should go too," Sasha added, looking suddenly exhausted. "Sorry. Weird day." She put her bag over her shoulder and then grimaced at it. "I might just throw this away, you know." Then she caught Kendal's expression. "Oh my god, I didn't even say thank you. Alex would have killed me for losing my phone." She leaned over and pulled Kendal into an awkward hug. "You're my hero, thank you so much." Nat looked on with a bemused grin. As she walked away, Kendal briefly imagined going on a date with Louis. She almost scowled at the idea. A lovely blouse and some goddamn lipstick. She didn't know why it made her instantly angry to think about.

Walking along the high street, she felt exposed. She saw the rockabilly mum appear in the reflection of a charity shop. She felt cars were crawling along as if to make a grab and could sense eyes on her. She would have liked to run immediate counter-surveillance but had an obligation to fulfill first.

She headed for a grungy alley adjacent to a hospital and found the kid ducked behind an industrial-sized bin. He had all the hallmarks of a fledgling addict. He was sitting on a low wall looking worried. When he saw her his posture changed, trying to project a sense of power. If anything, it made him look even weaker; he was all skin, bone, and swagger.

"I thought you said no repercussions," he muttered angrily. She pulled a fifty-pound note out of her pocket and handed it to him.

"Sorry, had to make it look real."

"You said quick snatch, fifty quid. You didn't say anything about getting jammed in the fucking teeth."

"I didn't mean to hurt you. You should have let go of the bag."

Kendal looked at him—just a teenager, not a proper criminal—and saw she had bust his lip. "I'm really sorry." She pulled another fifty out of her pocket and handed it to him, which seemed to cheer him up a bit.

She held her hand out to help him up, but he ignored it.

"Crazy bitch," he muttered, walking away into the alley and toward the hospital entrance. Kendal watched him go.

Once he was out of sight Kendal called Rico.

"96! How's hags, nags, and bags?"

"Nailed it. New best friends, got a nickname and everything. And I dropped the bug, but she might ditch the bag."

"Ooh nice, a bit of progress. Anything juicy?"

"She said Alex hasn't been home for a week, but according to Joel, he's rarely in the office, might be worth a look to see where he's spending his time."

Rico released an aggrieved sigh. "You're still paddling in the kids' pool. Get in the deep end with the big boys, 96. There's talk of a beta launch for Cadu, it would be good to know it's all going smoothly."

"Copy that, boss, let me do my thing. Hey, did you have a tail put on me?"

"Eyes on 96? I wouldn't dare. Why do you ask?"

Kendal hung up the phone, scanned the area, and turned to head home.

18

The days got shorter and the weather turned mean. But for the first time in Kendal's life, she had a routine. If it was dangerous to get comfortable, she took the risk, because it gave Rosie parameters, walls to push against, and a sense of stability that Kendal had come to realize was the thing she had most craved as a child.

During term time, the mornings played out the same way. Rosie got up first and took herself downstairs to let Joel into the house. Kendal arose shortly after and went running. She did a few miles most days, and twice a week she went to an underground boxing club and sparred with a partner or kicked the crap out of sacks of sand. When she got home, Rosie and Joel had usually eaten breakfast and Rosie would be getting ready for school. At the weekend they'd be watching TV or messing about in the garden. On weekdays Joel would pour Kendal a coffee, clean the kitchen, and unload the dishwasher, then leave for work, either at the office or in the basement.

At 5:30 PM, if he was working at home, he would come back upstairs and make dinner. If he was at the office, Kendal and Rosie would cook and dinner would be at 6:30 PM. They ate together most nights. Rosie believed that this was a situation she had subtly engineered, and she was very pleased about it.

After dinner Kendal did bath and bedtime. She would have loved to delegate this process occasionally, but Joel never went upstairs, and it was a line that felt unnatural to cross. Once Rosie was asleep, Kendal and Joel debriefed the day, updating the org charts, trying to establish the sway Alex had at management level, and discussing strategies to get closer to him. Despite Sasha's claim, Joel reported that Alex was rarely in the office.

Kendal worked hard to bury the sad fact that this period was one of the easiest and most comfortable she had ever known. She also had the self-awareness to stay wary where Rico was lurking in the background, and she frequently yearned for Khalil, a real relationship instead of this loveless imitation.

It was a drizzly, cold November day and Kendal was running around Highbury Fields. It wasn't a massive departure from her usual route, but this time she kept the Shapiro house in her eyeline. When a cab pulled up and Alex Shapiro emerged wearing a suit and carrying a briefcase, Kendal decided to follow. It was rush hour, and the combination of roadworks, buses, school run, and bad weather meant the cab couldn't go much faster than she could run, and more than once she had to pause and wait for it to catch up. London had always been a stupid city for driving. She followed the car all the way to Old Street, where Alex hopped out and disappeared into the Glo-Tech office building. Kendal returned home at a sprint. The wind in her hair as she picked up pace felt like a liberation. She had stopped running about halfway through her pregnancy, and, with each day of this seeming normality, she felt the sometimes suffocating bond between her and Rosie start to slacken and ease, just enough that she could enjoy being alone, that it felt earned and valued instead of stolen and corrupt. Kendal wondered if everyone felt parenthood was a prison—from the mean guard and solitary confinement to the beige food. Or whether it was her particular style and circumstance that made it so. Either way, the freedom to run felt as fresh and gratifying to her as it would to an inmate in a supermax.

As her pace increased, the city flexed around her, fluctuating between Georgian terraces and brutalist estates, primary schools and parks, canals and traffic. She was a couple of minutes from the house when she noticed a familiar vehicle, unremarkable except that there were two people in it. She caught a fleeting glimpse of a lens glare and felt sure it was a surveillance op.

Heart pounding, she shifted gears. A sense of calm ensconced her mind. This was well-trodden territory. She cut across the road and ducked down onto New River Walk, then doubled back so she could see the vehicle from behind. Emerging into Barnsbury, she took a street parallel to the vehicle and jogged around the block, pausing to take off her hat and hoodie and put on sunglasses. On the road where she'd seen them she slowed to a walk, keeping close to the cars as if she were about to get in one of them. She got a picture of the car, the back of a head, and the license plate before they clocked her approach, revved, and zoomed away. Men, one white, one Black, both under thirty, not police, not Albanian mob either, and if they were on a mission to deliver a message, why run away when she was right there? There was a long list of bad people who might have an interest in her whereabouts, and the persistent feeling of being watched was rarely paranoia.

At the house Rosie instantly detected Kendal's anxiety, so instead of getting ready, she spent the next thirty minutes running around, naked and screaming. Kendal gave herself a time-out, sitting at the bottom of the stairs and recalibrating her system so that her stress would be undetectable to Rosie, who was like a bloodhound for bad moods, a finely tuned machine to increase agitation. It was as if a shift in Kendal's aura created in Rosie some equal and opposite action. Kendal didn't care if Rosie was late for school, except she wanted to run extra levels of countersurveillance. If they could use an SDR—one of their established surveillance detection routes—she might be able to figure out who the men in the car were working for. It didn't add up, none of it was adding up, and it was that, more than anything, that had Kendal worried. Rosie was more concerned with evading her uniform. She wanted to go to school in a dinosaur jacket, swimming goggles, and a silk scarf she must have unearthed from Kendal's wardrobe.

Once she had relaxed her endocrine system, Kendal went into the kitchen and put the kettle on.

"You okay?" Joel asked gently

"Yeah, fine. Rosie's being a knob."

"I heard you!" Rosie shouted from the hallway.

"GOOD!" Kendal shouted back.

Rosie trounced up the stairs and miraculously reappeared wearing her hat and jacket. She had kept the scarf and the goggles dangling out her pocket.

"Ella said no scarves," said Kendal, feeling guilty for weaponizing Ella's authority, having been expressly instructed to never do that. Rosie ignored her and stood petulantly in the hall, shoving various articles into her schoolbag: a letter from the council, some batteries out of a bowl on the side, and a framed picture of herself in a hat. Joel and Kendal watched in amused silence. When she was finished Rosie stood by the front door and tapped a coin on the side table. She looked about seventeen years old, and although she was irritated, Kendal also felt a wave of love and sadness. She was growing into an absolute rascal, and so quickly.

"Joel's taking me to school today," Rosie proclaimed in a haughty voice, without making eye contact. Joel shook his head at Kendal to show he had no part in this plan.

"Do you want to?" Kendal asked. It was a good idea; she could flush out her tail this way. Joel's delight at being asked was adorable.

"I'd love to!"

"You know where it is? Her classroom and everything?"

"She can show me. You can show me, right, Rosie my bro-zy?"

"Yes, sir," Rosie replied, trying to be cool, clearly astonished that her ruse had been successful. That this was a new level of trust wasn't lost on Joel, and he looked concerned. "Are you sure, is everything okay?"

"Yeah, all good. Use your training. If you see anything sus take evasive and remember the details. Don't let her go more than a yard away from you, never farther than you can reach, until she's right outside the classroom. Take a weird route back and change direction suddenly at least once, just for fun." Kendal smiled.

"Copy that, will do." He squeezed her shoulder on his way past and then blushed.

She followed them to school, watching their backs, the windows, the vehicles. She didn't spot anything. Once she had seen Joel drop Rosie at school, she headed back. No signs of anyone watching. She called Fini. "Have you heard of an app called Cadu being built by a company called Glo-Tech?"

"Good morning to you too, bestie."

"Sorry, small talk, niceties, kind regards."

Fini giggled down the phone. She had audibly taken a seat and started typing. "Lemme see. Oh yeah, the education thing. I have heard a bit about it. Dicey as fuck."

"How so?"

"Like, why is this dirty gambling-tech firm making a major education platform for the government? Reeks of backhanders."

"It's where my pet nerd works."

"Hmm, nefarious. Do you trust him?"

"I do actually, yeah. Like seventy percent at least."

"Go, team! Well then, better make sure he's careful. If they find out he's undercover, they might literally terminate him."

"Will you look into the tech for me, see if anything flags?"

"Anything for you, KC, as ever."

"Love youuuuuuu."

Joel rang the doorbell a few minutes later and then followed her into the kitchen.

Kendal handed him a device. "This connects to the bugs in Sasha's bag and studio. Will you go through them daily and see if Alex comes up? It's a bit of a long shot. It would be more useful to get inside his office, or maybe his house if he's not at work that much."

Joel took the device and slipped it into his pocket with a nod.

"Do you know the school closes for Christmas next week?" he said innocently.

Kendal frowned at him. "What?! They just had half term. It's November."

"And there's a parents' evening straight after the holiday. Ella leaped out at me and said she hoped to see me there because Rosie talks about me all the time."

He had the good sense to look embarrassed about it. "I'm not trying to gate-crash your family. I'm happy to help. I know there's a line."

Kendal softened her features, but for the briefest moment she felt sick. How had this person entwined so deeply into their lives? "No, I know, it's not your fault, I appreciate you. I didn't get the memo."

"Maybe check your spam?" Joel pitched unhelpfully. "Ella called it the progress, objectives, and perspectives meeting."

Kendal's mouth fell open. "That's what the POP is? Why is everything coded? They're worse than Rico!" She plucked her phone from her pocket and opened her calendar and added "POP." She could see now that the school had color-coded the three-and-a-half-week Christmas break in a very slightly different blue from term time, and cursed whoever made that decision. She turned her attention back to Joel, wondering what they would do for almost a month of childcare.

"Did you see anyone following you?"

Joel bit his bottom lip and looked edgy, and, not for the first time, Kendal thought his face was expressive as an emoji's, as round and silly.

"Well, there were people following us, but I think they were just also going that way so I'm not sure."

Kendal shrugged. "Doesn't matter, just try and be vigilant. I think I might have a tail. It's probably nothing, but might as well make them work for it."

She put the kettle on to make him a green tea. "What the hell are we gonna do for Christmas. Are you going home?"

Joel looked up from his own phone, confused. "Home?" He looked around the room. Kendal flinched at his innocence. Did he really think of this as home? She found herself jealous, that he was able to drop roots so readily. She still thought of it as a safe house.

"Canada?" she clarified.

"Oh. No. I was hoping we could spend it together." His face suddenly flushed with color.

"Us three?" Now they were both blushing. Kendal had been thinking about Christmas with Rosie. She wanted to share some of her history, maybe create new traditions. Joel wasn't an obvious choice to join, but maybe it was better to bring someone neutral.

"Do you want to come to Suffolk with us? I thought Rosie might like a change of scene."

He nodded eagerly. "Oh wow, yes please, sounds amazing. Just like *The Holiday*. Only if you're sure. Why Suffolk, is that where your family is from?"

"It's just a nice part of the world. There's a cottage on the beach in Aldeburgh that I used to like." A visceral flashback of Khalil made her temperature briefly flare.

"Amazing! I'd love to. Thank you for inviting me."

Something inside suddenly clicked in Kendal. She was warmed by the thought: a family holiday to a countryside cottage. A real Christmas, like a movie. It was an experience that was completely absent from Rosie's life, and she felt a swell of pleasure that here was a normal situation. Sure, it had been their secret, but Khalil was dead and the thought of a Christmas spent sitting around thinking about him was too depressing. At least this way they'd have someone with them who could cook.

19

Fini was on the doorstep with her mouth in a comedy "O."

"Whoa, momma, what a spot," she said lustily.

"I know, right? Welcome."

"Is this a Bon Temps joint? They've really come up."

"Yeah, he said it was a leftover from some high-end op."

Fini was standing in the doorway. "These are Banham Unbreakables," she muttered, examining the deadbolt plate set into the door and scouting the doorjamb. "But there's an override? Seems silly."

Kendal nodded, impressed she could tell so much at a glance. "It has facial recognition?" Fini asked.

"Fingerprinting."

"Both, by the looks of it."

"How easy would it be to hack?"

Fini was running her fingers along the surfaces and taking her time wandering through the hallway, visibly impressed. "It's not easy to hack a system like this really. It's not networked, so there's a finite number of people with access. And there's always the physical locks, those are hard to get through. It's probably about as safe as a house can be."

Kendal thought of Lula, Rosie, the cars she'd felt following her, and the big picture she wasn't able to see.

Fini saw the concern in her expression. "But I'll see what I can do." She had lost interest in the house and sat up on a stool at the kitchen island. She pulled her laptop from her bag and opened it, dropping her satchel unceremoniously at her feet. "Can I have a Coke?"

While Kendal bounced around in the kitchen, Fini went into her screen.

"Where's the nerd?" Fini asked without looking up.

"He's at work," Kendal said vaguely.

"How's it going over there?"

"They're prepping the launch, permanent sprint mode, all hands on deck."

"Yeah, they're talking about Cadu on the message boards. Lots of conspiracy theories about it."

Kendal frowned. "Like what?"

"Like what are Bro-Tech doing developing an education app for the government." She shrugged indifferently, but Kendal pressed. "Why shouldn't they?"

"Because everything they've been involved in so far has been high-profit, sin-stock garbage. Gambling, porn, and memes, the lowest bastion of the internet. They're famously not nice guys, so why the sudden interest in kids? Not a lot of profit in those pockets. And the pitch is no ads, no in-app purchases, free to schools everywhere. Pure altruism? Seems fake. They haven't launched the beta yet, but as soon as they do the hackers will be all over it. We'll know if there's anything really ropy going on."

Kendal frowned, but Fini had moved on. "How's jumpy Joel holding up?"

Kendal shook her head. "He's trying to get close to the project lead but not having a lot of luck." Fini looked up from her screen. "Is his gear here, shall we jack it?"

Kendal yawned. "He's got a setup downstairs, but I doubt it has anything useful on it."

"Let's find out," Fini said, and Kendal shrugged okay. Fini disappeared into the basement for twenty minutes. When she reemerged, Kendal put a Coke, a glass with ice and lemon, and a coffee on the counter and pulled up a stool to sit opposite Fini, who eyeballed the offering. "Got any sweets?"

Kendal found some packed-lunch chocolate biscuits in the cupboard and handed them over.

"Your man downstairs has a serious setup."

"He's a gamer."

"No, I mean he's got military-grade security, not Rico's usual matchbox nonsense, couldn't get into it." She muttered, "Anyway, I'm gonna copy your door code and confuse some of your appliances."

"Thanks, babe."

"Pleasure. I'm also giving myself a key."

"My door is always open."

"You sound like my therapist."

"You're in therapy?" Kendal was surprised.

Fini looked at her, bemused. "You're not? Where do you put all the trauma your mother gave you?" Kendal shrugged. Fini muttered what sounded like "yikes" but Kendal let it slide. "You don't seem yourself though," Fini said softly.

"It's a different game with the kid in the house."

"Ditch the kid, loser."

The hark back to the language of their teens made them both chuckle.

"Mustn't grumble though."

"Heaven forbid."

"Say, how good is your access to government intel?"

If Fini was concerned about the question, it didn't show. "Fairly good. It's still a sieve. What do you need?"

"Just curious. My leaks have all dried up. It's like they see me coming and run."

Fini was about to speak, but there was a gentle tap at the door. Fini looked up at Kendal, who leaned backward and through the mottled glass could see the outline of two familiar women.

"Random."

"What?"

"It's the mums."

"You want me to vanish?" Fini asked quietly.

"No, stick around, take a read on them. Check out my schoolyard laugh."

Fini winked and looked pleased, closing her laptop and adjusting her posture while Ken headed for the door.

Nat gave a big grin. "Hi, Ken, sorry for the drop-in! You're not replying to the group!"

"But you know where I live?"

"Yeah, got it off the school spreadsheet."

Kendal swallowed the fury she felt at this invasion of her privacy and made a note to find and destroy it.

"Well, it's a nice surprise, come in."

"You sure we're not interrupting?" Nat asked, already in the hallway.

"Not at all. A friend of mine is over for coffee. Come in, say hello." Sasha stayed on the doorstep, as if she genuinely didn't want to intrude. Kendal held the door wider and smiled her into the house. She was carrying a different bag from the one that was bugged.

"Shoes?" Sasha asked, and Kendal smiled at her. "Shoes on today, the cleaner hasn't been."

From the kitchen she heard Fini smirk.

Nat was peering around the house like a surveyor. "Gorgeous place."

"Thanks."

They went through to the kitchen, where Fini was perched looking like "grown-up" was a Halloween costume she'd just thrown on. Nat and Fini eyeballed each other possessively, and Kendal put the kettle on. Nat pulled her phone out of her pocket and swore under her breath. "Sorry, got to take this." She disappeared into the hall and spoke in hushed tones. When Sasha walked into the kitchen, Fini sat bolt upright.

"I know you!" Fini said suddenly, staring at Sasha. "You used to be Sasha Nova!"

Sasha gave a polite if mirthless laugh. "Used to be."

Fini seemed to realize what she'd said. "Oh, sorry, I didn't mean . . . that you're not anymore." She recovered herself. "But you're not making work, are you? I would know. I'm a massive fan."

"Thanks," Sasha said sweetly. Natalie came back into the room and introduced herself, her hand outstretched. "I'm Nat, nice to meet you."

"Fini."

"Oh, interesting. As in Fiona?"

Kendal smirked from across the room.

"No," Fini replied with a contemptuous glare. Then dismissed Nat and explained to Kendal, "Sasha Nova was a digital artist, like a proper originator." She turned back to Sasha. "Didn't you make a shit ton of cash on NFTs?"

Sasha laughed again; she seemed to be a completely other person. "I did okay. I got in and out really quick."

"You did the bubbles!"

"Ironically."

"Oh man, yeah, genius. Sasha Nova! What are you doing now?"

"I retired Nova, and I'm a sculptor. I've got a show coming up, you should come." She turned to Kendal. "You should bring your friend," she said nicely.

Fini looked fiendishly pleased and stuck her hand out to Sasha.

"Fini Meridian, very literally at your service."

Nat's mouth was agape and Kendal smiled. It had taken Fini less than a minute to find her a way in to Sasha's life. "Coffee for anyone?"

"We brought wine," Nat said, rummaging around in her bag and bringing out a bottle of prosecco. "Arts and crafts is no fun sober, mate." Her voice was regular but her enthusiasm seemed uncharacteristically phony.

"Arts and whats?" Kendal asked, watching Fini pack her kit away in a hurry.

"You're signed up for the nativity scene team, babe. Rosie is a sheep. Sam's a shepherd, obviously, fucking farm boy."

Fini laughed loudly, then blushed when all eyes turned to her.

"I'll leave you to it," she muttered. They waved goodbye and Fini slammed the front door, as Nat emptied what looked like a lifetime's supply of glue and feathers onto the table.

"*Wizard of Oz*–themed nativity play. Don't you sometimes wish you'd sent them to a normal school? Just keep it simple, mate, couple of angels, bit of myrrh. What the hell are dog sheep? Why so many Totos?"

Before they could answer, both Kendal's and Sasha's phones pinged. It was odd timing. They looked at their messages, and then they looked at each other. Sasha said, "I've been called to pick up because Lily's had an altercation with another student."

"Me too . . ." said Kendal slowly.

"Fight of the flower girls," Nat said gleefully. "Not to be smug, but it's always a win when it's not Sam who's in trouble." She held an invisible glass of champagne to the sky.

20

Sasha and Kendal walked awkwardly to the school, where they were met by Ella at her most fierce. She was pink with tension as they slipped through the classroom door, while the TA played with both girls in the other room. They seemed to be getting on fine.

Ella sat them down as if they were children. "Both girls have a tendency to get angry and lash out. Children this age have poor impulse control, so it's not unusual for them to experience intense reactions, but for some reason, this week they've taken to winding each other up. This afternoon Lily threw Rosie's workbook across the room, and I'm sorry to say that in return Rosie hit Lily quite hard, then threatened to kill her."

"Jesus, really?" Kendal was genuinely shocked. She turned to Sasha. "I'm so sorry. I don't know why she would say something like that."

Internally, she replayed her conversations with Rico and Fini. Had she talked about work in front of Rosie?

She looked contrite and directed her line at Ella. "There's absolutely no violence in our house, I don't know where that would have come from." She turned to look at the kids. "Is Lily okay?" Ella looked from one to the other. "Both girls were very upset by it. Rosie seemed as surprised as Lily that she had lashed out and she has apologized. I do think though that it might be good to have them spend some time together to try and patch things up a bit. Whatever the root cause of their friction, I think good ol' communication is the answer."

"As always," said Sasha sanguinely. Kendal could not believe her luck. Sasha turned to Ella. "Thank you for bringing this to us, we'll take it from here." She gave a wink and a smile and got up, and Kendal followed her lead. In the playground, Sasha glanced at Kendal, who flushed. "I'm really sorry."

"Don't worry about it. Lily can be an absolute bastard. She probably earned it."

Kendal looked surprised, and it was Sasha's turn to look guilty. "You know what I mean, sometimes," she said, then added, "Come over tomorrow if you like? I'll clear it with Alex. He'll just need a bit of a heads-up. We can pick up the arts and crafts."

"Sounds great," Kendal said neutrally.

"I'll message you later."

She called for Rosie to join her, and they headed off.

"Why did you hit her, Ro?"

Rosie scuffed her shoes along a wall.

"She's rude." Rosie didn't offer anything further, but she looked upset.

"Ella is furious. What did she say to you? I've never seen you hit anyone, you know better than that."

Rosie glanced up at her with a face equal parts fury and sadness. "She thinks she's so great just because she has a daddy and I hate her she's stupid."

Kendal stopped in her tracks. "Is that what this is about? What did she say?" But it was too late. Rosie was in meltdown. She sobbed and held her arms out. Kendal picked her up and carried her home.

They had a subdued evening. Kendal asked if she wanted to talk, but she shook her head. Rosie ate only a little bit of pasta at dinner, got out of the bath early, and, unusually, went to sleep in Kendal's arms. She hadn't even asked to watch TV. It was cuddly and delightful. At 10:00 PM. Kendal went downstairs and had a glass of wine and did some heavy background on Sasha Nova. Fini had, without needing to be asked, sent over a deep-dive file attached to an email she had titled "your sexy mate." Fini's file included info about Alex, who had been early in his career, developing pioneering technology, when Sasha met him. He faded out of her file after the wedding. Kendal replied and asked Fini to do a deep dive on Alex Shapiro. Bon Temps intel hadn't shown any red flags, but Kendal had a creeping feeling that Rico was holding out on her.

At midnight, Kendal turned off the lights and went up to bed. She found Rosie mewing, hot as fire and glassy eyed. Her skin was flushed and covered in sweat, and her breathing was raspy. Kendal picked her up off the bed and held her against her body, horrified at the heat coming off her. She yelled for Joel, but he obviously couldn't hear her. She keyed in the number for emergencies but then hesitated. It was so profoundly ingrained in Kendal that it was not okay to enlist the help of The System that although her thumb hovered over the green button to call, instead she texted Joel, "SOS please come up," and gave him the code for his door. He was there in moments, clutching a baseball bat and looking around wildly for danger. "What is it?" He was sweating and looked crazed with fear.

"She's burning up, her breathing is haywire."

Kendal moved aside, and Joel bent over Rosie and felt her head. He listened to her chest and took her pulse. Her wheezing made Kendal frantic. "Should I call an ambulance?"

Joel looked at her doubtfully. "I think it's croup. This happened to my sister and she had a panic attack and crashed her car." But Kendal couldn't hear him because her mind was racing. Joel pressed her shoulders. "It's okay, it's not as bad as it looks, honestly. Have you got any paracetamol?"

"In the medicine cabinet," she answered as if in a trance. He rushed out and came back with a cold compress and the kid's medicine plunger locked and loaded. He lifted Rosie tenderly off the bed and gave her the medicine, then laid her down and put the compress on her forehead.

Kendal remembered suddenly who she was, as if Rosie were separate to her. She went on autopilot, op mode.

"I'm taking her to A&E." Her pulse returned to normal. She had frozen, a panic response she hadn't had since she was eleven years old. She could examine the feeling now as if it were external to her.

Joel didn't notice the switch. "She's probably better off resting here. I think if her breathing gets worse or her lips go blue, I'll drive her in. Are you okay?"

"I was just drinking fucking wine. I wasn't checking on her or anything."

Joel chuckled, but it wasn't patronizing. "You didn't do anything wrong. She'll be fine. It's a dramatic cough, honestly. Give it a few minutes. I'm right downstairs if you need me, okay?" She nodded glumly, and he left the room as if he couldn't wait to get out of there. It was his first time upstairs and it clearly made him uncomfortable.

Kendal lay awake, listening intently to Rosie's breathing, which started to ease back to normal as the meds kicked in. It was the longest wait of her life, and her mind spiraled into all the ways she was letting her daughter down: raising her in a city, sending her to a school full of strangers to learn skills she wouldn't need in postcapitalist society; too many white carbs and ultra-processed foods; no siblings, no father, no grandparents. The list went on and on. Then she remembered that she had a crucial meeting with Sasha and that she would have to cancel. She considered inviting them over anyway, which threw her into another guilt spiral. She felt a deep fury at her own mother until she realized that that line of thinking was just her mind deflecting the guilt away, and turned it back on herself.

She held Rosie close but tried to keep her cool. She was already so big, her hand rested on Kendal's forearm and she stroked the fingers and the tiny fingernails and could remember with absolute clarity the feeling of those little fingers gripping hers when Rosie was a baby. She felt a tangible sense of loss, a wave of deep grief for the tubby, weighted bundle that had grown away. She longed more than anything to look at pictures and videos of the baby years. They were images she had never taken, videos she hadn't flimed, files she hadn't stored except in her head. She couldn't believe how many baby things people put online, their birthdays and full names and weights, every major milestone. She had never understood why parents felt the child's life was theirs to share, but in this moment, briefly, she got it and she envied them. She wept at her lack of a record of Rosie's life so far. It was safer, but it felt like a loss. Instead, she held that little hand and searched her mind for the memories.

Once Rosie's temperature had reduced, Kendal crept downstairs. Joel was waiting anxiously at the table and when she appeared he stood up and hugged her tight. She let him hold on to her for a few seconds and then mumbled into his T-shirt.

"I'm all right. Thank you."

He let her go. "That was more for my benefit, that was scary. She's okay though, right?"

"She's okay, I'll keep checking on her. We should have a debrief. Did you get any face time with Alex this week?"

Joel grabbed a beer and sat down. "No. They're going to beta launch Cadu any day now, so everyone is heads down. Hard to get any gossip at all when it's like this. Headphones on and lunch at the desk is the norm. It's a bit boring, sorry."

"Have the bugs shown anything?"

Joel shook his head. Kendal was distracted by Rosie, but something wasn't right. Joel got up to go.

"I can work from home tomorrow in case you need a break, and I can watch Rosie?"

"Thanks, Joel." He disappeared down the stairs.

At 8:00 AM, red eyed and exhausted, Kendal texted Sasha. "Rosie's been up all night, think it's croup, can we reschedule Nuremberg? Sorry!"

Sasha texted back almost immediately. "Oh no, croup's the worst! Hope she recovers quickly." There was nothing in the words to imply it, but Kendal could definitely sense that Sasha was relieved.

Kendal sighed and threw the phone on the table. She felt bored, stressed, and helpless, which seemed an apt synopsis of motherhood in the early years. She wondered when it would change, and what it would change into.

In the increasingly frenetic buildup to the Christmas break, croup spread through the school like a flame through kindling. Attendance at the pantomime hit an all-time low. The WhatsApp group was awash with hand-wringing and banal advice: "Hot-water bottles for the win!" and "Have you tried lemon on the chest?" The school sent a memo asking anyone with a cough to stay at home.

On the penultimate day of term, Joel arrived back from work late. Rosie was already in bed and Kendal was reading when he tapped on the door. He entered the room looking tired and anxious.

"What happened?"

"The bag bug picked up Alex going bananas at Sasha. It's a bit glitchy but I thought you should hear it."

He pressed Play on the device, and scrolled through scrunching that sounded like the bag moving around.

Sash, I swear to god. You don't understand.

Sasha's side of the conversation was inaudible and Alex's was glitchy. Joel stood over the device chewing at his thumb.

You can't just bring people in. They're fucking watching everything I do.

There was a sense that Alex had moved farther from the bug. Their voices matched now, a low murmur.

I can't. Baby, I can't. It's not up to me anymore.

Sasha must have picked up the bag because she was suddenly crystal clear.

Yeah well, maybe I can't do this either.

There was a final grappling of material against a hard surface and then a door slammed and neither was audible.

Kendal frowned at Joel. "He sounds scared."

Joel nodded. "That's what I thought. But of whom?"

"Was there anything else?"

"No, I think she must have ditched the bag after this, because there was a bunch of crunching and the bug died."

"Damn. How about the studio?"

"Nothing, she's barely there and it doesn't pick up anything other than Radio 6."

Kendal tapped at the table in thought. Dead bugs and a scared Alex. She wasn't sure what it was all adding up to, but it didn't seem good.

21

Kendal rented an inconspicuous car under an old alias, and Joel drove down the motorway with Rosie contentedly singing in the back seat. She was newly into Motown, and Kendal was newly realizing how many songs from the era were about the problematic love of underage girls. Joel whistled along. Kendal kept a vigilant eye on the wing mirrors but couldn't see any signs of a tail. Joel picked up on her surveillance.

"You worried?" he asked quietly.

She nodded and checked Rosie in the rearview mirror. He smiled reassuringly. "Want me to take evasive?" He looked at her hopefully, and she chuckled. "It's okay, just keep your eyes on the road."

A few hours later, they were in a cottage in Aldeburgh, Suffolk. A log fire crackled and the air was heavy with smoke and salt from the sea breeze that battered the house around them. Kendal and Rosie sat cross-legged at a coffee table, both staring into the flames. They were spending Christmas in the countryside like normal people. Joel had gone for a walk, blown away by the sheer Englishness of the town. He bustled back in through the door, windswept and pink. "Dude, how did you find this place? It's amazing!"

Khalil had brought her here. To this exact cottage. It had been one of many weekends they'd organized for each other. Always trying to outdo the other in beauty and surprise. "I used to visit with a friend," was all she said.

It was a Christmas out of an Enid Blyton story; the Famous Five and Just William, postcard villages and day trips to historical sites. Joel wore khaki trousers and baseball caps and carried a water bottle and could not have been more Canadian. Rosie got bored and sticky and shouted "COW" at intervals along the roads. She saw her first Shetland pony and wept with joy that such a thing was real, bringing about a new game called Real or Made Up?, which had started simply enough, with unicorns, Peter Pan, and owls but got gradually more difficult—magic, TV, God. Ridiculously, for December, it was clement enough for walks on the beach. Joel bounced between classic comedy references that made Kendal smile obligingly, and leaping off the street into surprising if not very convincing hiding places.

He sought out local ingredients and got into long, enthusiastic conversations with shopkeepers about anything from fishing tackle to Roman cobblestones; there was nothing he wasn't interested in. He spent twenty-five minutes in a bakery in Woodbridge talking about cooking over fire, while Kendal and Rosie itched to get on with their day. Kendal told him he was a walking podcast and he took it as a compliment. He started meal prep early on Christmas Eve and spent hours at the stove. Kendal tried to help but was shooed away to play with Rosie.

"What's he making?" Rosie asked, bored of Kendal.

"He's putting a chicken inside a duck inside a turkey. I think it's a Canada thing," Kendal said quietly.

Rosie thought about it. "Does he hate birds?"

Kendal giggled. "I guess so."

At 6:00 PM on Christmas Day, with rain falling ("pretend it's snow!") and music playing, he delivered the finest dinner of their lives. Rosie, dressed as an elf, stuffed potatoes into her face until she was asleep at the table. Joel put her to bed and joined Kendal by the fire, which was still going with a comforting crackle.

"You are amazing at Christmas, Joel. Thank you," Kendal remarked as he sat down, topping up her glass and raising his for a clink.

He beamed at the rare compliment. "Thank you, ma'am. It sure is a pleasure to have a break from the norm."

That he spoke in clichés and platitudes didn't annoy her briefly. She had never had a Christmas like it, and didn't know how she would have provided it for Rosie without him.

On the last day of their trip, which seemed to have lasted several months, they woke up to tumultuous skies and distant thunder. As if reality were rolling back in to make each of them miserable. It manifested as silence in Kendal, who was coming to terms with a fresh kind of grief.

Joel was compensating for Kendal's quiet with a high-pitched, phony cheer, Rosie with outward belligerence. Try as they might, none of them could get a grip on the day. They went out for coffee and a walk and wrapped up against the weather, which wasn't freezing but wasn't friendly either.

They sat on a bench by the beach watching Rosie kick at pebbles. They seemed to have run out of things to say and even Joel was on edge.

"Do you miss Canada?" Kendal asked, thinking of her own lack of a home.

"Not really," Joel answered. "My nephews mainly. My mom. She doesn't understand what I do, so staying in touch is harder than I thought it would be."

Kendal smiled ruefully. Her own mother was a ghost and she wouldn't have it any other way.

"It's Shanghai I miss most," Joel said, staring into the middle distance. "Which is weird because I don't remember liking it that much at the time."

"What about it?"

"The energy of it. It's like nowhere else I've been. I find myself craving it sometimes."

"The busyness?"

"Yeah, I guess. Have you been?"

He didn't wait for an answer and went on. "It's frenetic, but it's always moving forward, a commitment to progress. It has momentum. I sometimes feel like the West is the opposite. Like they're trying to cling on to the past and stop things changing."

Kendal nodded in agreement. "Or so desperate to forget their history that they refuse to learn anything from it."

"Yeah. Yeah, exactly." Joel nodded again.

They heard the tinkling tune of an ice cream van before Rosie did and sat braced for the request. When her ears seemed to waggle and she looked up in response to it, they both chuckled.

"In December?" he asked incredulously.

"British seaside, innit? No such thing as weather. Fancy a Twister?"

Joel smiled at the callback and shook his head in response. "I'm good, thanks." There was a tenderness to his voice. He sounded genuinely happy.

Rosie wandered over, the picture of innocence. She was practically whistling.

"I wish we were allowed ice cream in winter," Kendal said wistfully. Rosie looked from her to Joel suspiciously.

"We could, though. There's a van." She looked around as if undercover. "No one would know."

Kendal laughed and stood up, reaching for Rosie's hand.

Rosie looked delighted. As they approached the van Kendal felt uneasy. The window hadn't opened and the engine wasn't running with the familiar, onion-fumed exhaust. She slowed as the window slid open and she could see a man within.

For a moment the world stood still. Her eyes were relaying a message to her brain that simply wasn't possible and her brain was trying to reject it. A surge of adrenaline kept her moving forward, and with a rush that must have been her mind catching up with the facts, she acknowledged the face she was looking into belonged, unequivocally, to Khalil Masoumi. The man she had left behind five years earlier. Rosie's dad. A dead man. She practically heard the gunshots echoing through time. This was not possible. And yet . . .

He leaned forward languorously and rested his chin on his hands, holding her gaze with a force that nearly toppled her. She had a swift and fierce internal debate about how to react, and settled on her default: act natural. She approached with a mild smile, raised brow, narrowed eyes. You would have to be standing very close to see the tears pricking at the corners. Somehow she had forgotten quite how beautiful he was; her whole body contracted as she took him in. Inwardly she cursed her cardigan, which was perhaps the ugliest garment ever created by human hand. She didn't let that thought into her voice. She scanned the area surrounding the van, but there was no one else around.

"Hello," he said brightly.

"HELLO!" Rosie yelled.

The smile he gave them made Kendal invisibly melt into a useless puddle.

Without taking his eyes off Kendal he said gently, "What can I get you, beautiful?"

Rosie had two fingers in her mouth and gazed up at Kendal, expectantly.

"In a bunch of trouble."

Khalil tore his eyes off Kendal and glanced down at Rosie. Could he see that she was his? Yes, of course, anyone could see she was his. Kendal saw the realization spread across him like a tidal surge; his aloofness momentarily dissipated and he looked at Kendal with searching eyes. She gave the slightest nod and a wave of pure joy crossed his features.

The smile he gave Rosie made her grin and stick the front of her tongue between her teeth. Kendal marveled at seeing them together. Rosie had his eyes, but more than that, she had his spirit.

"He means me, Mama." Rosie giggled in a voice she didn't normally use.

"I do mean you, baby girl. What would you like, anything you want, free of charge."

The desire to get in the van and somehow absorb him completely was overwhelming, and Kendal found herself lost for words. She reached up to the window and touched his hand; he closed hers in both of his and the warmth lit her up. Rosie took over. "Can I have two creams on the sprinkles?"

"Please," Kendal murmured automatically.

"Please," Rosie added quickly, lest this rare treat be taken away.

Khalil released Kendal's hand, took a sprinkle-topped cone, piled it high with soft serve, and poured some more sprinkles on top. He was surprisingly adept at making ice creams. He handed it down to Rosie with a flourish, and as he leaned out of the van Kendal smelled the warm honeyed scent she had longed for so many times over the last few years.

His skin brushed hers and he looked into her eyes as if searching for something. His smile said he'd found it. Kendal wished she wasn't at street level, gazing up at him like some teenager.

It wasn't just that he was alive, it was the relief of the information that really sent her soaring with joy. She'd been living in a Schrödinger world, never able to settle in either reality. Finding him alive meant she could discard half her questions, and she was shocked at how heavy a load that had been.

"Who's the spook?" He nodded over to where Joel was on the bench, chatting with a lady who was walking a dog.

"He's not a spook, he's a nerd."

Khalil paled. "What do you mean? Who does he work for?"

"That's Joel, he's from Canada," Rosie offered, her face already bearded with ice cream. "He's not my daddy," she added proudly. Khalil raised his eyebrows and smiled at her, but not before a brief glimmer of venom had crossed his features. Brief, but enough to ignite Kendal's indignation.

"Joel? You trust him?" He purred this at Kendal.

"Yes sirree," she chirped.

She didn't know why she'd turned into a lady from 1950s America;

maybe the cardigan had taken over. She smiled politely, but a wave of deep fury swept over her like the tidal breeze. Where had he been? Rosie turned and walked away. Joel had stood up to take a phone call. He gave them a distracted wave. Kendal and Khalil stared at each other.

"Kara," he whispered.

"No," Kendal replied firmly. "She died."

"It's not safe. We need to talk."

"I don't have your number," she said.

He scowled at her like she was a belligerent child and handed her a white card with a QR code on one side. She slipped it into her pocket, stared into his face for another moment, tried to wipe her feelings from her face as she turned and walked away.

The lilting jewelry-box tune started up again as the van drove calmly away, and as the distance grew, Kendal felt a part of her torn out and taken with it. She wanted to lie in the fetal position and groan. She wanted to run after it and tear its doors off and fight and kill and eat him. She wanted to hold him. She wanted Rosie to know, so strongly, that the handsome man in the ice cream van was hers too, he was theirs, he belonged to them. Surely now he'd found them, he wouldn't go far. She had an awful feeling that she'd let him go again, and that it was a terrible mistake. Rosie was oblivious, intent on her ice cream. Kendal scoped the area for surveillance, feeling newly vulnerable.

They walked toward the cottage and Joel caught up, tousling Rosie's hair and chuckling at her sticky face. "He was a handsome fella," he said timorously. Kendal looked at him from the corner of her eye. "Who?"

"The ice cream man. White T-shirt, no hat," he said teasingly. Kendal kept her voice steady, looking at her phone instead of at him. She murmured in response, "I know, right? So hot." Joel frowned at her, turning partly in the direction the van had driven away. Kendal couldn't shake the feeling they were being watched. She suddenly felt a long way from anything secure. Sensing the change in her mood, Joel lifted Rosie onto his shoulders and picked up the pace, looking at her with concern. "You okay?"

She was holding the card he'd given her so tightly she might absorb it.

Her phone rang: Bon Temps. The timing was unsettling.

"Yes?"

"Ken."

"Rico."

"Merry Christmas. How's the holiday?"

"Fine, thanks. Lovely."

"Excellent. Just checking in. See you soon."

She didn't like Rico being friendly. She scanned the town for flickering windows or cars full of creeps and hurried them along. Joel decided to clean the house, ready to leave the next day. Kendal said she had a headache and went for a lie-down. Rosie had found the TV remote and was indefinitely occupied. In her room, Kendal sat on the bed and stared at the card. She could hear Joel vacuuming. Rummaging in a locked compartment of her suitcase, she pulled out a phone she'd not used before. It had four-factor secure identity protocols, a souped-up Fini special. She unlocked it and scanned the code, sent a message, and deleted all trace from the phone. She shoved the card into the compartment she'd stored the phone in. She sat back and closed her eyes. It felt abstract—had she dreamed it? Her mind raced with images of her past life, playing and replaying the last time she had seen Khalil. What had she missed?

She'd slept with him under the guise of the op, although sex wasn't usually in her armory. She told herself it was necessary, but almost immediately it became something more. As if sensing the artifice in her, Khalil had used her body against her, weaponizing pleasure, disarming her and forcing her to be authentic, and in doing so, slowly, sensuously, and for the first and only time in her life, she had fallen madly in love. He was a consummate professional, but he was also funny and kind, and it was a combination she'd rarely encountered in her world. The day it began to detonate, she was standing in a silk robe holding a cup of coffee. He lived in a penthouse with floor-to-ceiling windows and a mildly ironic view of MI5. Maybe she had been staring at Thames House and that's why he said it, or maybe he was reading her thoughts.

"You'd make an excellent spy."

It was out of context, and she must have flinched, no more than the briefest flicker, but it was enough. Without moving, his body, the language of it changed, his lips parted in shock, grief etched in his eyes. They both knew she was burned; simultaneously they felt their hearts shatter and she saw that it had been as real for him as it had been for her. Neither spoke—how could they? Who knew who was listening? Not even Kendal knew. She was Kara, to him, and the sound of him saying it made her wish it were her real name.

"What makes you say that?"

"The way you stand. Like you're holding something dangerous inside." She turned back to the window and let a tear topple over the edge of her eye, wiping it discreetly from her cheek.

"Get back into bed, Kara." There was a new edge in the way he said it, like a swear word.

She walked back toward him, her eyes glistening. He stared at her, questioning, desperate.

They switched to sign language. He asked *who?* She said *sorry*. She wanted to signal that they were safe but she couldn't know for sure. That was the moment she realized what a mess she had made. Who *was* she working for? She couldn't save him from the unknown forces she reported to.

Her mind spiraled and he watched, seeming to read it. He pressed his face into her shoulder and she could feel the heat of his eyes and the tears he pushed against her skin. He leaned up on his elbow and smiled at her. With tiny movements he used sign language, a pointing finger across the chest that asked *why?*

And she had to shrug, hot with shame, labeling herself as a mercenary, a weapon rented to the highest payer.

"I'll get in the shower." She kept her voice level, packed her feelings back where they belonged, out of reach.

"Kara."

She didn't answer; she gasped against the wave of shame that coated her body like mud, seeping in through her skin. She had never in her life felt more repugnant.

He reached out and placed his hand on her heart.

"I love you."

He'd said it before, but it had been a game. Nonetheless, she gave the same answer she always gave; this time it was an apology.

"I know."

That should have been the end; that was a closing moment. But instead they toyed with fate, thinking they could keep up the pretense, live the IDs as if nothing had changed. But somewhere out of sight the mechanics of the op had shifted, and by the time it came tumbling down they were too far gone; they were in love.

He was cooking when she got a kill order from Rico. She looked up from the phone and Khalil saw the expression on her face. They were burnt, it was over. He was holding a knife, poised over meat. Then the power in the building was cut and they only had the moon to light the room. He put the knife down and took the gun from under the sink. She leaned across her chair and pulled a Glock from her bag. They clicked the safeties in unison. It was almost funny.

"Do it then," he said calmly, his eyes boring into hers.

"We could run. I have places," she whispered, but he shook his head.

"It's over."

He walked grimly over to her side of the room and stood directly in front of her.

"Do it," he said. She shook her head, desperate for him to move so that she could fight whatever was coming.

"I won't. I love you," she whispered, bracing.

"I know," he replied sadly. But as the door tore back, he pulled the gun from her grasp and pushed her from him into them. She lost her footing and fell, grabbed by armed men in black masks who hadn't uttered a word to identify themselves. She fought wildly, but there were too many of them. They dragged her out of the apartment and threw her down the stairs, a disposable piece of the puzzle. "Single-use spies" as Rico sometimes called them. The muted cracks of silenced weapons rang out. She was outnumbered and unarmed, her wrist shattered. So she ran, shamefully. She left him, because he was dead.

And now? She was lying in their room in Aldeburgh. She couldn't make sense of the scene. But she didn't have to. She could just ask him. She pressed the phone against her chest, feeling silly as a teen, light as a feather, and closed her eyes. She slept more deeply than at any other time in her adult life. When she woke up it was dark, and the clock on the bedside table said midnight. Rosie was in her pajamas and asleep next to her, her feet nuzzled into the small of Kendal's back. Joel must have got her ready for bed. The phone had slipped from her chest and was vibrating softly against the sheets.

She entered the code to answer the phone and pressed it wordlessly to her ear.

There was a long, loaded pause. She could tell the line was connected. She smiled, after everything. After EVERYTHING. They were still cat and mouse. He broke first.

"Kara."

"Sorry, the number you have dialed has not been recognized."

She could literally feel his smile in her body.

"Kara. You're alive."

"I think so. And you?"

"I am now."

The silence felt like arms stretching through time.

"What's her name?"

"Rosie."

"Beautiful."

"She is."

Kendal wished she could see his face. "Can I see you?" they said at the same time, and then smiled.

There was a commotion at Khalil's end, someone shouting in Arabic. Khalil swore gently. "I'll come to you," he said, and hung up.

Kendal slipped out of bed and put the phone back. Her bag was in disarray where Rosie must have been looking for her pajamas. Kendal lay on her back and allowed herself to believe that they might, maybe, the three of them, be a real family.

When they got back to London, Kendal went to the playroom at the top of the house. The window faced out onto the street. She placed a book, *Catch-22*, on the left-hand side of the sill. Each day, when the house was empty, she would move the book to the right. In this simple way she could let him know she was there, and waiting. She tried to keep the spring out of her step. She tried to stop gazing wistfully out of the window with a not-so-secret smile. She tried to think of a way to tell Rosie her father was back from the dead.

22

Kendal could not find her keys. Rosie and Joel were watching her search the house with the sort of detached disinterest you might watch an argument in the street. She was uncharacteristically flustered, as she had been on and off since the Christmas break. She couldn't seem to relax, she was snappy and distracted, and now her keys had gone.

"Are they in the bowl?" Joel pitched.

"The keys bowl, you mean? Where I keep my keys? Do you think?"

"Sorry," he murmured, giving a scared look at Rosie, who giggled naughtily.

"Ro, do you know where they are?"

"In the last place you had them!" she answered, as if she had been waiting her whole life for the opportunity.

Kendal thought, but did not say, *fuuuuuck*.

"Just ring the bell or text me when you head back," Joel said.

Kendal gave up. "Are you sure you don't mind watching her? I shouldn't be more than half an hour."

"Not at all, girls night in!"

Rosie giggled again.

Kendal marched up to the school for her meeting with Ella. They had ten scheduled minutes to talk about progress, objectives, and perspectives. That the school spoke in the corporate jargon of government was depressing. Kendal worried that Rosie was a creative child and neither the school nor she herself was equipped to support that side of her. She wanted to nurture the softness and beauty in her, where her own mother had been obsessed with languages and PE.

It was the first Thursday evening of the term they called "spring," despite the frosty darkness that sat on the city like a pillow on the face. She waited in the darkening playground for her turn, then took a seat on a comedically small chair while Ella perched on a table and towered uncomfortably over her, leafing through a thin pink folder.

"So, our lovely Rosie. I'm glad to say things with her and Lily seem to have settled down. Nevertheless, she's a bit of a loner. I'm hoping this is the term we can get her out of her shell a little bit with the other children, because around the teachers and TAs she's very funny and confident."

The image of Rosie alone broke Kendal's heart. Ella must have seen it in her face. "It's not a criticism, and Rosie seems very happy in class. She is popular and she plays well with others. Perhaps I shouldn't have said loner, maybe 'independent' is more accurate." She looked at Kendal as if for reassurance. But Kendal didn't know how to respond, so Ella went on. "She does seem a bit . . ."—she cleared her throat uncomfortably—"a bit unclear about her family situation. Have there been a lot of changes recently?"

Kendal almost laughed.

"We moved in at the start of the school year, so it's all quite new. We don't know many people yet. Both loners, I suppose."

Kendal felt a droplet fall into the well of shame within. She thought Ella looked embarrassed, and it made her hot with rage. Ella gave her a kind smile. "I don't mean to pry. She's very animated about all the people in her life. She seems to quite enjoy spinning different tales about her family, it's very normal. I only flag it so you know. Kids at this age are fascinated by different ways of life, different family setups, all the things they might not have been exposed to before . . . We have a lot of blended families. It's all perfectly normal." Kendal aggressively wished she'd stop using the word "normal." She let the perennial guilt she felt about Rosie's fictional life wash over her and away.

When the meeting was over, as she was leaving the school gates, she bumped into Nat and Sasha. They hadn't seen each other since before the holidays and it felt like an age. They greeted each other warmly. Kendal had genuinely missed them.

Nat was hopping from one foot to the other to stave off the cold. "How was it?" she asked. "Everything good?"

"Oh yeah, all good, thanks."

Sasha added, "Come for a drink?"

Kendal was surprised. "I texted you a bunch of times over the holidays."

"Urgh, sorry, super annoying, I had to get a new phone."

Nat patted Sasha on the back. "I've got to run in but it won't take Ella long to let me know what a fucking terrorist Sam is." Her hand shot to her mouth. "God, sorry. See you in the pub."

Nat took off and Sasha turned to Kendal. "Lily told me what she said to Rosie last term. I'm really sorry. She's got a nasty habit of finding the deepest wounds and sticking her salty little fingers in them. Please come for a drink. It's been ages and I'd like to clear the air. Between us at least. I understand if Rosie thinks Lily is awful."

"I'll text the babysitter. Reckon I can swing it for a swift one." Kendal pulled out her phone and texted Joel confirmation: "Eyes on target. Running a detail. You good to stay on the job?" She used spy language to make him happy. He texted back right away, "Copy that. Girls night is a go!" next to a selfie of him and Rosie on the sofa, a bowl of popcorn between them and *Hey Duggee* on the TV behind them, although Rosie looked half asleep already. When she looked up Sasha was waiting for her. "Got the permits?" Sasha said, smiling hopefully.

"Yeah, my neighbor is watching her. He says he's fine to stay." They fell into step toward the pub. "Is Lily with her dad?"

Sasha practically snarled. "Yeah, right. You know, I actually tried to get a male nanny so she doesn't grow up thinking men are an absent force."

Kendal didn't say anything, but Sasha's hand shot to her mouth. "Oh my god, I am so sorry. I don't mean . . . I didn't mean you. It's not that he isn't there, it's that he constantly disappoints her."

"That's okay. I've got my neighbor and he's a really good role model. I know what you meant."

"That's great!" Sasha was effusively grateful to be let off the hook. Kendal liked this game; it was like fishing, but instead of fish you dragged feelings out of someone and then threw them back.

"This is his first time doing bedtime though. I hope he can manage a story."

Kendal could feel Sasha looking at her out of the corner of her eye. "Are you divorced or . . . ?" she ventured.

"He left before she was born. I think I've handled it appallingly. For some mad reason I thought it wouldn't come up," Kendal replied.

Sasha's eyes widened and she flinched in apology. "Then Lily rubbed it in her face. I'm so sorry."

"No, it's my fault, we should have talked about it long before she started school. I didn't think they'd all be so wise so quickly," Kendal replied quietly, knowing it was the truth.

They were nearly at the pub, a classic Islington haunt. It was Thursday evening, so nice and busy. They were gearing up for a band to play in the back.

They reached the bar, and Sasha waved over the bartender and ordered a pint of IPA.

"I would have guessed white wine."

Sasha gave a knowing chuckle, though she might have been offended. "Instant heartburn." Kendal nodded knowingly. "Same." She ordered a vodka and soda and nodded to the far corner of the pub. "I'll get these if you grab that table."

When Sasha was out of earshot, Kendal told the bartender to skip the vodka, and he acquiesced with a wink. Sasha was sitting at a corner table with high banquette seating. She was staring out of the window, lost in thought. Her clothes were in muted colors, and although she wore loose cuts and straight lines, Kendal could see they were well made. Nothing about her was bohemian or shabby. The contrast between her and her studio was amazing. Kendal was finding it hard to get a read on her. This was her favorite kind of woman. "So why is your husband always away?" Kendal asked.

"Urgh. He's launching an app he designed. It's been literally years in the making. He's so excited about it. Or he was at least. He says it's all going to shit."

"Oh no. How come?"

"New management don't share his vision. He thinks everyone's out to get him. They go to beta in a couple of days, so I guess we'll see. Honestly, I think he's having a nervous breakdown. That's what happens if you don't sleep for four years. I've tried to tell him, but he just says I don't understand." She shrugged. She looked like a woman who'd had enough.

At that moment Nat rolled up, and she had such a commanding presence that all attention was drawn to her. "What don't you understand?" She didn't wait for an answer. "What's everyone having?" She looked at the table. "One IPA and one . . . what is that?" she asked Kendal.

"Vodka soda."

Nat rolled her eyes. "Jäger bomb? Jäger bomb? Yeah? They've got the nice glasses."

"No," they replied in unison.

"No, *thank you*," Nat scolded, turning to face a woman standing behind her. "Jäger bomb?"

"God no," the new woman replied, as Nat went to the bar.

"Hi, I'm Priya," she said. "Boy Noah's mum." She lifted herself up onto the seat next to Sasha. "Bane of my life that there's a girl Noa in their class." She seemed to be detaching herself from a hundred layers and there was an aura of chaos attached to her. She spoke with a broad American accent. Chicago, Kendal would have guessed. "How did everyone do under Ella's arbitrary scrutiny? Like, what metrics are they using to judge four-year-olds? How many ducks they can point at? How many times they can shout 'airplane'?" She looked around the table. "Don't get me wrong, I'm sure she's a good teacher, but one time Noah came home wearing someone else's clothes. They didn't have PE, I asked. Not just a hoodie or something, the full set. I never even found out whose stuff it was, just disappeared it back in with him."

She looked at each of them, shrugging earnestly. She was beautiful but unkempt, her hair all over the place, stains on her top and collar. She talked fast and loud, but she seemed genuine and alive, and they were appealing qualities. She trained her gaze on Kendal. "I don't think we've met."

"Kendal, Rosie's mum."

"Rosie! Ah, Noah loves Rosie. How did she get on?"

"Yeah, she seems fine, likes making things up apparently. She must get it from her dad."

"Storyteller?"

"Something like that."

Priya nodded sagely. Sasha pressed her lips together and gave Kendal a sympathetic glance, snared into her confidence.

Nat slammed down a tray with two pints, a glass of wine, a vodka soda that was definitely a double, and four glasses that were half full of Red Bull and had shots of Jäegermeister nestled within. To be fair, they were nice glasses. Kendal hadn't seen such a thing since university. It was positively transporting. Nat hoisted herself up onto the chair next to Kendal and distributed the drinks, raising her glass. "To us, the mothers, and those we bore. May they soon stop boring us too!"

Reluctantly they each downed their drinks, and immediately the atmosphere turned jolly. After two more shooters, Nat and Priya decided to try and beg cigarettes from a table sitting nearby. With some success they disappeared outside, leaving Sasha and Kendal alone.

"It's nice to meet the other mums," Kendal said.

"Yeah, it's Nat, she makes friends so easily. I wish I could be like that. Sometimes it feels like there's a club I'm not part of."

"The Perfect Mums' Club?" She nodded sagely. "I haven't been invited either."

"Maybe this is just how we all feel," Sasha mused.

"No, I think there's an actual club," Kendal replied and they both laughed. "I don't think you're missing much having a nanny at pickup. It's completely excruciating," Kendal said. "The chitchat." She mimed blowing her brains out.

"Wouldn't the school gates be so much better if everyone went high-concept? No more, 'how's your weekend.' Just straight into big talk. 'Morning, Rosie's mum. What do you think happens when we die?'"

Kendal thought about it. "Might be too far the other way?"

"Yeah, maybe."

Kendal gave Sasha a cheeky grin. "So, how has motherhood messed with your sense of identity? I've found it's totally undermined nearly all my core values . . . Lol," she added with a goofy smile. Sasha had her drink resting on her lip and took a long drink, then she held the glass aloft. "Hear hear."

She walked home after four rounds of drinks. It was a fifteen-minute walk, but she made it take twenty, meandering in the dark, allowing herself some time and space to think about Khalil. Where was he, where had he been, his lovely arms. At the door she took a moment to shake him away, fumbling for her keys for a while before remembering she didn't have them. She went to ring the doorbell, but it was nearly eight and Rosie might be asleep. She texted Joel instead and waited a couple of minutes for him to appear in the doorway. Once inside, she caught herself in the hallway mirror, grinning foolishly. She stared at herself and thought she looked beautiful and really truly understood what beer goggles were. She hadn't been tipsy for years, and had forgotten the wonderful warmth it brought.

"She's only just dropped off," he whispered, and Kendal giggled with relief.

"Don't worry," she said at a regular volume. "Once she's gone she's gone. Good work! I was sure I'd be watching *Hey Duggee* all night. Do you fancy some wine?" She glanced at her watch. It was 7:55. "I can't remember the last time she went to sleep before eight."

He smiled at her. "She was on her best behavior," he said quietly, still whispering, despite the distance between Rosie and them. She clapped him on the shoulder as he passed and followed him into the kitchen. He poured them both a small glass of wine and brought her a large glass of water, placing it down with a wink. "You might need it."

She felt patronized, but she said thank you and downed it.

"Was it fun? Get any intel?" Joel loved a debrief and she chuckled at him. "She says Alex might be having a nervous breakdown. Thinks he's being sabotaged. My alcohol tolerance is very different than it used to be though. Must be my new mum bod." She hiccupped gently and smiled, feeling genuinely happy.

"So she talked?"

"The trick is to lead with information that changes the intimacy parameters. So we slagged off our husbands, the school system, the existential crisis of parenting while being cool. It's amazing how nosy mums feel authorized to be. I got grilled on Rosie's dad. Those broads do not operate on a need-to-know basis, you know what I mean?"

"What did you tell them?"

"Told them he ghosted me." She gave a forlorn hiccup. "Literally." Joel poured more wine and frowned at her while he took a sip.

"What?" she asked. She was being defensive and emotional and was beginning to feel properly smashed. She should have eaten something. "He's dead," she said petulantly.

"Is he though?" Joel said, but simultaneously the room spun out of control and Kendal realized she was going to be sick.

23

She woke up fully clothed with her tongue stuck to the roof of her mouth and a headache akin to having rusty nails tapped into her temples. Rosie was gone, the house was quiet. The clock read 11:20. She made to leap off the bed and toppled against the wall. She tried to yell for Rosie, but her voice was hoarse and her throat was parched. On her bedside table there were two tablets, a glass of water, and a cold coffee. Kendal squinted at it. *He's a vampire.* She had invited him in, and the realization made her cold with dread. She tried to piece the evening back together but it was fractured. She'd had maybe two hundred milliliters of vodka and a couple of shots. She was out of practice but she wasn't a total lightweight, and she'd never in her life been blackout drunk.

Kendal had to focus her thoughts to establish what day of the week it was. Friday, a school day. They should have been up more than three hours ago.

Her phone was in her pocket and she had a message from Joel. "Took Rosie to school. Happy hangover!"

Kendal made it to the bathroom before she puked chaotically into the toilet. How could she have been so stupid?

Kendal dialed Rico.

"Woddup, 96?"

"Joel spiked my drink. He's not who he's playing."

"You got drunk without me?"

"I had a couple of beers with the mums, nothing to warrant this. It's not right." Her head spun fuzzily as if to confirm.

"Sounds like you just hit the bottle a bit hard. You can't do that in your forties, it'll mess you up."

"I'm not in my forties." The room swirled again, and she leaned against a wall, trying to clear her mind. The fog was maddening.

Rico snickered, and she could hear him tapping at a keyboard. "Semantics, KC. Joel's at work like a good boy. Can you be sure it wasn't one of the mums slipping you doubles?"

"I know the difference between a cocktail and a toxin, Ricky, it's not my first rodeo."

"It sounds like you're putting two and two together and getting tooty-two. Come to Bon and have a catch-up? Let's do lunch like we work in marketing. Hair of the dog."

He was so irritating it made her head ache more. "No. Come to the house, bring a sampler. I bet there's Rohypnol in my system . . . If I'm wrong I'll buy you lunch."

"Okay, that's a bet."

She could practically hear him roll his eyes and hung up the phone. She pressed her head against the cold of the bathroom wall, trying to collect her thoughts through the fugue. She turned the shower on, undressed, and stepped in, letting the water shock her back to life, running through the last seven months. *Seven months!* How had she not seen it sooner?

She got out and put on her running kit, threw Joel's pills in the bin, and rummaged in the drawer for paracetamol from a pack. She spotted a note from Rosie behind the cold coffee—love hearts and unintelligible writing she must have made over breakfast. Kendal felt a pang of regret for the family life they'd been living, even as she pictured breaking Joel's neck.

She let herself into the basement and listened for Joel, but all was quiet. Down the stairs the air felt charged, like a server room, hot and humming. It was still devoid of personality, and luxuriously tidy compared to the rest of the house. He'd made his bed with hospital corners and, except for the computers, you wouldn't know anyone lived there. The ick she got from the room was intense and inspired a wave of nausea that forced her to pause and take some deep breaths of the stale air. She waggled a mouse and three screens came to life. Two were password protected with an interface she'd never seen, and the third opened the Firefox browser on the Google search page. She clicked the history tab and scrolled through, but it was all Canadian news sites and Reddit. Not really surprising that a computer guy wouldn't have all his secrets in an internet tab, and what had Fini said? *His kit was impenetrable.* She stood up straight and turned slowly on the spot, surveying the room. His watch was on the desk next to the computer. It was overpriced and showy. That was a clue she'd overlooked, and his military-grade phone. She almost groaned, thinking of the training drills she'd put him through. She had trusted him, truly. It was painfully naïve. She had never, in a long career of dealing with liars, players, crooks, and criminals, ever once fallen for a line or been duped by a double. There was rusty, and then there was a personality transplant. She would have kicked herself if it would have made any difference. She went methodically through the room looking for pill bottles, weapons, spy toys, anything that would give her further insight into who Joel was, beyond the absolute pencil case he presented as. Everything was clean, but she could see now that it was contrived. She was looking at his bookshelves for anything out of place, when she heard a soft clunk and turned to find Joel standing at the bottom of the stairs. He was holding her keys. He kept his benign smile in place, although he wore a questioning frown across his forehead. Seeing him in the room made her head spin again. The effects of whatever drug he had used surged and then subsided as her body fought back. She was dizzy and wanted to sit down.

"Hey! How are you feeling?"

"I feel like garbage, Joel, as you probably know."

He circled the room and she mirrored his movement, keeping the distance between them. He stood behind the sofa and she was by the door to the garden. She considered making a run for it, but it didn't solve the problem. She patted her waistband for a weapon she already knew wasn't there. Not even a pocketknife in her Lululemons.

He turned to face her, his eyes searching the room. "What are you talking about?"

"Why did you spike my drink?"

He threw up his arms. "You can't blame me because you had one too many cocktails."

"Who are you, Joel, really?"

He flushed angrily. "Holy smokes, you have some serious trust issues."

"No shit, Wizbit."

"You came home super drunk. We had a nice chat, then you lurched up to bed. I don't know why you're acting so crazy. Are you feeling okay? Did you not take the pills I left for you?"

"Of course I didn't, you mad bastard, what were they?"

"Paracetamol! Jeez Louise!" But a shadow flickered across his face, and whether he meant to or not, it blew his cover and they both knew it. Before her eyes, his whole posture changed. He somehow got taller and better looking, and then he gave her a truly wicked smile.

She sighed. "Ah, man. Really? We had such a nice little game going."

In a voice that was more confident and lower pitched, he said, "I knew you'd be tipsy and since you never, ever relax, it felt like the perfect opportunity to find this . . ."

He perched on the edge of the sofa, his hand feeling about for something in his pocket. She held her breath, but he produced a white business card. She stared at it.

"What is it?"

"The hot ice cream man's number, I believe." She laughed a hollow sound. "You're welcome to him." A sense of doom passed over her like a cloud.

Joel put the card in his pocket and backed toward the bookshelf. He pulled a book from the shelf and opened it to reveal a gun. Kendal released a tiny groan of disappointment, and Joel acknowledged it with a pained nod. "I was hoping it wouldn't go like this." He released and checked the cylinder, then clicked it back into place. He handled the weapon like a pro, and Kendal knew that this was going to end very, very badly. He moved back to the sofa, perched on the arm of it, and pointed it at her, signaling that she should sit.

"Ah fudge." She slumped onto one of two chairs at a sad sort of dining table and rubbed her temples. She was genuinely sad. He held the gun at his hip, pointed at her stomach. She had forgotten how much she hated guns pointing at her. She looked from it to him and back and shook her head, resigned. He gave her a smile that bordered on sympathetic. "You should have trusted your instincts. Living with an asset is insane with a child in the house."

"It's true. You're very good though. Must have been tough to keep up."

"Not really. I'm a nerd at heart." His accent was distinctly debonair.

"Don't tell me you're fucking British?" If it wasn't for the malicious glint of the metal in his hand, she would have laughed.

"I'm a citizen of the world."

"Alex Shapiro was a runaround. Very clever. Is Cadu even real?"

He was watching her carefully. With his act dropped he was unrecognizable.

"That's classified, I'm afraid. But having you bug the only person who was on my case was genius. If I say so myself."

He was completely relaxed and it was incredibly irritating.

Kendal's mind was fizzing. She could tell he was intending to shoot. She had seen this look in men's eyes before. A protective panic was rising, and she scoped for a way out. She was utterly without weapons down here. It was soft play.

"Classified by whom?" she asked, both curious and buying time.

He laughed. "You really don't know anything, do you? Driving blind is a very dangerous hobby, Kara."

She looked up sharply at the use of her old name. He went on, nodding toward the business card on the desk. "Imagine our delight when we realized my handler was Kara Corelli."

"Whose delight?" She was completely confused now. "Who do you work for?"

"Cadu is more powerful than any of you seem to understand. Khalil Masoumi knew it, and I thought Shapiro might have got to you but you're all just chasing your tails. It's been a lot of fun to watch."

"Joel, babe, I don't give two hoots about Cadu. My assignment was to help you. Why don't we join forces? No one gets hurt, and we both get paid."

"Yuck. You sound like Rico. I don't need his money, but you're a real prize." He raised a sneering eyebrow at her.

"Well, thanks, I guess. Always nice to hear."

He grinned, watching her trying to catch up, his familiar freckly smile replaced by something wolfish and dark.

"What do I have to do with any of this?"

"You were the last person to see Khalil Masoumi alive. Whoever has you has a way to him, and he has been a problem for longer than I'd care to admit."

"But he's dead," she said weakly. The gun pointing at her was about Khalil, again.

"No, he's not. He's a terrorist driving an ice cream van in the middle of winter. What a ridiculous cover, is he an idiot?"

She was rumbled. She leaned forward in her chair, elbows resting on her knees and her chin on her hands, examining him anew. She answered him in a voice that was audibly colder and more dangerous. No more Mrs. Nice Guy.

"That was the first time I've seen him in five years."

"Regardless, now we have his number . . ." He waved the card. "And we have his daughter. One way or another we'll pick him up."

"What do you mean you have Rosie?"

Kendal stood and a brief moment of fear flashed over Joel's features.

"Relax, Momma Bear, she's at school. I'll pick her up, he'll come for her. Chill your boots." He gestured at the chair, and Kendal reluctantly sat back down. While they were conversational, Kendal was checking her mental file on Joel—his weaknesses, his physicality. He was strong but was he merciless? Had he mentioned any injuries or weaknesses? There was something wrong with his knees, she recalled, some high school injury. He was probably not that much heavier than her and not taller either. He had a gun though, and in the end, that was the main thing. She didn't know if he had the capacity to kill, but based on the last sixty seconds she guessed he probably did, and for a fleeting moment, she felt sad for him. It seemed a shame he wasn't the nice boy he'd played.

"What has Khalil got to do with any of this?" she asked, genuinely curious.

Joel frowned at her. "Do you not know why you were assigned to him in the first place? He's been trying to kill the Cadu contract for years. Everyone hates a whistleblower nowadays, pain in the butt."

"I was assigned to watch him, nothing more."

Joel shook his head. "Ha. Always chasing tails, classic UK government. I can see why Rico calls it the clown factory. He's not wrong."

The room felt cold and heavy.

"Are you actually planning to kill me?"

"I am. Sorry."

"Just seems a bit drastic after everything we've been through. Rosie actually likes you."

"She'll probably prefer it. She told me yesterday she wants me to be her daddy."

"She'll forget you ever existed by next week."

"Boo-hoo." He shrugged.

"You think you can beat me in a fight?" she asked with a swagger that was mostly phony.

"I don't need to fight you, I have a gun. I don't think you can beat bullets, can you?"

"It has been known."

He smiled at her. "You know, it's funny. When they gave me the file on you, it said you were a stone-cold psychopath. I was braced for a real game, and all I got was this nice old lady looking after me."

"That's files for you. Yours said you were a clean-living Canadian with a heart of gold, and yet." She gestured to his hands.

He pointed the gun toward the closed door next to the kitchenette. "I was thinking you could go in the safe room. Nice and soundproof and wipe-clean."

She really did not want to do that.

"Seriously, why don't we team up? You can have Khalil. He owes me quite a bit of child support since, apparently, he's been out there living this whole time."

"I think you might be lying though, because you went all misty-eyed talking about him last night. Sounds like quite a wonderful romance."

"It was nice," she admitted ruefully.

Joel smiled at that. "Oh well, better to have loved and lost, right?"

"I honestly don't know if it is."

"No, me neither."

For a moment it felt like the fake family they had created was back. This brief stint of domestic bliss would be missed.

"Did you dope Rosie last night?"

He gave a tiny, maddening chuckle. "A teeny pinch of midazolam in her milk."

"Dude, she's four years old. Could you seriously not handle a bedtime story? I know it's a slog but drugs is a bit much."

Joel shrugged. "She liked it. She was tripping balls."

Kendal's venom changed color. "You shouldn't have told me that, Joel. I can't let that slide."

"Big talk from Little Miss Unarmed."

Kendal pulled her phone from her pocket and scrolled her contacts. She pressed to call, mildly surprised that Joel allowed it.

It rang twice, and the school administrator picked up. "Hi there, it's Kendal Carter, is Rosie in school today?"

Kendal kept her eyes on Joel while the administrator checked. Joel held her gaze with a smug smile. After a few moments, the administrator came back with a cheery if confused confirmation, and Kendal hung up and tried to keep the deep relief from her face. Her mind cleared another degree.

"You know, a good mother would have done that first."

"We're all just doing our best, Joel, no judgment."

Kendal felt cold calm descend. The shifting reality had mentally settled. Joel was a hostile with a gun, he was strong, but they were gym muscles, not fight muscles. Not the kind of muscle a mother has when her child has been threatened and her parenting insulted. She allowed the rage to build into a plan.

"Shall we get on with this?" she asked.

He smirked again. "Sure. After you." He waved the gun across the room.

She walked toward the safe room, closing the distance between them. He didn't flinch, she noticed. He was reflected in the glossy sheen of the kitchen cupboards, and she kept the reflection in her peripheral vision as she passed him and turned toward the door. He was holding the gun—a little black snub-nosed .38—aimed at the small of her back. She stood in front of the door as if looking for the handle. With a microscopic tut, he leaned around her to press the button that slid it open. First things first, the gun had to go. She stepped slightly to her right and butted it out of his hand so that it skittered across the floor.

Next she wanted him contained. She turned so they were facing each other and, with a wink, jabbed him in the gut as hard as she could.

Now she had time to think about how it's silly to wear a tie to a fight, because she took hold of it and pulled him toward her as she stepped backward into the safe room. This move he saw coming though, and he barreled into her, knocking them both to the ground. He landed heavily on top of her; their legs were intertwined, which she noted was weirdly intimate, inspiring her to bring her knee up to his groin with all the force of her newfound fury.

He released the unmistakable *whoomph* of a man getting hit in the nuts, but he also reached up and grabbed her by the throat, pressing painfully into her jugular. She felt her airway compress and with it a surge of anger that powered her to push him heavily to the side, and with a grace she was mildly surprised she still possessed, she swung over, pinned his elbows with her knees, and wrapped his tie firmly around his neck. Finally, she wanted him dead.

As she tightened her grip around his throat, watching him fight for breath, she thought that had he been better at his job he'd be able to get out of this hold. He fought like an analyst and had that same nerdy swagger, like he'd read the books but never had to defend himself. As he struggled and bucked, she wanted to whisper that it served him right. But instead she had a vivid image of his mother, sitting in Canada, waiting for the phone to ring, and she loosened her grip just a fraction. Not dead, then, but very sorry.

Behind her she heard the distinctive click of a firearm safety catch. She glanced back to see Rico standing in the doorway, pointing Joel's gun at her.

"Let him go."

"No, he's an agent."

"Even more reason to not have his corpse in your house, Ken."

She loosened her grip slightly.

"It's your house, Ricky."

She released the pressure and moved so she was sitting next to him. Joel didn't move.

Without looking at Rico, Kendal said quietly, "Stop pointing that gun at me."

Rico entered the room and sat down but didn't lower the weapon. "Is he dead?"

Kendal looked at Joel's face appraisingly, then nudged him gently with a toe, looking up at Rico with an apologetic flinch. "At least I didn't shoot him. He was waving that piece at me like he meant it."

"Goddamn, this is a mess now." Rico was sweating.

She looked up at him and frowned. "Have a little think about who you're pointing that gun at, boss. Didn't go so well for the last guy." She nodded toward Joel, whose eyes had closed. She reached over and held her finger under his nose but couldn't detect a breath. "Anyway, you love a mess. Isn't that why you're constantly making them?"

"What is he doing here? His tracker said he was in the office." He was uncharacteristically nervy, Kendal noted. They'd seen bodies before. She pressed Joel's neck to feel for a pulse. His arm shot up and grabbed her wrist, and he lurched upward toward Kendal, who leaned back with distaste. Without hesitation, Rico raised the gun and shot him in the head. A clean black hole appeared right between the eyes. Joel fell back, never to rise again.

Kendal glared at Rico, her ears ringing with the terrible noise of a .38 mm bullet exploding in an enclosed space. From experience, she knew it would take days for the tinnitus to stop.

"I'm not cleaning that up," she said inadvertently loudly. She looked at Joel's broken body and felt sorry. She didn't want him to die. She didn't want anyone to die. Rosie was going to be gutted. "At least mine was self-defense. What's your excuse?" She stopped when she saw the look on his face, like he wanted to shoot her too.

24

Mechanically, both Rico and Kendal stood up and stripped to their underwear, leaving their bloody clothes near Joel's lifeless body. Kendal went first and used the basement shower, and once she was wrapped in a towel, she went upstairs, got dressed, and waited for Rico to join her.

She poured two cups of coffee and noticed her hangover, which had taken a back seat during the action, was lingering still, making things feel very complicated and uncool. She plucked a packet of Pom-Bears from the drawer and ate them in two goes. Her hands were shaking, and as she waited for Rico, the vivid image of the hole appearing in Joel's head played over in her mind like a bloody, horrible GIF.

Rico emerged using a hand towel to run over his hair, looking mildly stressed. "Well, this is a bag of maggots now, man."

"You owe me lunch," Kendal replied.

He ignored her, perched at the island, and took a sip of coffee she placed there for him, tapping furiously at his phone.

"How do we proceed?" she asked.

Rico looked up as if he'd forgotten she was there and frowned at her. "We?" Then he puffed out a long, overly dramatic sigh and put the phone face down on the counter. "What did he say? Was he trained? I don't like having this many questions, K. Questions is not where the money is."

"He's been sabotaging Cadu. He knew my Kara Corelli ID. He made it sound like I was a perk."

"No offense, K, but when have you ever been perky?"

She watched him closely. "He thought I could get him to Khalil."

Rico looked genuinely pained and cracked his neck and knuckles. "Why the christ would he think that?" He tilted his head like a velociraptor. "Since Khalil is dead and buried."

"Joel seemed to think that he is neither dead nor buried."

"So I'll ask again, Ken, yet another question, why would he think that?" Kendal took a deep breath. She could see Rico's brain working at triple speed. He was holding something back.

"How did you not know Joel was an asset?"

"I did know. He's *our* asset."

She fiddled with an envelope on the counter, trying to understand what had just happened and why. Suddenly it clicked. "You double-booked it. Didn't you? 'Course you did, you daft bastard."

Rico rubbed his eyes as if he were exhausted but was actually buying time.

Double-booked: Rico had a nasty habit of selling the same set of intel to more than one buyer. He argued that gatekeeping information was antidemocratic and had created counter accounts that meant cases could be repackaged and sold twice.

"Do you have any sense of loyalty at all, Ricky, or is it just you and your wallet and the Wild West?"

Rico looked at her with a hangdog expression. "Glo-Tech were the client first."

Kendal shook her head. It was so typical of him to be playing all sides. "And then you clued in the Mounties?"

Rico had the grace to look guilty. "Glo-Tech booked a routine background check on Joel. I thought the Mounties might like to know what their boy was up to. It sold itself."

"But what? Because you didn't just ice an asset by accident."

"I called the Mounties on my way here." He looked at her sheepishly and put on a pair of black-rimmed glasses. Possibly to guard from getting punched. "I spoke to his handler, who said there was a possibility he's been tapped by the Chinese. They wanted eyes on him to confirm."

Kendal's mouth fell open. "I genuinely wasn't expecting that."

"Same. I thought they were in it for the tech, but they wanted someone watching Joel."

"A heads-up would have been nice."

"Not really the nature of The Game, is it."

"Jesus Christ. I've had a tail for weeks. It would have been good to know it might be the People's fucking Republic."

"Why would Joel have you tailed, he lives in your house?" Rico asked, not unreasonably.

Kendal had a headache. "What are you going to tell Glo-Tech about Joel?"

Rico picked up his phone again, his attention disappearing into the screen. "How often did he work from home?"

"Couple of days a week."

"I'll get the temps in to clean up. Maybe we can *Weekend at Bernie's* him and buy a bit of time while you am-dram some MIA backstory. Joel can quit by email and go back to Canada. I don't think Glo-Tech will care that much if he's AWOL now that the beta is ready to go."

"And the Chinese?"

"They placed an asset on UK soil, so they can't be that surprised if he comes home in a bag." He said it with a practiced confidence they both knew he didn't feel. They sat in silence for a moment, working through some of the ramifications. Kendal thought about Joel's mother; Rico thought about invoicing.

When Kendal picked up Rosie from school, she looked tired but fine. "Is Joel home?" was her second question after asking for a treat.

"Joel's gone away for a bit, Ro. It's just you and me, kid."

Rosie shrugged. She still had the TV.

25

Life after Joel was terrible for Kendal and Rosie both. They were tired, their routine was shot, they had all but forgotten how it was done. Rosie grumbled and asked repeatedly when Joel would be back. Kendal casually swept the questions away—at work, back soon, on holiday—and although Rosie took these answers at face value, it hurt Kendal to lie to her and it made his death weigh on her heavily. She also just straight-up missed the guy. He made cereal better, he made mornings better, he definitely made better coffee. The house felt haunted. The combination of Joel's death and Khalil's reappearance had Kendal believing in ghosts. She doubled down on surveillance detection, she was never without a weapon, and she did not signal Khalil. Her initial pleasure at seeing him had changed into something more cautious. He was a man who seemed to be trailing danger and she was wary of its proximity to Rosie.

Rosie kept changing. Sometimes it was incremental and sometimes it was sudden. Overnight, the baby would fall away and a new set of emotions would be installed. Kendal thought of these changes as software upgrades, and they were tough on them both. A new slew of feelings for

Rosie to cope with and a mental adjustment for Kendal, her baby another step further from her. When Rosie did what developmental experts would expect her to do, it threw a stark reminder to Kendal that she had no model for "normal" parenting. She had nothing to corroborate her memories, but she believed her own mother had treated her as an adult from the day she was born. She'd never had any inkling of a father figure, had no idea what her origin story was. Her mother had refused to give her any details; she'd made it seem as if this information was none of her business, and had leaned on the concept of "need to know" for as long as Kendal could remember.

How old had she been the first time her mother had answered a question with "that's classified." Kendal had utilized all of her network skills, Fini's hacking prowess, even Rico's access to redacted files, but never once unearthed a clue as to her father's identity.

Kendal's journey through parenthood was littered with fresh revelations that hers had been a terrible mother. It wasn't just the danger she had been in, or the violence she had witnessed, it was the little things. The independence she should not have had, the language she should not have heard. Parallel to this was an appreciation for how hard it is to be a parent, just straight-up hard work.

Mornings were tough but bedtimes were not much better, so it was with a groan that Kendal answered her phone at 2:30 AM on a school night. It was Fini.

"Dude, you have a problem."

"Is it people calling me in the middle of the night?"

She heard the creak of Fini's gaming chair.

"Oh shit, sorry, I didn't realize the time. They launched the beta of Joel's project. I thought you might like to take a look."

The following morning, Kendal dropped Rosie at school and headed to Kentish Town. She found the shop shuttered, so she gratefully bought a coffee and pushed through the secret door to Noisy Buttons, where she found Fini unmoved in her gaming chair behind the counter. She had a headset dangling across her shoulders, and without taking her eyes off the screen, reached over and rummaged blindly at an empty packet of Skittles. She was surrounded by the sort of detritus you would expect to see at a teenager's desk.

"Did you bring sweets?"

Kendal frowned at her. "Why would I bring sweets?"

Fini shrugged grumpily. "Mums have sweets."

Mildly stung by the implication, Kendal patted her pockets and had a scan through her bag. "I've got a fruit roll-up."

She threw it over, and Fini unwrapped and unfurled it. She popped it in her mouth and turned up her nose. "Tastes healthy."

"What are we looking at?" Kendal peered over her shoulder at two active computer screens.

"Cadu in beta. My mate Zahir has been rummaging in the backend. He's in Pakistan, let me introduce you."

Fini wiggled the mouse and the left-hand screen cut to a picture of a boy, no more than twenty years old, wearing a New York Yankees baseball cap and a black T-shirt and staring intently at the screen. Without moving his eyes or giving any indication that he was aware their screen had changed, he said, "Nice to meet you, Kimberly Carbonara. I'm Zahir."

"Very funny, Fini, Zahir, ap se mil ker khushi huwi," said K, earning a glance and a small smile at the camera, which revealed him as even younger and with a cheeky gleam in his eyes.

"And you, friend," he replied.

"Show-off," muttered Fini under her breath.

Kendal smiled. "So. Cadu, what's the story?"

Zahir glanced up at the screen and then back to whatever he was looking at. He had flawless English that he spoke with a strong accent.

"First up, the whole thing is about as secure as using the word 'password' as a password, so if they think they're even close to being ready to roll out they must either be nuts or they don't give a damn about the user security. But even assuming they patch that up, I looked at the Ts and Cs and there's some very wobbly wording around the AV permissions. Considering Glo-Tech are usually making apps that handle money, and considering even further that this is for children and made with government funds, I have to say, something has either gone very wrong inside that company or else . . . Actually I don't have an or else. It's a mess. And I believe from insiders that it's run up a bill of nearly nine hundred million pounds sterling, which is getting pretty ha-ha, no?"

Kendal rubbed her face and wished she had more coffee in her system. "So, what? It's an expensive piece of shit, is that the punch line?" Kendal addressed them both.

"That's just the headline. The real problem, if you care about such things, is that Cadu is essentially data-gathering spyware that they're offering to put in schools for free. Best-case scenario is your government is inadvertently building a tool to keep tabs on your children, and it's so poorly built that any hacker, hostile nation, bad actor, or kid with a grudge can access that data."

"Worst case?"

Across screens, networks, and oceans, Zahir and Fini shared a look. "Worst case is that it's intentional." He said this with an indifference that was eerie.

"Brilliant. And can we kill it?"

Zahir bobbed his head uncertainly. "Maybe. That's ironically the only thing about it that's secure. You'd probably need someone right inside Glo-Tech to fully take it apart."

"Of course you would," Kendal muttered.

Fini frantically clicked at her screen and then threw her headset onto the desk. "It's gone offline."

"It's just a beta, they're probably stress testing. Okay, I am off back to the grind. Bye, my friends."

Zahir logged off and disappeared, and Fini turned to face Kendal.

"Cool kid though, no?" Fini's glib response was making Kendal edgy.

"Can you guys keep an eye on this? Let me know if it looks like they're going to release it into the wild. Find out what we might need to kill it?"

Fini turned back to her screen and pulled up a new window. “No sweat, boss.”

“But, Fini, babe, have a nap first, no? And maybe some vitamins.”

“Okay, Mum.”

26

The air con in Alex Shapiro's office was too high, or too low, whichever setting it was that made the room really bloody cold. His phone trilled, and he picked it up before the end of the first ring. He wiped sweat from his upper lip and listened.

"Joel Ayre is no longer an employee of Glo-Tech. However, you are not authorized to remove his belongings or access his terminal. If at any point anyone attempts to interact with his space, they must be detained, and you will contact me. Do you copy?"

Alex wanted to piss and moan; Joel was essential to their delivery schedule, his terminal was full of vital work, and he, Alex, the BOSS, was sick to the teeth of taking orders from this supposed security service. What he said, however, was: "Yes, ma'am."

27

With Rosie safely at school, Kendal sat at Joel's machine in the basement, clicking through the apparently endless facets of Glo-Tech. It wasn't just games they made, it was news outlets, discount designer stores, chat rooms, betting apps, and meme generators. It seemed relentless and impenetrable. Her phone rang, and she put it on speaker. It was Rico.

"How's my favorite agent?"

"Not bad, just trying to figure out what Joel was up to. Can you send me the access codes for his kit?"

"Probably not, 96, since he was a primo tech guy and I'm about as savvy as your nan. Send it to the breakers. Meanwhile, I've got the Mounties up my ass. I've told them their boy went back to China, but I'm not sure they're buying it."

"Sounds like a you problem."

"Does it? Because it's your name on the memo I'm looking at."

In the pause that followed, Kendal heard a movement upstairs. She hung up, and with a flick-knife tucked into her sleeve she made her way silently to the top of the stairs, where the door was open. She could smell cologne and the air felt disturbed. She stood statue still and listened. They pulled up a chair and sat at the kitchen table, just out of view.

"Hi, honey, I'm home."

She rounded the door into the kitchen to find Khalil sitting at her kitchen table as if he lived there.

They took each other in.

"How did you get in?" She stayed close to the wall.

"Where's your boyfriend?" he countered with a sly smile.

She walked past him into the kitchen and poured herself a coffee, glancing into the hallway in case he'd brought backup. Satisfied that he was alone, she clicked the scrambler on and leaned against the counter with the coffee in her hands. He watched her closely but stayed seated, his legs crossed, looking much more relaxed than he had any right to be. He was real, and it made her equal parts furious and thankful.

"Where have you been?" she asked quietly.

"I was trying to keep you away from a dangerous situation. Somehow you found yourself in it anyway."

She considered the absurdity of his response, walking around him to take a seat at the opposite end of the table. "I thought you were dead," she said with more composure than she felt. "Because eight gunmen stormed your house and broke my arm."

He tapped the table. "It was an exfil. They made it look like a kill. I'm sorry about your arm."

He seemed to think that was enough information; her silence made it clear it was not.

"My team shipped me back to Iran. I did try to reach you. I tried many times. Not even Ortez had a line."

"You contacted him?"

"Not directly, but his organization has holes."

Kendal wasn't surprised. Bon Temps was a high-turnover circus; leaks were inevitable. "So you *were* a double."

"Is that what they told you? I was at the Ministry of Defence. I flagged everyone's favorite tech firm as a glaring security risk, and I was removed from my post, scrubbed from their systems, and placed under surveillance. They chose their contract with Glo-Tech over their national security. And then they sent their most astonishing woman to infiltrate my private life."

"Very smooth."

"Thank you."

Kendal's temperature rose. If she'd been wearing a Fitbit it would have registered unusual heart activity.

"And now what? You're a terrorist?"

"Psh. An ugly label from a racist organization that negates the fact that they are risking the security of their own population to save face on a bad investment. Your government is corrupt at its core."

Kendal was only half listening; her mind was replaying the day he was killed. "They're not my government," she said softly.

"Ah, I almost forgot, no point bringing it round to loyalties here." He leaned forward and booped her on the nose. "You who have none."

"I have one," she said.

"Is she here?" With this question his entire face softened, the warrior left his eyes and was replaced, with love, with beauty, with magic.

"She's at school. I haven't told her. She's so like you."

"Kara. I'm sorry."

They held each other's eyes for a moment. The fight in her twisted and turned. She pictured an alternative universe where they lived happily in this big, beautiful house, raising their daughter. She'd work in publishing, he'd be a civil servant. They'd have coffee together in the morning. The basement would be Rosie's playroom. They would cook good food and drink cold wine on warm days. Instead, here was a man wanted as a terrorist. Their daughter was an asset, the safe room was recently covered in blood, and she had a tech scrambler plugged into the wall. *Who am I?* She screamed internally when she realized: she was her mother.

The more she played the series of events, the less they made sense.

"Why now?"

"There was an incident. MI6 realized I was alive. I knew once they found out, they would try and get to you. I had a contact let me know if they found you, and once they did, I tried to get a message to you."

Kendal stared at him with disbelief. Of all the scenarios she'd considered, it was never this. She spoke slowly, hoping she was wrong. "*How* did you try and get a message to me?"

He leaned forward and rested his hands on his knees. He looked stricken. "They were supposed to give you a rendezvous code, nothing more. But we thought it might be a trap, so I couldn't send a known associate. I used a random connect. When they realized she wasn't you . . . I fucked up. You must have been terrified. Kara, I am so sorry. I planned to leave you alone, I didn't want you in the middle of this. But then you left the signal, and I knew I had to see you. Can you forgive me?"

She let it wash over her. Lula's death was his fault. She looked at him, aghast. "But we had systems in place. You could have contacted me. You could have set a drop. You let me believe you were dead, and then you murdered my only friend. This is beyond ridiculous. This isn't a game. An innocent woman died for a rendezvous code. Can you hear how insane that is?" She shook her head. "I have no idea who you are."

He reached for her hand but she moved it away. "I'm the father of your child."

She did not want to believe that Khalil had been the catalyst for everything that had happened, a stupid relationship putting others in danger again, with Rosie at its center. She wished she had never met him. And she wished he wasn't in the house. He went on. "I wanted to contact you, but I assumed you were MI6. I needed to know whose side you were on."

"Did you find out? I'd love to know."

Khalil laughed gently. "Mine?"

She looked into his eyes. Was he right? Could she choose him?

"So what happens now?"

He pulled a thumb drive from his shirt pocket. "This is a virus tailored to kill Cadu. It needs to be destroyed. If there's even a slight foundation left they'll try and salvage it."

"I don't have access."

"Your Canadian is inside Glo-Tech, no? Get him to do it."

"He's China. And he's dead."

"Ah. That complicates things."

Khalil paused. She could see his mind working the angles. The urge to kiss him was intense, and extremely unprofessional. She moved closer to him, and he held her gaze. She could feel the heat from his body. And then the doorbell went.

"Damn," he said quietly. Kendal paused for a moment, then walked to the hallway and glanced out. She made out the profile of two suited men through the glass.

"You expecting anyone?"

"No."

"Is there another exit?"

She was in the kitchen in a blink. She swiped the trapdoor, which swooshed open inches from his feet, and he arched an eyebrow at her. "Cool."

"I can buy you sixty seconds."

She glanced at the front door. One of the suits was testing the locks. Khalil adjusted his cuffs as if they'd been in some office meeting.

"Please allow me to see Rosie."

She paused. "Maybe."

"I'll arrange a meet. It will be safe, I promise. She's my daughter," he whispered urgently.

"Yes, but you're a dead man." The doorbell went again followed by an urgent banging on the glass. "I'll think about it," she said simply, and turned toward the door. Khalil reached for her arm and pulled her roughly back toward him so that they were inches apart. His eyes held hers for a moment, and then he smiled. He pulled her again, closing the final fraction of space between them. A tornado was loosed in her body, his warmth enlivened her, his smell enveloped her. She kissed him, and five years of building torment, aching, and desire was finally, blissfully released. He kissed her back, his hands on her neck, brushing her cheek.

And then stepped away, and holding her gaze, dropped through the hole in the floor.

She gave him ten seconds, then opened the door to two young men, one holding a clipboard and the other in a branded T-shirt and jeans who was wearing a tool belt for effect. Behind them, a van with British Gas branding sat idling at the curb. Kendal nearly laughed at them.

"Hello, miss, there's a gas leak in the area, we need to check inside for your own safety."

"Really?"

"Yes, ma'am."

"Sounds like a scam, fellas."

He held eye contact, pulling his lanyard up to show her. "Here is my identification. It's a five-minute check."

Kendal could tell from the way his eyes moved that he had an earpiece and someone was talking to him. He turned to look at the road.

"Sorry, ma'am, we do need to come into the house at this time."

He was holding up the act but had obviously lost interest in convincing her.

The tool belt kid was glancing left and right. A newbie, Kendal thought, or just poorly trained.

"There's no entry here today, lads. Sorry about that." She closed the door, and when the guy stuck his foot in to obstruct it, as she'd known he would, she bought her heel down on the tip of his toe, opening the door wide enough to shove him backward, so they were both forced down the stairs.

"Next time, send adults." She slammed the door and heard the van screech away. She checked the house and basement for Khalil, but he was gone. Her desire to find and protect him was surprisingly fierce, considering everything was his fault. She spared a thought for Lula, collateral damage for a cheap trick. There would be no revenge and no justice. The impotent anger that rose up in Kendal in defense of her friend was a long-familiar feeling. *Not fair* was a phrase her mother had banished from her usage as a child—"*If you seek justice in this world, you'll live a lifetime of disappointment.*"

A powerful lesson for a preteen. *Thanks, Mom*, Kendal thought bitterly.

She called Rico. "I've just had a visit from two spooks dressed as gas men."

Rico muttered an expletive. "What did they want?"

"Trick or treating?"

"I'm coming over."

She set about wiping all traces of Khalil away.

Rico rang the bell twenty minutes later, his eyes wide as if to signal *huh?* Kendal was unmoved. "This house feels about as safe as a coach station. By the way."

"Put it on your feedback form."

They sat in the kitchen.

"Do Glo-Tech know Joel's closed?"

"They think he's skiing in the Canadian Rockies."

"And the Mounties?"

"None the wiser."

"Sounds like a shit sandwich you've made for yourself."

He looked exhausted but not sorry. He poured himself a whiskey from the liquor cabinet that had been gathering dust since Kendal moved in and raised his glass in an unconvincing salute. Kendal watched him closely. "Khalil is back."

Rico let out a long groan and rubbed his temples. "For fuck's sake. What does he want?"

"He wants me to kill Cadu."

They both rested their heads on their hands and took each other in. The Game had changed shape again. Kendal reached over and finished his drink. "Who paid for Prom? Because I thought he was selling secrets to Iran, but now I'm led to believe he was wrapped up in this Glo-Tech dumpster fire you seem to have thrown me into."

"Prom was a portrait op ordered by some new tech department in the MOD. The kill order came from an anonymous black box. It was a big price. I thought it was gov outsourcing their wet work to cover their asses. I swear to you, 96, apart from the fact that it blew up like fucking Etna, it was totally standard."

"The KO was Khalil throwing up a smoke screen. Something very weird is going on inside Glo-Tech."

"No shit," Rico replied. "My contact inside has gone dark. Most of my temps have been switched out and there's a fresh intake of graduate scumbags doing god knows what."

"And MOD don't care?"

"They're either in too deep or there's something shady at the top."

"So either corporate incompetence or a state-sponsored threat?"

"Or the Christmas combo of both." Rico added with a sigh, "They're rarely mutually exclusive."

"Now what?" Kendal asked. She had a headache.

Rico refilled the glass and led them outside. Sitting in the chairs on the balcony, they looked out at a bright day. Kendal wondered how far Khalil had got.

Rico sipped his drink. Kendal had a sneaking suspicion that despite the danger and the chaos, he was enjoying himself. "Let's do a head count. We have one dead Chinese asset, two spooks playing dress-up, an inaccessible Glo-Tech, big gov money in a very bad app, a resurrected ex, and a small group of confused Canadians. Am I forgetting anything?"

Kendal's alarm went off on her phone. "A woman who is sick of your bullshit, and a kid who needs collecting from school." She put her stuff together, picked up a banana from the fruit bowl, and led Rico to the door. Once they were outside, Rico scanned the street and lowered his voice. "Listen, 96, Khalil is not just your smoking-hot ex, he's wanted on terrorism charges on several continents, and whenever his name comes up, yours is never far behind. He's nuclear. I know you like him, but you should stay away."

He walked off, and his car picked him up on the corner. He didn't look back.

Ten minutes later, Kendal was waiting awkwardly in the playground, with images of Khalil playing on a loop in her mind. It felt almost like grief. She couldn't stop thinking of things she wished she'd said, questions she still had. His face, his hands, his smell. It was grief's opposite, if such a thing had a name. Parents with better social skills stood in huddles and talked about the weekend; the others looked at their phones. There was no sign of Sasha or Nat. Louis was flanked by year 6 mums, and when he caught her looking at him, he sent her a seductive wink that she found annoying. She looked around for Priya, but she was late every day, and Kendal was grudgingly jealous that she missed out on the loitering.

Eventually Ella appeared with her trademark cheery grin and called to the kids whose parents were present. When Rosie emerged she was visibly agitated. Ella gave Kendal a bemused shrug and Rosie a soft pat on the head. They set off without comment. The gated entrance to the school was at the end of a long driveway that fed onto a main road. As Kendal and Rosie walked toward the street, a clean black Mercedes-Maybach GLS slid into the spot directly in front of the gate and stopped, the engine purring. Lily Shapiro squealed behind them and, with a few glances from parents and a yell from the TA, came running past, knocking Rosie's bag off her shoulder. Rosie didn't bother to lift it up, and instead dragged it along the concrete. The back door of the car opened, and Alex Shapiro stepped out. He seemed bigger and more aggressive than she remembered him. It was his stance, hips forward, chest splayed—*compensating*, she thought. His head was shaved, but his eyebrows and stubble were dark, his features slightly bulbous, his eyes hard. He was smiling widely as he saw Lily run toward him, the grin of a man who thought picking up his kid once a term meant he was winning at Dad. Kendal wanted to be kinder, but she was a good judge of character and he was giving Grade A Dickhead. He wore a lavender polo shirt with jeans and shiny shoes that matched his belt. He slipped his phone into his back pocket as Lily neared. With the car door still open and no regard for the traffic trying to squeeze past, he held his arms wide and picked up Lily in a big, performative cuddle, checking the other parents' faces for their approving smiles.

"DADDY!" Lily yelled, wrapping her arms and legs around him and clinging on. She turned to look at Rosie, who was watching closely. "See!"

Rosie pressed her lips together and walked past without acknowledging the comment or the scene, but Kendal stopped to talk to him.

"Hi! We haven't met. I'm Kendal, Rosie's mum. Is Sasha okay? She's not been around for ages. She missed arts and crafts!"

Shapiro put Lily down, but she held on tight to his leg, looking past Kendal and sticking her tongue out at Rosie.

He looked Kendal up and down with an expression that would have had him in grave danger in any other situation. "I think she has more important things to do than arts and crafts."

Kendal held his gaze with an amused smile. "Don't we all."

"Isn't yours the one that threatened Lil?" He indicated Rosie with a glib flick of his chin.

"They had an argument. I think the blame was shared." If Kendal had been operational she would have pinned him to the car and put pressure on his jugular. Instead, she simply smiled.

"Please can you move away from my vehicle, I've just had it cleaned." He gave Rosie a filthy look.

"Okay, great to meet you. What a . . ."—she narrowed her eyes, as if trying to find the right insult—"rare treat."

Kendal briefly allowed a violent fantasy to emerge and disperse before turning to Rosie. "Well, now we know where Lily gets her manners!"

Rosie smiled, but it didn't disguise the tears at the corner of her eyes or the line of snot that betrayed her despondency. Kendal picked up Rosie and her bag and walked away, eager for more distance between them and the car.

"Ro . . . do you want me to beat up Lily's dad?"

She knew it wasn't appropriate but Rosie giggled wickedly in her ear and she couldn't help it. "Do you want me to smack his bum, baby? Cos I will. If they upset you, Ro, I will go to their house and I will poke him in the eye."

Rosie howled with laughter. "DO MORE."

"What made you sad, Ro?"

Rosie's demeanor changed in a flash, and she looked downcast. In a broken whisper in Kendal's ear, she said, "Everyone has a daddy except me."

"Did Lily say that?" Rosie wrapped her bottom lip over her top one and nodded with abject shame. Kendal could have screamed.

"Well, that's a stupid thing to say."

"Smack her bum!"

"I will smack her daddy's bum and maybe her mummy's bum. I won't smack her bum though. Just cos she's a kid and that would be really weird. What do you think Ella would say if I walked into your school one day and was like, 'Hi, I'm here to smack Lily's bum'?" Rosie cackled at this image. In her arms, Kendal could feel the tension leave her muscles, and she made a mental note to Google a more constructive way to deal with this. They were nearly home. Kendal's arms were screaming under Rosie's weight, but she was reluctant to put her down. Instead, she said softly, "You do have a daddy, Ro. I'm sorry we haven't talked about him." Rosie didn't answer but she held on a little tighter, so Kendal went on. "He's very tall, and he's very, very strong. He has your curly hair, and your sparkling eyes, and your sense of humor, and your wild, wicked spirit."

Kendal paused, holding Rosie tight, and made a rash promise. "You can meet him, if you'd like."

Rosie leaned back in Kendal's arms and searched her face. "For real life?"

"For real life." Kendal was expecting a barrage of questions, but instead, Rosie wrapped herself tighter around Kendal and sniffled her tears away. "Thank you, Mumma," she said, and something inside Kendal broke a little bit more. Rosie was so like Kendal sometimes it made her feel insane. She had been expecting endless questions, but instead, Rosie sat with this new intel. Quietly digesting, turning over and contemplating her thoughts in the solemn secrecy of her mind. It wasn't until bedtime, when the lights were out and Rosie was being the little spoon, that she whispered, "Can you tell me a make-up story?"

"Which one?"

"With my daddy." She said it with a nervousness that made Kendal ache.

"He was a knight of the realm. He was the bravest, most intelligent knight in the queen's castle. He was the queen's favorite and she chose him for all of her most dangerous jobs and she always picked him when there was a dragon in the kingdom. Unfortunately, all that glory made some of the other knights quite cross."

"Why?"

"Because even knights get jealous. And because your father had a better way of doing things. See, knights are supposed to kill dragons, but your father wasn't a dragon killer. Instead, he would find the dragons, and he would honor them with respect, and gifts, and all the stuff dragons like."

"Bones," said Rosie, sagely.

"Sure. The dragons loved him, and so they protected the kingdom and no one got hurt. But the other knights couldn't compete, so they lied to the queen. They said he was a traitor and that he must be punished. And so, punished he was."

"Who punished him?"

"I'm not sure, but when I find out, we'll have a massive battle and all the best dragons will be on our side."

"And we'll win," Rosie said in a small but satisfied voice. "And then we'll be together," Rosie added, and Kendal murmured nothing in reply because Rosie was nearly asleep and Kendal was trying not to cry. The fantasy of the three of them being a family was so close, and so desperately far away.

28

The floodgates of fatherhood questions had opened. Kendal discovered that until Lily had enlightened her, Rosie had thought girls had mothers and boys had fathers. Now she knew the truth, she wanted to know everything. She would appear at the school gates each day looking for new ways to contextualize him. She wanted to know how tall he was, how fast he could run, when his birthday was. At no point did she think to ask his name or where he came from. Kendal was braced for those, and for the inevitable "where is he," but she was happy to wait for them to appear organically. Everything that was asked, she tried to answer as honestly as possible.

Wanting to keep Rosie close at all times, Kendal had signed up for every opportunity to be at the school. She had chaperoned the hat parade, baked for the cake stall, sold tickets at the popcorn social, manned the jumble sale, and played backing tracks at the year 6 breakdance show (Louis's daughter, Violet, was the star because she could convincingly do the helicopter, he'd confided proudly, as she tried to figure out Spotify playlists). She had hung bunting, watched assemblies, painted corridors, joined book clubs, and marched back and forth from the school until every aspect of the journey was deeply embedded and she felt a kind of radical boredom that was an entirely new sensation.

It was a muggy Thursday afternoon, and Rosie was on the beanbag watching cartoons.

Rico, Fini, and Kendal were looking at Joel's kit. Rico had requested Bon Temps breakers but Kendal called Fini instead, limiting the number of random men in the house. Fini was looking at a page of code only she could understand.

"I don't think this has access to the Glo-Tech network. He was using it to communicate with his handlers. This won't help us kill Cadu."

"Why don't you come and work for me, Ms. Meridian?"

Kendal laughed. "She's not motivated by money. You've got no chance."

Rico rolled his eyes. *Hippie nonsense.*

"Bon Temps is famously without scruples, Mr. Ortez," Fini answered Rico with a grin. "And I identify as scrupulous."

"Psh, everyone has a price."

"Mine isn't monetary though," Fini said. They eyeballed each other with mutual admiration.

"Another angle into Glo-Tech then?" Rico turned to Kendal. "What about getting Alex to give us access. How's things with Sasha? Could she get us a line?"

"I think she got spooked."

Rico took on a tone of faux sympathy. "No, hun, I think Sasha is incredibly cool, while you look like one of those sad sacks that had a kid instead of a life. Now she doesn't want to be friends with you, because you suck."

He said all this while looking at his screen, where he was scrutinizing a press release from one of Sasha's past art shows.

"Rude."

He wasn't finished. "You played it all wrong, Ken, you should've gone for the tortured artist angle . . . Have you seen her work? It's like being a mum is the worst thing that's ever happened to her."

"This was your angle."

Rico tutted at her, and she turned her attention back to her phone. "I'd forgotten how long it takes to get any damned action in this game. One day it's all brains on the pavement and the next it's sitting on my arse for months scoping for a meet. Was it always this tedious?"

Rico cracked his knuckles and then his neck and then his back, seemingly coming to a decision. "Let's make it happen, then. Let's crack open Glo-Tech and kill the app. You need some action and you've got a poison drive, let's plug 'er in."

"Oooh, a black op?"

"Why not? Shake the cobwebs off. It's an office full of dorks, not a military base, nothing you can't handle."

Kendal thought about it and eventually nodded. "Let's finish this."

"Fun time!" Fini added gleefully.

Since the Easter holiday stretched across what felt like centuries and Kendal's childcare solutions were basically none, they set up a limited operations hub in the house. Rosie was thrilled to have the company. She was drawn to Fini, but stared dreamy-eyed at Joe & Pete, giggling into her fist and hiding if they tried to engage her. Joe asked her serious questions about school safety protocols and her ambitions. Pete made googly eyes and fart noises. Rosie seemed entranced by them both equally. Nobody ever raised their voices or encroached on her space, and that made Rosie feel like royalty. She wasn't ignored or belittled; in fact, her presence in the room seemed to have a dominating effect on everyone in it. She would leave and sneak back in, like trying to catch the fridge light going out, to see where the lines of her power were drawn. For the first time in her life she called Kendal "Mum" instead of "Mumma," a transition that hit Kendal right in the gut. If it occurred to her that her house was full of strangers, she never said it out loud. She had forgotten Joel completely.

Rico briefed Joe & Pete, and Fini did what Fini did, and within a couple of days they had a full floor plan, schematics, and seating arrangements for the Glo-Tech offices and the companies immediately surrounding them.

After days of intensive research and planning, the team gathered in the kitchen for dinner.

Over the years, Kendal had known Rico to claim his heritage to be British, Colombian, Egyptian, Tunisian, German, Kazakhstani, and Albanian. Today, he said his mother was from Rome, and seemingly to prove it, he had spent the afternoon kneading pasta dough, rolling out long, thin ribbons of tagliatelle with a pasta maker Kendal hadn't noticed they possessed. He stirred a vat of rich red sauce, chopped like he'd been a chef all his life. He had Rosie pluck basil leaves from their stems and peel the skins from garlic. He stood close and showed her how to hold a knife and cut up tomatoes. She concentrated with the intensity of an assassin, her tongue halfway down her chin. Kendal watched from her spot in the lounge and loved him for it. He baked focaccia and shook a vinaigrette, and every time Kendal looked up from her work he was working on another element with a different process. The room filled with the warmth and comfort of home cooking that hadn't been known since Joel's exit. While Rico prepped, the rest of them hunched over screens and pored over pages, a portable printer churning out documents relating to everything from Glo-Tech's caterers to the dress code to the CCTV.

Rico fed Rosie early, a plate of simple spaghetti and sauce that she ate with gusto. Kendal took her to bed and she quickly fell into an easy, happy sleep. That Rosie was a social animal, thriving off the company of others, gave Kendal a physical ache, and she felt bruised by the guilt of the isolated childhood she'd provided. That even now, the best she could offer were colleagues. She wondered if Fini, as her oldest, closest, most trusted, possibly only friend, would agree to be a godparent, whatever that meant.

When she got back downstairs, at Rico's behest the dining table had been cleared of all operational kit and was set in the style of an Italian bistro.

"I didn't know you were house-trained." She marveled at the room. He'd lit candles.

"Yeah, well." He shrugged. "All work and no pasta is una vita non degna di essere vissuta. As my mother used to say." *A life not worth living.*

They pulled up chairs, poured wine, cut bread, and watched incredulously as Rico served a first course of Tuscan ribollita.

He glanced around the table at the wide eyes and mouths agape. "What? It's brain food. I can look after you guys, stop looking at me like my hair is on backward."

"How many IDs do you have?" Kendal asked, slathering butter on homemade bread and dipping it in the soup. Rico pulled his chair in at the head of the table and paused to think about it. Joe & Pete shared a look like they couldn't believe they were sitting with the boss and his best agent.

"No IDs on me. I've got myths and tricks. And I've got this, of course." He gestured around the table. He was trying to be enigmatic, but it was laced with lassitude and they all just felt sad for him. Kendal wondered where his kids were, and if he ever saw them. She could imagine not; his priorities had always leaned toward money over all else. Foolish man.

He cleared his throat, unused to either examination or pity.

"The butter's infused with garlic, sea salt, honey, and thyme," he said gruffly, gesturing at it.

Fini cleared her throat and picked gingerly at her bowl. Kendal smiled, remembering that her friend had the palate of a twelve-year-old, and a chunky bean broth was probably her nightmare.

Fini broke a piece of bread in half but didn't eat it. "Speaking of time," she began, "Glo-Tech appears to be in sprint mode. I think it works in our favor. There are lots of freelancers and unfamiliar faces in and out every day."

Rico nodded. "Copy that." He took a sip of wine and turned to Joe & Pete. "What are the headlines from your team?"

"The main problem we haven't cracked . . ."

"No, Joe, lead with the good news, we're running the positives. Problems are for pudding."

Joe & Pete shared another look, and Joe looked stricken. Pete stepped in. "Alice has access to company calendars, and we've cracked their base-level security, so we can print a pass and access CCTV. Anything deeper than that though . . . Um . . ."

"All out of good news?" Rico asked.

"Yes, sir."

"Who's Alice?" Kendal asked with her mouth full.

"The temp on reception. She's good, but she's playing dumb, so not a lot of seniority." Rico turned to Kendal. "What do you think?"

"Keep things legitimate. Get Alice to add a meeting to the company calendar and grant access. I can go dark once I'm inside."

"And what do we know about the location of the tech?" Rico directed the question to Fini.

"Alice confirmed that Joel's machine is dormant. I've scraped his passwords from the kit downstairs but it shouldn't be any more difficult than logging in, plugging in the virus, and killing a couple of minutes."

"And we're absolutely sure we need to be in the building? There isn't an easy way we're not seeing?"

Joe, Pete, and Fini answered "no" in unison.

"Right." Rico nodded as if something had resolved in his head. "Pens down for tagliatelle and then let's get a kit list together. By tiramisu we'll have a plan."

29

It was a dusky, clement evening when Kendal emerged from Old Street station onto the unfortunately coined Silicon Roundabout and walked toward the Glo-Tech offices. She was dressed in the trench coat and trouser suit of an office body. The Bon Temps Salon, as Rico liked it to be known, had altered her appearance enough to confuse any facial recognition tech. The makeup artist had made her skin slightly darker, her nose and lips slightly bigger, and her hairline slightly lower. He'd changed her eyebrow color and contoured her cheeks so that her face was a different shape. It might not have fooled her mother, but at a glance she was unrecognizable. She wore horn-rimmed glasses and a long, wavy auburn wig and carried a briefcase. She had the swagger of someone with an important job they were good at, and late for. She caught her reflection on the way in. The most convincing part of this disguise, she thought, was her age.

Pete was babysitting Rosie, and Fini and Joe were in a black VW transit van that had been refitted as a comms center and parked in the car park of an adjacent building, tracking Kendal's movement through the office. Rico was in a bar across the road, plugged in to the comms link.

Glo-Tech had two receptionists. One of them was a fastidious worker. She followed protocols, she logged visitors, she never authorized deliveries without confirming recipients. She was the kind of employee that was precious among big firms. The other was Rico's temp, the diametric opposite of her colleague. Alice was well trained, her haplessness a carefully cultivated cover, so that when she did "balls up" it would be attributed to her gullible personality and not an act of corporate espionage. Alice had a timed absence for plausible deniability. She had dead-dropped an all-areas access pass for Kendal to pick up from behind a vase on the reception desk. Kendal continued purposefully past the desk and into the glass-monolith office and beeped through the barrier and into the waiting elevator. "Smooth," Fini said in Kendal's ear. "Floor fourteen. Joel's desk is in the northeast corner."

As she rose in the glass elevator, Kendal looked out into the muted banality of the building. All the activity of Glo-Tech happened in code, on screens and servers, in realms almost entirely out of physical reach. It addled Kendal's brain how intangible everything had become, how unsatisfying she found it. Everything from the collective acceptance of a digitized world, the cashless cafés and self-serve checkouts, to the disconnection between what was real and the illusions created online. Not for the first time, she had a strong urge to move herself and Rosie out into the wilderness, to live in nature with people who connected to the living world physically and spiritually.

"Oh shit," Fini muttered in her ear.

"What?"

Fini tutted. "There's way more people in the office than we expected this late on a Friday. Mostly coders, so they'll be plugged in."

Rico piped in on the comms, "Easy, 96. Remember you're there for a meeting."

The elevator doors beeped open. The corridor was empty, but beyond, the office had the low hubbub of people working, hunched in chairs and connected by headphones to their inner worlds.

Kendal walked toward Joel's cubicle. A couple of staffers looked up, but no one reacted to a stranger in their midst. She took a seat at Joel's desk. A picture that Rosie had drawn was in a small frame resting against his console. It took Kendal by surprise, and she stared at it for several seconds before discreetly dropping it into the pocket of her coat.

She pulled the USB key from her pocket and clicked it into the keyboard, her work was done, it was all down to Fini now. Without making a sound, someone had approached and was standing behind her. Kendal froze the mouse. Had he seen her do it? In the black mirror of the computer Alex Shapiro's reflection came into view. *This guy*, she thought. She hadn't expected to see him somehow, had thought of Glo-Tech as Joel's realm. Now that he was here, the op shifted gears. She doubted he would recognize her, but the thought that he would connect her to Rosie sent a cold shiver across her neck. This was followed by a deep calm. She was operational, and a clown like Shapiro wouldn't faze 96; this was what she was born for. She knocked on the desk for luck and spun around in the chair to face him. He looked angry, and more than slightly worried, but he kept his voice level and spoke with authority.

"What do you think you're doing?"

She took a black baseball cap from her other pocket and pulled it low over her face.

"Just leaving."

She stood up, was a little bit taller than him, not as broad but a lot more confident. He was nervous, beads of sweat forming at his hairline. She knew she was on borrowed time, but she was curious to see what he would do.

"Stay where you are. Security is on their way." He grabbed her arm roughly.

With her free hand she pulled a black handgun from her waistband, and stepped closer to him. With it shoved hard into the soft underside of his chin, she spoke in a low, threatening whisper, right into his ear. "And what will they find when they get here, Mr. Shapiro. Is it your brains all over the wall?"

The color left his face and his mouth hung open, his tongue lolling about in surprise. She pressed the barrel against his forehead and then gave it a nasty tap. No real damage, just a bruise in a stupid place. She wanted to go harder, she wanted to pistol-whip him out cold. He grabbed his head and threw himself back against the wall. "Why did you do that?" he wailed.

Running low so she was obscured by the cubicle partitions, she made for the door, swerving left away from the security team that were heading toward Alex with a collective look of confusion. "She's over there! Get her!" he screeched, pointing in the wrong direction. Another security guard rounded the corner between Kendal and the lifts and she ducked into a cubicle that was occupied by a girl in a baseball cap, with pierced eyebrows and a tattoo of Totoro on her upper arm. The girl caught a glimpse of Kendal in the reflection from her screen, but when she turned around, there was no one there. She took off her headphones and peered over the partitions at the hubbub from the corner. She saw Alex Shapiro, a man she found intolerably creepy, clutching his reddened face and demanding that security "catch that bitch." She turned to see Kendal disappear in the lift. She sat down and put her headphones back on. Sprint weeks made people craaaaazy.

Kendal was out the door of Glo-Tech and removing her cap, wig, and coat, dumping them in a bin on her way out.

"That was easy," she said into the comms link.

"No, it wasn't—" Fini started but was interrupted.

"Oh shit," Rico muttered in her ear.

"When did 'oh shit' become our signal, guys?"

"There's spooks here," he said quietly.

"Where?"

Kendal pulled open the door of the VW and hopped in next to Fini with a wink. Fini looked at her aghast, her head shaking. "They got to it, they aborted the program, it didn't work."

Joe was watching three screens, camera links surrounding Glo-Tech. Kendal's radio buzzed in her ear. "Why does it sound like someone's using our channel?"

Joe was frowning at the middle screen. "What is that?"

A van had pulled up outside the Glo-Tech office, and they watched as what looked like a SWAT team emerged and ran into the building.

Rico reappeared on the comms link. "The whole area is crawling with teams," Rico whispered urgently. "Secret service all over the place."

Joe was frantically tapping at the keyboard in the back of the van with Fini and Kendal watching. Their comms speaker crackled. "I'm trying to pick up their channel," Joe murmured. Suddenly it burst into life: "Repeat, Casio only."

Kendal's mouth fell open. She took the earpiece out as if it were infectious, dropped it on the floor, and crushed it with her heel. Fini looked at her with eyes wide. Keeping her hand close to her chest, Fini signed, *Is that Jenny?* And Kendal nodded, her face ashen.

"Kill the comms, Joe. I've got to get out of here," she said.

"Yeah, for sure, we just need to pick up the boss."

"Go dark, Joe. Now." He caught the look on her face and tapped the side of the van between him and the driver. Instantly, the van moved, pulled away down City Road, and Joe powered down half the screens.

"What the hell is going on?"

"The government's all over the place," Joe answered. "Might be fun to send them on a mess-around though."

He'd spent too much time with Rico.

"There he is," Joe said, tapping a screen. They pulled into a cab rank on the side of the road, the door slid open, and in one fluid motion Rico stepped in and Joe stepped out. They were wearing identical outfits and were of a similar build. Joe kept his head down and stepped into the cab in front, which took off. The van followed more slowly.

"Why did you guys cut comms? Let's give His Majesty's monkeys a proper run, shall we?" Rico grinned at them. "That was fun, I haven't been tickled by an A team in years."

"What were they doing there?" Kendal attempted to bring his boyish exhilaration back into focus.

"I have no idea!"

Kendal had time to wonder what percentage of sounds that came out of Rico bore any resemblance to the truth.

Rico checked his phone. "Got you a drop-off in T minus twenty."

"Copy that," Kendal answered. "Ping me a spot for the debrief. Make it swift."

The van pulled up outside Angel station so that Kendal could drop down into the Tube system and disappear.

30

The next evening, Joe & Pete were babysitting again so that Fini, Rico, and Kendal could sit at the bar in a long-closed restaurant, nursing drinks that Rico had mixed with the vim of someone who knew the difference between bourbon and rye. A punter wouldn't know, but the bar was a Bon Temps secure-sound room, where they could talk without fear of being overheard. The confirmed presence of the UK's Secret Intelligence Service made each of them anxious, albeit for very different reasons: Fini was operating miles outside of both UK and international law, Rico was worried about pissing off one of his most lucrative clients, and Kendal was newly aware of a presence she had hoped to avoid, forever. Their stirrers tinkled in crystal rocks glasses.

"So. His Majesty's finest out in force. What a catastrophic waste of time."

Fini tapped the bar for attention. "Two important things. One, I copied the virus, so all is not lost. And two, what the unholy absolute hell, Kendal Carter, is Mummy dearest doing in town?"

Rico tapped his stirrer on the edge of the glass as if he were about to make a speech. "What are you talking about?"

Kendal took a long drink and looked at Fini. "You said she was still in The Game?"

"Not SIS!" Fini smirked into her glass. "She wouldn't!"

"Who wouldn't what?" Rico demanded.

Fini gave him her dirtiest grin. "Have you ever met a woman called Jenny Corrin?"

Rico looked from one to the other. "*The* Jenny Corrin? She's the new deputy director at the NCPSA."

"'Course she is." Fini smirked.

"What the hell is the NCPSA?" Kendal asked.

"Some new techy gov department. National Cyber Protection Security Assholes. Something like that. They put Jenny in to head it up. I know her well." Rico made a lascivious face, and Fini let out a barking laugh. Rico frowned. "But what's she got to do with the price of fish?"

Fini beamed smugly. "KC? Should I do a drumroll?"

Kendal gave her a steely glare as she said, "She's my mother."

Rico did a spit-take, sending an inelegant sprinkling of Negroni across the bar. "You have got to be kidding," Rico muttered. "For fuck's sake, Ken. Who are you?"

"She's 'Casio.'" Fini giggled; she may have been tipsy.

They could practically hear the cogs in Rico's brain whirring. "Wait, why would she put a team on you? And why are we sitting around speculating like a bunch of punters? DM her, ask her what gives. Get her on FaceTime, fuck it, let's all say hello." Rico had recovered from the surprise and switched smoothly into piss-taking. "Oh my god." He laughed, a hearty, gloating sound, while he gazed at Kendal with an awestruck smirk. "I can see the resemblance. You have her mouth." Fini snickered behind her hand.

"I have her right hook as well," Kendal replied coldly. "But I won't have her anywhere near me or Rosie. She's an agent of chaos. She'll only appear when she wants to. I have no power over her." Kendal disappeared into a dark place, a feeling, a memory that she boxed back up immediately. She turned to look at Rico. "You need a different angle."

Rico adjusted his tone back to operational. "So you don't know what she wants?"

"If she's gov, maybe she wants Khalil. It's very on brand for her to try and murder my boyfriend."

"Or maybe they're just protecting their investment?" Rico added, sounding mildly sloshed.

Kendal gave him a long, hard stare. "Are you in contract with them?"

"Classified." He hiccupped, but it was phony.

"You're a snake, Ortez."

Kendal finished her drink, checked her watch, and stood up to leave. Speaking directly to Fini, she decided. "We need another way to kill Cadu. None of these people can be trusted with this tech. None of them give a shit about kids, or safety, or anything beyond their own disgusting pockets. We can't let it get out."

Fini held up her glass. "Amen."

Rico shook his head, defeated. "It's not our monkeys, Ken, not our circus. Let the clown factory clean up their own mess."

"When have they ever cleaned up a mess? If you're worried about your clients and your cash flow, that's fine. We can do it without you." She slammed out of the bar, but not before she heard Fini say to Rico, "You haven't actually boffed her mum, have you?" Thankfully, the door closed on his response.

31

Rosie was sitting at the dining table folding strips of green crepe paper into what she had confidently asserted were magic worms. The infant years' final assembly was coming up and parents were supposed to "support and facilitate but not project manage" creating costumes for their offspring. Rosie's character was "Juice." Kendal wondered if she could help her fashion an apple out of scarves. She didn't know if the magic worms were associated with the show or if it was a side project. Rather than improving communication, Rosie's exponentially growing vocabulary had just made their conversations more abstract. All the information she had was a pack of crepe paper strips and the word "juice."

Letting Rosie get on with it, and remembering that at age four, whatever they were doing was unlikely to be either important or professional, she made a drink and picked up her phone. Rosie looked up from her crepe paper. "I need a tail," she announced.

"What for?"

"FOR MY BUM!" She laughed herself off the beanbag.

"Ro, who else is in your group in the play?"

"Lily and Ariel."

"Shall I text Sasha and see what Lily's wearing?"

She had already made a pretty radical decision, and this fortuitous moment firmed it up. It was time to break cover.

"Hi, Sasha. Do you fancy arts and crafts at mine? Just making Rosie's outfit. Have wine!"

She played it soft. If Sasha didn't respond, she would force the issue. She waited.

Rosie picked up a small, crocheted rabbit that she had become obsessed with. She carried it everywhere, and its ears had been sucked into oblivion. She called it Woolly and said it was her best friend. She claimed it would bite anyone but her. For some reason, this made Kendal incandescently angry, a feeling that welled up from somewhere buried deep within her own childhood. The end of the school year was a mixed bag of emotions and responsibilities. The school calendar went from demanding to apparently just full time. There were plays, fundraisers, class parties, petitions, donations, food banks, excursions, productions, and teachers' gifts funds . . . The WhatsApp group was on fire. Kendal took any and every opportunity to stay close to the school.

She was walking back one day when she glimpsed a tall, bald white guy whose nervous eyes she'd seen in reflections before. She stopped abruptly and he continued walking past her, bumping her shoulder nervously. When she got home she found a balled-up chewing gum wrapper in her pocket. On it was a code number she recognized as a connect to Khalil. He was setting a meeting. Kendal left the curtains of the house closed until 11:00 AM the following day, confirming the meet. She stayed even more alert after that. She didn't see the bald guy again, but there was a pair of young women who were so bad at surveillance they were either fresh temps in training or bona fide locals. When she was alone, she ran counter-surveillance as a force of habit and always carried layers for quick changes, slight disguises, and an exit strategy wherever she was. When she was with Rosie, however, they were sitting ducks. Kendal couldn't remember a time in her own life when she would have been allowed to explore every brick, bush, and wall on the way. The best she could remember was running counter-surveillance as a child. In her earliest memories it was hide-and-seek, with a ten-second head start. Before she had turned ten it became more sophisticated, and Kendal had to find gaps in surveillance to slip away unseen. Kendal was nine when she first turned her coat inside out and disappeared professionally. She had doubled back and followed her mother to their door. Then she had stayed hidden for an extra half an hour until her mum seemed genuinely worried. Kendal had a deeply vivid memory of emerging from behind a neighbor's wall, cold but pleased with herself, feeling like she had finally achieved an impossible task. She walked proudly into the house, her coat and schoolbag dragging behind her in the hallway, tall with her tiny triumph. But Jenny couldn't stand to lose. She waited until Kendal was inside and said after her, "Next time put a hat on. I could see that ponytail from a mile away."

Maybe that was the moment that young Kendal realized her mother was not a generous person, that victories would be hard won, and rarely worth it. Maybe Jenny had intentionally programmed the competitive spirit out of her, knowing it was a weakness in their trade. *Their* trade, she thought. She was a spy before she could spell it.

Now, when they walked she would dawdle, watching Rosie drag a stick noisily across a railing, waving at vehicles and picking up random tat: old hair bands, leaves, and rocks. If Kendal felt they were being watched, she would take evasive, ordering cabs through ghost apps, switching phones and scrambling routines. But she also knew that ultimately a bad actor who knew where Rosie went to school would be able to pick them up. Instead of hiding, her plan was a display of innocence. They had nothing to hide, and no one to hide from.

Lost among the memories, she had cut a piece of cardboard into a tail. She was sticking cotton wool to it while Rosie inexplicably but enthusiastically dabbed at it with red paint. The result was a horror show, but Rosie liked it. She painted her nose black and put a worm on her head.

"I'm Juice!" Rosie screamed, delighted, and ran upstairs to show her toys and pose in the mirror. Kendal checked her phone and chuckled at the parents' messages; at least she wasn't alone.

And then Sasha finally replied "yes."

It was a pleasing scene. As the sun dropped behind the alder trees, the kids were sitting on a blanket on the lawn wearing matching white cotton tunics that Sasha had put together at home. Dressing them as twins seemed to have bound them together, at least for now. Kendal and Sasha sat at the table on the deck with large glasses of white wine, surrounded by scraps of paper, constructing increasingly complex flowers from elaborately folded squares.

"Who is Rosie playing in this epic they're putting on?" Sasha asked.

"She says she's 'Juice.'"

Sasha stopped cutting and looked up. "What do you mean?"

"Juice," Kendal repeated, feeling foolish.

Sasha stopped short of laughing at her, but only just. "They're doing Greek myths. Lily is Hera and Abdul is Poseidon . . ."

They looked at each other with the same face, the universal expression of cogs turning. It clicked for Kendal first. "Is she saying *Medusa*?!" She shouted over the garden, "Rosie, are you Medusa? With snakes for hair?"

Rosie looked at Lily as if she had the dumbest mother in town and Lily dutifully rolled her eyes. Sasha was grinning broadly. "How were you going to make a juice costume?"

"I was just gonna paint her green and give her a straw to hold."

"I kind of wish we had let that play out."

Sasha resumed her scissor work. "I love crafts," she said happily. "Anything handsy." She went on, "Switching from digital art to making real things was like a personal renaissance . . ."

Sasha let her eyes close lustily and shook her head as if it was some lost fantasy. "Do you ever wish you could resign parenting like you could an office job?"

"God, yeah."

"Me too. I wanted a baby so much. I went to such extraordinary lengths to have her that it feels ungrateful to regret it. Not that I do regret it!" She looked guilty. "I love her, but I didn't know how hard it was going to be."

Kendal took the opening. "My thing is the boredom. I used to take risks, and now I have to make sure everything is stable and reliable and consistent . . . Exhilaration definitely hit an all-time low."

Sasha laughed and sighed. "Not a lot of thrills it's true."

"I do have something that's sort of exciting though."

Sasha put down her scissors. "Well, thank god for that, what is it?"

"Before I say, can I just caveat that it's very sensitive information and I really need to know it won't go any further."

Sasha looked mildly confused, and Kendal could tell she wasn't particularly worried.

"Cross my heart," she said, as if Kendal were being silly. Kendal took a deep breath, her hands on the table and her eyes on the kids.

"My real job is investigating corporate malfeasance for an intelligence agency. There's a reason I asked you to come here today. It wasn't arts and crafts."

She watched Sasha's face carefully. She was turning over the information and frowned. "What reason?" she asked suspiciously, looking like she might bolt for the door. Kendal felt terrible that the kids were here. This was the sort of meeting that should happen in noisy bars or under railway bridges.

"Glo-Tech is developing an app that is covert spyware. It's aimed at kids, at tracking and manipulating them. I think Alex might be the only person with the capacity to shut it down and I want you to help me get him to do it."

Sasha's mouth hung open and she shook her head, part horror, part anger, part awe. "You have been consistently surprising, I will give you that."

Kendal held up her glass, and Sasha obliged her with a clink. Kendal let Sasha sit with the idea. Eventually she seemed to have digested it. She then spoke with a quiet, sad authority.

"I knew he was doing something bad. His whole persona has changed in the last couple of years. You know when you can tell someone is being awful because of how they feel about themselves? Ever since he started at Glo-Tech he's been impossible to live with. He did honestly used to be one of the good guys."

"Good people do bad things."

"Yes, but then what does that make them?"

It was a fair point, and Kendal stayed quiet.

"What do you need from me?" Sasha asked. She had a brave face, but Kendal could see questions starting to bubble up under the surface.

"Ideally I need a few minutes alone with him and network access to Glo-Tech."

"Why does it have to be Alex?"

"We need someone senior, someone who knows the program. And we don't think anyone else at Glo-Tech has ever been one of the good guys."

"What does he need to do?"

"Log into their system and kill the app before they do the rollout."

Sasha looked utterly woebegone. "He said it was going to revolutionize education," she said quietly.

"Maybe in another iteration it will, but this version has been hijacked and corrupted."

Sasha looked up suddenly, her mouth slack. There was real fear in her eyes.

"They've started the rollout already! They gave it to year 6 to test."

"We need to act fast. Let me run some scenarios with my team and see if we can disconnect the school from the Cadu system. Don't worry. If it's still just a trial, we're not too late."

Sasha bit at the nail on her ring finger and spoke with a dull melancholy. "I knew they'd ruin it. He wanted to build something that anyone could use. He sold it to them thinking it was the only way to achieve scale. I told him they were toxic, and he swore he could control it."

"He lost control, I guess."

Sasha's contempt was written in bold capitals across her brow. The eternal *told you so* of women for millennia. The world's most unsatisfying victory.

"How can I help?"

"I need a cover to come over and get a few minutes with him. We need to lay out a believable reason for me to be there at the same time as him so it doesn't raise any eyebrows. He's being watched, and most likely, so am I."

Sasha sucked her teeth in thought.

"He's never home."

"Do you have access to his calendar?"

"Only his personal one, but he never sticks to anything."

"Well, don't worry. We'll figure something out."

Sasha mulled it over. "He can be a bit slippery if he's under pressure. There's a knack to managing him if you want him to behave a certain way."

"How so?"

"Like if you want him to do something new or exciting, you can't pitch it too far in advance. You must wait until the latest possible moment and then just gently let him know it's about to happen. And you can't ask him loads of questions. His limit in one sitting is three or four, if they're answers he doesn't have to think about too much or easy decisions, you know? But if you go in with tricky decisions, he'll just sort of seize up."

Kendal was listening incredulously to Sasha and wondering why anyone would invite a person like him into her life at all. It seemed unlikely he'd ever been a nice enough person for her. She seemed to read the thought and glanced, embarrassed, at the table between them. "He wasn't always like this. He was an artist when I met him. Groundbreaking technology, a true dreamer. Life got to him. It's not his fault. I swear Cadu was about democratizing education. It was only ever supposed to be a force for good."

"Do you think he'd kill it, given the chance?"

"I think so. If it's the right thing to do."

On the lawn, the kids were squabbling over a music player. Kendal and Sasha watched to see if it would escalate.

Dreamily Sasha said, "Most of the time I can remember that these years are precious and I'll miss it when they're gone. But just occasionally I do wish they'd just hurry up and grow."

"Amen," Kendal replied, and they went back to cutting the paper. "How many of these do they want?" Kendal asked, adding a raggedy flower to the pile.

"A zillion dillion, I think."

Kendal smiled, happy with company, feeling unusually secure with Sasha. It was the fact that they both had kids in play, it leveled the stakes. It gave them a fundamental priority. It meant they understood at least one thing about each other, and that was more than most of the relationships Kendal had had in her professional life.

32

On the day of her meeting with Khalil, Kendal felt a mixed range of emotions. There was a hark back to her old life, the clandestine actions that happened in plain sight. She felt twinges of excitement and fear. She was desperate to see him again, but desperation and desire made for risky decisions and bad ideas.

Despite this, at midday on a bright Saturday morning, there she was sitting with Rosie on an overground train destined for Shepherd's Bush. Nearly everyone stared at their phones. Rosie was on her knees on the seat counting houses. Squeaking with delight at the gardens and lives they swept past. They swapped trains a few times, switchbacks and false starts, but Kendal was hyperaware that if they were under observation, there were no CCTV dead spots on public transport. She considered getting a car but again, roads were easily monitored. No, she had given it a lot of thought, and their best chance was to keep it simple and travel by train. Khalil's code had indicated a location in Westfield. It was a place that came preloaded with opportunities to subvert any surveillance. There were cameras, yes, but simple ways to flush out anyone watching as well as a multitude of hiding places, crowds, corners, and costumes.

Six years earlier, Kendal and Khalil had been to Paris. They were walking the Champs-Élysées talking about CCTV. It didn't bother him, he said; the tech was too basic, the management too chaotic, and the purpose overall was deterrence, not engagement. The real boon to privacy, he said, was addiction to phones, "the portable puddles of Narcissus." He had gestured to the people around them, mostly absorbed in screens, only the tourists looking up, Khalil's arm sweeping them all into the generalization. "If I make drama, they film me, but the small moves, the sleight of hand, anything requiring the payment of attention, they will miss it all."

Kendal glanced at the camera in the roof of the train. Maybe he was right.

Rosie was absolutely delighted that they were going shopping. She had the spending power of a venture capitalist; her love of shiny new things was surpassed only by her love of sugar, and Westfield mall was crammed to the gills with both. Kendal hadn't said they were going to meet Khalil in case it went awry.

"Where first, Ro?"

"ICE CREAM."

They entered the center via a single-file escalator that delivered them directly to high-end shops: Tiffany, Gucci, Chanel. These had security guards and soft lighting and felt completely incongruous with the otherwise unglamorous destination. Rosie was tugging her along with absolutely no interest in diamond-studded handbags.

The security guard standing outside Jimmy Choo looked through Kendal as if she were a window. Just another mum dragging some brat through the poorly lit heart of capitalism. In the melee that was shopping on a Saturday, Kendal realized Khalil had a point. The cameras were only as useful as whoever was watching them and could be outmaneuvered by a baseball cap, but literally everyone in her eyeline was on a phone. She was having this thought and concentrating on the reflection in the window of Urban Outfitters when a large, bustling woman in a hijab, also glued to her phone, collided painfully with her shoulder.

Too painful, Kendal realized, more a sharp pain than a bump, and she felt Rosie's hand slip from hers as her legs gave way.

"Rosie . . ." she tried to say, but her mouth was slack. She reached her arms to grab at reality but found herself powerless to resist the closing circle of black. A scream failed to form, as any remaining fight dissolved under the drug. There were no reserves to call on. The last thing she saw was several phones pointing at her as she was pulled backward into the darkness.

She woke up in a small room that smelled of cigarettes. She was lying on an overstuffed two-seater sofa made of a rough synthetic material. Her mouth felt like velour. She sat up as quickly as she could. A swivel chair with its back to her was facing a bank of screens that showed twelve different angles of the shopping center in grainy black and white. Within a few seconds Kendal's grogginess started to fade and she leaped from the sofa, reaching for the door behind her. Her legs betrayed her and she tumbled painfully to the floor.

The chair turned and a boy in his late twenties looked at her with a smug disdain. He was blond and had the pale whiteness of someone who didn't get outside enough. He glanced at her hands, which was when Kendal realized that it wasn't the drugs making her hands hurt, it was cable ties.

"Calm down," the man-boy said, turning back to face the screens. The back of his head was familiar. Where had she seen it before? She rolled up painfully from the floor and leaned against the sofa, trying to clear her head, her thoughts lolling around uncontrolled and hard to grasp. She had walked them into a trap and now Rosie was gone, but she wouldn't be far. How did she know this? She felt it in her bones. This wasn't so much a dangerous situation as an orchestrated one.

"Who do you work for?" she slurred at the boy. He turned in his chair and gave her a cocky look that she would have liked to physically pull from his face. He obviously wasn't going to answer.

The room swirled with an annoying psychedelia.

"Hey, fucko. I don't mean which organization. I can smell that secret service cologne. What is it, eau de hubris?"

She fought against a wave of nausea. "Your boss. Is she an old woman? A real pain in your ass? Gets your name wrong a lot?"

The boy, Taylor, né Jonathan, couldn't help the muscles in his neck answering the question for him. Despite herself, Kendal laughed. "You poor bastard."

He still didn't say anything, but this time his face told her everything she needed to know. He was a poor bastard and he did work for Kendal's mother. He turned back to the screens.

"You were following me, by the canal. I recognize the back of your head." He didn't speak or move.

"Where is my daughter?"

"She's safe." His voice was more adult than she was expecting. He'd been given lines he was allowed to say, she realized—no more, no less. Classic Jenny.

"Who is she with?"

"She's with Khalil Masoumi. They're allowed twenty-three minutes. Then you can go."

"What do you mean *allowed?*"

The boy tutted. He was enjoying knowing more than her. Having the upper hand was probably a rare treat.

"He handed himself in, as long as he got to meet the kid. He set it up himself."

He muttered something else under his breath, but Kendal's mind was busy processing the information among the swirling lights.

"What did you knock me out with?"

"Ketamine."

"Why?"

He turned to face her and splayed his legs, a manspread. She hated him a touch more. "They didn't think you'd let him go. They said you're a weapon."

"Rude."

He didn't smile; he looked like he hadn't smiled in years. He gave her a look of such pure contempt that she stopped feeling sorry for him completely.

It took fourteen minutes for Kendal's brain function to return to normal. She knew this because the time was displayed across the bottom of all the screens. Rosie's absence was like the high-pitched tone of tinnitus; it was making her crazy. Her brain raced with worst-case scenarios. Rosie had an AirTag in her jacket! She grasped for her phone and tried to get it to light up but it wouldn't. Jonathan watched her. "You can go in six minutes. Chill out."

"Where is she?"

"She's in KidZania."

"What is that?"

"It's an interactive play center for kids. She was escorted there. The target followed her. They are allowed twenty-three minutes together, then you can go and get her. No harm, no foul." He shrugged as if he hadn't abducted her only daughter, cuffed her, and called her a weapon.

Kendal noted the time and subconsciously kicked off the countdown. She watched the boy's hands tapping at a keyboard, shifting the monitors to cameras around the mall. He had long, bony fingers, his forearms sinewy and strong. He was exactly the type of assistant her mother adored. She liked the arrogance; she enjoyed using it against them. "I can see why she chose you." They both knew it wasn't a compliment. They watched the clock countdown. When it hit 13:42 he cut the cable ties. She considered taking a couple of seconds to break his face, but it wasn't worth it. She disappeared from the room before he'd had time to consider his luck.

She couldn't tell if it was the flooring, the lighting, the layout of the place, or the embers of ketamine in her system, but traversing the mall was like running through syrup. Every time she turned a corner the compass points seemed to shift, as if the whole place were sitting on a slowly spinning disc. Even once she had spotted the giant airplane sticking out of KidZania like the aftermath of a terrible crash, she had to double back to find a staircase that took her closer. She ignored the half-hearted yelps of the receptionist and ran inside. It was a stuffy nightmare of happy children, screens, and undersized versions of milk trucks, laundromats, and banks, weirdly defunct concepts in the modern world. She felt like she was in an awful dream. Eventually she saw Khalil kneeling next to Rosie, who was on a bench. She was fine. As she approached, Khalil stood up and looked at her. Apology and regret were etched into his face; he hadn't shaved, dark stubble and tousled hair adding to the drama behind his eyes. Rosie saw Kendal and ran toward her. "Mumma, that's him! That's my daddy!"

"I know, honey. Isn't he lovely? Did you have a nice time?"

"He's my daddy," she repeated, holding her arms up to be lifted and bursting into tears. Khalil approached them, and Kendal turned her shoulder so that she and Rosie could both see him.

"It was so beautiful to meet you, Rosie. Thank you for speaking with me and for being so sweet. I will try to see you again soon. The very moment I can. I promise." He held Kendal's gaze and her heart broke again. It wasn't a repeat injury, it was a return to form. He was going. It was her fault. He looked past her, and she turned. They could see beyond the body of the broken airplane into the mall. The tall guy who had passed Kendal the code was cuffed and encircled by suits. Kendal looked desperately at Khalil. "There'll be a fire escape. You can run, I'll cover you."

He put his arms around them both. "No, Kara, it's better like this, it's safer for you if they know where I am. Once Cadu is dead, they won't care about me anymore. Please, Kara . . . I'm so sorry. We should never have . . ."

"I won't let them keep you." But they both knew it was an empty promise. "I'll do it. I'll kill it. We'll see you again."

Holding her gaze, he leaned forward and kissed her tenderly. His lips held hers for a few moments, and Kendal's heart swooped skyward, and then he stepped back with a smile that killed her. He booped Rosie's nose. Then, without a backward glance, he walked toward the suits. Kendal hoped he might duck and run at the last moment, but he went quietly instead.

"Who's Kara?" said Rosie.

"No one, my love. She's gone. Let's go home."

"Can I watch TV?"

They took a taxi. Rosie was subdued; she had aged again.

"What happened, Ro? When I fell?"

"Gee Gee was in the airplane."

"Who is Gee Gee?"

"Gee Gee."

Kendal looked at her daughter's confused face, which was more worried than a four-year-old's should ever be. She didn't question her further.

33

Kendal, Nat, and Sasha were sitting around the breakfast bar while Lily and Rosie put dolls in lines, and Sam tried to assassinate a beanbag with his hands, feet, face, and teeth.

"You want gender to be a social construct," Nat said over a steaming cup of coffee, as they watched Sam's progress with varying degrees of concern. "And then a boy comes along, and lives up to every cliché you can think of."

"I think that just means that he fits the paradigm," Sasha mused, "not that it isn't a construct."

"All right, Einstein."

Sasha shrugged defensively. "Kant, if anything."

"Who are you calling a Kant?" Nat snickered.

"You're both being very highbrow for a coffee morning," Kendal said.

Nat turned to her wearing her dirtiest grin.

"So, Karate Ken, Sasha tells me you're an actual undercover assassin."

"Natalie!" Sasha blushed vermilion. "You promised!" She turned to Kendal. "I didn't say that."

Kendal noticed her fight response surge. Blown, again. She kept her tone light.

"I wish it was that much fun. It's a corporate malfeasance case, nothing glamorous. Technically classified though." She gave Sasha a small, admonishing glance.

Nat said quickly, "I absolutely won't breathe a word to anyone." She looked genuinely contrite. "I just wanna be in the gang." She made karate hands.

Sasha grimaced. "I haven't told anyone else. I was scared. Nat's who I call when I'm scared."

"Yeah, it's okay, I get it," Kendal answered, distracted. The hole in Joel's head appeared momentarily in her mind. She looked from one woman to the other. These were her friends. If anything happened to them it would be on her; more collateral damage, wreaking havoc on people's lives. But as she worried about them, they looked at her eagerly, excitement in their eyes and visibly keen to help. It made Kendal smile. A team of women with skin in the game was extra protection for Rosie, from people who understood what was at stake in a way that Rico and even Fini seemed oblivious to. Reaching for her phone, she sent a request to Joe & Pete for a background check on Nat, and weighed the case . . . An unvetted, untrained circle of trust this close to Rosie was either good or very, very bad. She looked from one to the other. Nat was an open book, smart, aggressive, and raw, yes, but a straight shooter. Sasha was harder to read and harder to trust. She had a murky background, multiple identities, and her loyalties were ambiguous at best. She was clever, cloaked, and until this, had seemed to be discreet. She was the one to watch. The fact, Kendal reflected, that Sasha had been frightened and had shared her intel with a mate was reassuring. Pros don't gossip. Kendal rubbed the four-inch scar on her forearm and noticed a stretch of stress across her sternum that hadn't been there five minutes ago.

"What's the op?" Nat asked gleefully.

"No, don't say op. I'm not allowed to talk about it. Seriously, I'll get in trouble."

They looked suitably abashed.

Nat sniffed the air as if she'd just received an olfactory alert. "Wait . . . Are you baking?"

"Oh shit!" Kendal raced to the oven and pulled out a Le Creuset Dutch oven with what was supposed to be a loaf of bread in it. She dropped it on the counter with a heavy clang, and lifted the lid to reveal a flat, steaming mess.

"What is it?" Sasha asked

"It's meant to be bread."

"Focaccia?" Sasha suggested hopefully.

"No. I dunno, just white bread." Kendal tried to keep the sulk out of her voice. She wasn't accustomed to failure.

"Are you doing fucking sourdough?" Nat smirked. "It's not 2020, mate. We're allowed out."

"I saw a thing about ultra-processed foods," Kendal said, dropping the unreasonably weighty pan in the sink with a forlorn puff of breath. "I thought it would be better for Rosie."

Nat patted Kendal on the back. "You gotta get off the TED talks, they'll ruin your life."

Nat pointed at the steam rising from the sink. "And your pans."

There was a delighted scream from the lounge, and suddenly it was snowing. Sam had won—the beanbag was dead, its guts exploded into the air.

"Oh shit, sorry." Nat rushed over and tried to gather them together in what was maybe the most futile exercise the world had ever seen. The girls were throwing handfuls at each other. Sasha calmly picked a bobble out of her coffee and stayed seated. With the rest of the room distracted, she said quietly, "Sorry about telling Nat."

Kendal, happy that the noise would be adequate to cover them, replied, "Did you say anything to Alex?"

Sasha shook her head. "I can keep secrets. It's just Nat, she could tell something was up. And we might need her."

Nat sat in the middle of the room shaking her head and looking like the disgruntled star of a snow globe, while Sam screamed and ran into the wall on repeat.

"Wanna see a magic trick?" Nat looked up at Kendal and Sasha with a twisted grin, reaching into her back pocket.

"Hey, Sam," she yelled in a voice she didn't normally use. "Wanna play Cadu?"

Kendal glanced at Sasha; she had blanched white, but she didn't move.

Sam, on the other hand, stopped what he was doing and walked toward Nat with his arms outstretched and an affected look of bliss. "Yes please, Mummy."

Nat shook her head at them. "Zombieland, right? Kids on phones."

She chuckled and unlocked her phone before handing it to him. He sat down, dropping like he'd been shot and disappearing into the screen.

The two girls took seats either side of Sam to watch; it was a covenant. None asked what was happening or for a turn. The silence that fell on the room was as peaceful as it was bleak.

"What's Cadu?" Kendal asked Nat. Sasha stared out of the window as if lost in thought. Kendal noticed that this was bang on brand for her, and pegged her as a listener. Another quality that was either an asset or a weapon.

Nat looked at her like she was about to reveal winning lottery numbers. "It's a learning app that was given by a software company to Jemma's class as a trial run. The year 6 kids use it for everything."

"Since when?"

"Couple of weeks. They can point the cameras at anything and it will tell them like, what it is, when it was invented, by who."

Whom, thought Kendal, and had a pang of desire for Khalil. For a partner in crime.

"And then, like, ah, I can't even describe it, you can go anywhere and do anything, but real time. Connect to a tour of the pyramids in Egypt. Do a hike in Appalachia. It's amazing for Sam, because he thinks he's playing a racing game or some shit, but then they'll pause to make sure he's learned stuff." She looked over at the kids, tuned in to the invisible frequency only they could see. Simultaneously all three kids shouted "RED" and squiggled in delight. That they were quiet and united should have been nice, but somehow it absolutely wasn't.

Nat's nose crumpled as if reading the room. "I don't let him look at it a lot," she said guiltily.

"They use the camera though?" Kendal asked.

"Yeah, they interact with their surroundings . . . honestly, it's so good. They're giving it to the schools."

As if on cue Sam raised the phone and pointed it directly at Kendal, then panned slowly around the room. Then the kids giggled and went silent again. Kendal grimaced, wanting desperately to kill it. Nat was oblivious. "They reckon it'll be standard tech for all schools within a couple of years. I hate screen time as much as any anti-vaxxer but shit, this works."

Kendal sipped her coffee and tried to signal Rosie to get away from the phone, but Rosie was absolutely engrossed. "Someone must have read the Ts and Cs, right?"

Nat had the good grace to look concerned.

"If it's schools they'll have people checking that stuff, won't they?"

"Will they?"

They were silent, because it was the UK, and no one in politics had authentically cared about the greater good since . . . when? July 5, 1948, the founding year of the NHS, was what Cadu might have said.

"They have lawyers," Nat said, somewhat wretchedly.

Kendal glanced at Sasha, who looked nauseous.

"What's with all the looks between you two?"

Kendal decided a clued-in Nat was going to be more useful than having her half informed and playing guessing games. She agreed with Sasha that correctly handled, Nat could be a valuable addition to the team. "It's Alex's app. We think it might have been hijacked."

Nat blushed burgundy, stamped across the room, and snatched the phone off Sam. She deleted the app and glared at the screen. "What does it do?"

Sam screamed from his seat while Rosie and Lily looked on fearfully. "You snatched!" Sam screeched. Lily and Rosie nodded judiciously—the witness testimony was correct, what would the judges do?

Nat went back to the kids and crouched so she was at eye level with Sam, who was actively weeping. "Sorry, kiddo. Here's a tenner."

Sasha tutted. Kendal's mouth fell open and she laughed. Sam gleefully grabbed the tenner and the girls seemed to agree that a fair trial had been had and the correct verdict delivered. They turned back to the TV. Nobody seemed to care that the room was still very much covered in beanbag bits.

"So what's the plan?" Nat asked quietly.

"I need a meeting with Alex away from Glo-Tech," Kendal admitted.

"He's so slippery," said Sasha, then added, "I can't guarantee he'll do anything he says he's going to socially, so we're trying to find a way to pin him down to a room without it being too blatant." Sasha chewed her lip. "We could have a party?" she suggested.

"Will he go to a party?" Kendal asked dubiously.

"If it's for Lily he'll have to."

"Smart," Nat added.

"It's good, right?" Sasha asked, hopefully. Kendal smiled at them. "I like it. Perfect cover."

Nat put her fist in like a Ninja Turtle. "Let's go! TEAM!"

"For god's sake, Natalie," Sasha scolded.

"Be cool," Kendal added, but Nat didn't care.

34

The Shapiros' house was among a row of Georgian terraces that faced out onto Highbury Fields. Number 20 had a dark green door and smartly polished brass fixtures. It was framed by a colorful front garden and enclosed by a wrought iron fence. They could hear delighted screams from within and paused to brace themselves. Rosie held Kendal's hand tightly and looked up at her. "Trust your insects," she advised.

"You too, kiddo."

They rang the bell, and the door was answered by a woman in full Elsa-from-*Frozen* regalia who welcomed them with a pained smile. She was giving it her best shot, but her wig had seen better days and she was visibly hungover. "Welcome to Arendelle," she trilled, waving a wand toward the back of the house. Rosie hid behind Kendal and glared at her. "Elsa doesn't have a wand."

Elsa did not care. They walked through to the kitchen, a testament to Sasha's impeccable taste even with all the party accoutrements. A tray of champagne had been placed by the door and there was a waiter in the garden handing out apple juice with curly straws. "Wow, they really went for it," Kendal muttered. The garden was long and narrow with hedges on either side and grapevines climbing up trellises. A stone terrace extended from the kitchen, where a bubble guy was dunking a net into a bucket.

At the back of the garden, a sleek glass studio had been repurposed into a party hub. At the edges of the grass, a man was dressed as a rotund farmer in such vivid colors he looked computer generated. He was leading a Shetland pony wearing antlers, which was pulling a small wagon across the lawn with a pleasing wooden clatter. There were adults milling about in small groups. Priya from school was trying to coax Noah onto a trampoline. Louis, wearing a sharp blue suit, was deep in conversation with a guy wearing cargo shorts. Kendal would bet her bank account that they were talking about crypto. There were about fifteen kids providing a backing track of delighted squeals.

"Whoa," Rosie said quietly, holding Kendal's hand tighter. It was an ode to fun and color; it was magical. Sasha approached them with a bright smile. "Hi, guys! So nice to see you. Rosie, what would you like? There's ponies or bubbles or something to eat?"

Rosie moved closer to Kendal and whispered "bubbles" but much too quietly.

Sasha ignored her and examined Kendal. "You okay?" The question coded.

"Absolutely. I've never seen anything quite like it."

"I know, right?" Sasha looked around the kingdom she'd created. "I was getting really stressed about what we'd do next year and the year after that. And then I remembered eventually she'll probably want darkened rooms and boys and alcohol, and I thought, you know what, *Hey Duggee* while the sun shines." She gave Kendal a cheerful wink, then squatted so she was at eye level with Rosie. She changed the timbre of her voice so it was just the two of them. "Do you want to meet the bubble guy? He is SO cool, he's got a net that literally makes a gazillion bubbles." She held up a hand for a high five. Rosie responded with a gentle palm, and Sasha stood up, linking arms with Kendal. "Bubbles all round!" She winked.

"Gorgeous garden," Kendal noted, with a pinch of envy. Sasha's life was real. This was her home, she tended this garden and was friends with these people.

"Thanks, I love it."

They perched on the edge of massive planters on the decking surrounding the studio. "Alex is in his office, it's on the top floor. I don't know if he'll come down," Sasha said quietly. "There's a magician starting in about ten minutes, so the kids will be distracted. I can keep an eye on Rosie." Nat appeared from the kitchen and made her way toward them, clutching a champagne flute and looking happily if sloppily drunk. She caught Kendal's glance at her glass and winked. "Haven't touched a drop, mate, consummate professional." Then she downed the rest of the glass and hiccupped. She plopped down on the decking next to them and spread out. She was wearing a floral shirt, jeans, and sunglasses. Kendal admired her style. She looked great. Louis spotted her and headed over.

"Hello, ladies. Looking lovely today. What a great party, Sasha." He raised his glass in a silent toast. He moved to stand next to Kendal, but she gestured to the house. "Just popping to the loo."

Kendal passed Rosie staring transfixed at the bubbles and looked back. Sasha gave her a thumbs-up and Nat made a two-fingered *eyes on* gesture toward Rosie. Kendal slipped into the house behind a waiter. The kitchen was alive with the bustle of a catering team who were operating like a well-oiled machine. Catering meant temps, which meant if Alex was in real trouble, these guys might be the ones starting it. Kendal paused in the hallway, scanning for pros, but they barely glanced at her. They were mostly teenagers, and no one stood out as incongruous.

Along the hallway she peeped through a door into a family room with a large TV, two rubber trees, and some luxurious low-slung sofas, all immaculately tidy apart from a group of older kids watching a movie. Kendal stepped gently on the parquet floor, passing noiselessly through the house. Her phone beeped in her pocket and she silenced it quickly. Up one flight of thickly carpeted stairs she found a bright landing with a massive arched window pouring sunshine onto blocky, primary-colored artworks. She passed Lily's room and glanced in, impressed by the sophistication of the layout and decor. Wondering how much was Lily's choice and how much was designed by Sasha or some well-paid specialist. She thought of Rosie's chaotic space and felt the familiar stab of guilt. Not a great look that Rosie was downstairs and she was running an op.

Another flight of stairs took her to the top floor. This was a more grown-up hallway, adorned with books and framed maps. As if the decor were maturing as she climbed. Here was a door that she sensed was an office. She pressed her ear to the door and heard the tapping of a keyboard.

She pushed the door open to find Alex at a desk surrounded by a bank of screens that showed various areas of the house. He must have watched her ascend. The office was sparse. A sorry-looking fern stood in one corner, and two filing cabinets and a bookshelf were piled high with folders and paperwork. There was no art or color to it. Alex pulled the headphones off his head. He didn't seem surprised to see her, maybe thinking she was staff.

"What do you want?" he asked without looking up.

"I want you to kill Cadu. Today. Now."

He pushed back from his desk with a surprised grunt and looked at her, utterly incredulous. "What are you talking about? Who are you?" He took her in, a long, impolite examination. Then he narrowed his eyes. "Do I know you?"

"Cadu has been hijacked and you need to kill it."

Alex glared at her. "It hasn't been hijacked. Cadu is fine. Get out of here!" He turned back to his computer, and reached for his phone, but she leaned over and spun his chair back to face her. She leaned in close.

"Do you remember Joel Ayre?"

Alex furrowed his brow. "The Canadian guy? He was in charge of debugging . . ." Alex frowned more deeply. "He left . . ."

"He's a foreign asset who was working against you. If you release it, you're fucked."

"I knew there was something off with that guy."

"Well done. You were right."

"We can just clean it up," Alex said weakly. "All that work. We'll just undo whatever he did."

She pulled a thumb drive from her jeans. "No. The board at Glo-Tech approved the spyware. They knew what it was. They left you in the frame for it."

"No. That's not right. I've done everything they wanted."

"Yeah, exactly, and they'll blame you for everything that happens next. If you release Cadu, it's treason."

He rubbed his temples and stared at the CCTV screen showing his kid's birthday party. "I can't help you. They'll kill me."

Kendal felt sympathetic; he had the face of a life's work dashed by greed.

"We can protect you. But only if you do the right thing. This is a virus that will wipe them off the map, without implicating you. Sasha told me that you were one of the good guys. Be the good guy. Now."

He looked at the drive as if it would bite him.

"Alex, these are dangerous corporations who don't give a shit about your kids. You can stop them, only you. But it has to be now. Do it for Lily. You can either be the victim of this whole thing, or the hero. Which is it?"

He held his hand out and took the drive, then turned to the screen and opened a series of log-in windows, skipping rapidly between profiles. Kendal watched anxiously, aware that these were minutes Rosie was out of her sight. She tried to find her on the monitor. The magician was in full swing, using the decking around the studio as a stage. Kendal couldn't spot Rosie among the crowd. In her pocket, Kendal's phone buzzed again, and she pulled it out. There were two messages. The first was from Rico: "There's a KO for Shapiro. Big $ if you want it." The second was an encrypted message from Joe. She went through the requisite rigamarole to unlock it. "Background on Natalie Atkins has come back red. Possible hostile." Kendal went cold. "Hurry up," she hissed at Alex, scanning the monitors for Nat, every one of her senses on high alert. She was coursing with adrenaline. In the old days, this was her favorite feeling. Today, it made her ears ring and her heart stop. Alex was moving at a casual pace that made her want to kill him, big bucks or not.

Behind them the door clicked gently open.

"Hi, guys." Nat's face peeped around, followed by her shoulder, followed by a hand holding a Jericho 941, a black midsize, semiautomatic pistol with a steel frame.

"Hope I'm not interrupting." She pointed the gun at Kendal. "But I'm going to need you to stand down. And I'm going to need him to stop doing whatever he's doing." Staring beyond the barrel that was inches from her face, Kendal focused on Nat's eyes. Was she a killer? Nat's pupils were dilated, her eyes almost completely black, and Kendal understood that right now Nat had the capacity to pull the trigger. Kendal licked her lips and nodded. She'd underestimated Nat, because she was fun, and a mum, and a woman. The exact disguise she was wearing herself. She wasn't angry, she was just disappointed.

"What are you doing, Nat?"

"My job." In those two words her accent flickered, still a generic London lilt, but now there was something else among it. Calm as a meadow, she released the safety and cocked the gun. Alex flinched at it with a wary frown.

"That's a nasty bit of kit," Kendal said, maintaining eye contact, wanting Nat to see the cold fury the gun had unleashed inside her. A flashback to the last time a gun had been pointed at her. And the time before that, and the time before that. It was a scenario that seldom ended well, but here, in this scenario, loosing a bullet was unthinkable.

"Who do you work for?"

"Glo-Tech, babes. Freelance! Keeping an eye on this asshole." She nodded toward Alex. "They knew he was a weak link."

Kendal took stock.

"You're not going to shoot a guy on his kid's birthday, so put the gun down and tell us what you want."

Nat lowered the gun slightly but kept it held tight, trying to see what was on Alex's screen without dropping Kendal from her peripheral vision.

"How's your friend Fiona?" Nat said with a sneaky look. It took Kendal a second to realize she meant Fini.

"Don't let her hear you call her that."

Nat sneered. "Why? What's she gonna do, reset my password? She's at the kiddie table, Kendal. From what I gather, you both are. Although I must admit, you had me fooled at first. Your legend was tight. But Fini Meridian was a dead giveaway. No way you're clean with her sitting in your kitchen. Wasn't that hard to unpick your nonsense after that."

Rico's legend would have been built layers deep. Kendal smiled at Nat and flexed her shoulders. "Your sources may have been misleading."

Kendal glanced at the cameras again.

Nat smirked. "She's with Louis. And if either of you press anything other than the Off button, that is the last picture of her you're ever going to see."

Kendal saw Louis standing next to Rosie while the magician juggled fruit. He placed his hand on Rosie's shoulder and turned to look at the camera with a smile.

It was a step too far. Kendal stepped into Nat's space and twisted the gun out of her hand. Then she smashed her forehead into Nat's face with her whole body weight behind her. Nat slid to the floor, her nose exploding with blood. "Jesus," Alex muttered from behind her.

Nat was unconscious, but it would be brief. Kendal turned and pointed the gun at Alex, walking the two steps to him and placing the barrel exactly where the bruise from their last encounter was.

"Kill Cadu. Right now." Then she donked him, exactly as she had before. His eyes widened in recognition, and he turned to the computer and plugged in the drive. One of his screens was already open to Cadu on the Glo-Tech server. She watched as he copied Fini's virus over to it. The code visibly glitched and started to change and disappear. The virus would work its way backward through Cadu and destroy everything Glo-Tech was running. He put his head in his hands and watched his life's work disappear through the gaps in his fingers. "It's done," he croaked.

Nat groaned awake and pulled herself up into a sitting position against the wall. With her eyes on Louis and the CCTV, Kendal pulled a tissue out of her sleeve and handed it over.

Kendal's phone rang. On the other end was a voice she hadn't heard for more than two decades.

"Hello, darling."

"Hello, Mother."

"You have a situation."

It was so on brand for her mother to either know what was going on, or convincingly pretend to, that Kendal was tempted to hang up and take her chances alone.

"Do I?"

"There is a team outside the property who will escort Mr. Shapiro and his family to safety. Tell them to gather their things. They need to leave now."

"And why should I trust you?"

Her mother sighed, and the noise sliced through every hackle in her body.

"Listen carefully, my dear, because you are about ninety seconds away from a major diplomatic incident. Shapiro needs to move. Now. Hand him over and go back to your little party. Your work here is done."

From the floor, Nat wiped a thin line of blood off her nose. Before Kendal could stop her, she leaped up, aiming for Alex's machine and the Stop button that had appeared as a safety protocol. Kendal pulled the thin metal lipstick from her pocket and pressed the button. Everything in the house was knocked out with an audible clunk. The cameras, screens, and phones died. Outside, car alarms wailed and the music had stopped; in the distance a kid cried. Kendal turned Alex to face her. "Is it done? Did it work?"

"It's already in the Glo-Tech servers. The whole company will be dead in maybe twenty minutes."

A brief silence was broken by one of the catering staff nervously calling out, "CAKE TIME."

The door of the office opened to reveal a woman in her late sixties wearing a very garish jumper. She spoke with a strong Congolese accent.

"Mrs. O?!" Kendal said, unable to hide her shock at seeing a childminder from a Swiss housing estate appear like an apparition in the middle of the day, in Highbury, at a birthday party. "What the . . ." But she stopped talking as the answer clicked into place. Of course, she was a plant. Her mother had her pegged the whole time. It made absolute sense.

Mrs. O ignored Kendal and Nat and directed her attention to Alex. "We leave now."

Nat stood up and in a voice muffled by her broken nose tried to address Mrs. O. "Who the fuck are you?" Mrs. O turned her attention to Nat with an expression that would have turned a lesser woman to stone. Nat shifted testily where she stood.

"You are not needed here . . ." She slowed down and made sure Nat felt each syllable. "*Ozali mwana moke.*" No one in the room spoke Lingala, but they all knew what she meant.

Nat tried to hold her ground but withered under Mrs. O's glare. She brushed awkwardly at her jeans. She looked at Kendal with an angry shake of her still-bleeding head. "No skin off my nose, I get paid either way. Glo-Tech will have a backup. All you've done is wasted a tiny bit of everyone's time." It would have sounded more serious if she hadn't muffled it out of a broken nose.

"You should get some ice on that face," Kendal suggested.

"Yeah. See you next term anyway, yeah?" The message was coded—no hard feelings, professional courtesy. Kendal gave a tiny nod of acknowledgment and Nat slunk out of the room.

"Am I supposed to let her go?" Kendal directed the question at Mrs. O.

"Yes, she's irrelevant." She pointed at Alex. "You, come with me."

Mrs. O pulled up Alex by the scruff of his shirt, and Kendal handed her Nat's gun, which she disappeared among her clothes. "You did well, lovely girl," Mrs. O said to Kendal with a proud smile, bringing her in for a quick but strong hug. Giving Kendal something she hadn't known she needed.

Sasha was standing on the first-floor landing, poised as if on her way up. She saw them emerge, and confusion seemed to gather around her. "It's time for cake," she said weakly. Nat walked past clutching her bruised nose. Sasha reached out, but Nat shrugged her off. "I'm fine." Sasha turned back up the stairs, utterly flummoxed by the presence of Mrs. O, who was imposing at the best of times.

"What happened?" she addressed Alex. He stopped in front of her, as Mrs. O carried on to the ground floor and checked her watch.

"Sasha, grab the bags. We have to leave with this woman now."

Sasha's look of incredulity almost made Kendal laugh. "But I've got a show." For a moment, Alex looked truly broken.

He seemed to be trying to find the words but eventually, having lost some internal debate, he simply nodded. "I hope it goes well." He kissed her on the cheek, and Mrs. O led him out of the house. Sasha and Kendal followed them to the door. Waiting outside was a black unmarked car. Alex got in with a final glance at Sasha.

"He didn't say goodbye to Lily," Sasha said quietly. "On her birthday." She looked beseechingly at Kendal. "I mean, that's not normal, is it?" They watched the car pull away, and Kendal suddenly missed Rosie viscerally. "Let's go do the cake."

"I never wanted to be a single mum," Sasha said, ignoring her. "But I already was."

"He did the right thing though, in the end. He fought back."

They watched the car disappear around the corner, and Sasha seemed to shrug him completely away. Her shoulders straightened, and she looked searchingly at Kendal. "What happened to the electrics?" Sasha asked.

"Power cut," Kendal answered, knowing it wasn't enough information.

"What happened to Nat's face?"

"I think she was trying to help."

Sasha didn't look any less confused, but she had run out of questions. In the kitchen the staff were working around the lack of power. Someone was playing a guitar and a three-tiered ice cream cake was being set alight. Squeezing past the caterers into the garden, Kendal found Rosie.

Louis had disappeared, but Nat hung back in the corner of the garden where Sam was having a sugar-induced meltdown. At the gate, a staffer in a bow tie handed Rosie a blue silk party bag embroidered with her name and gave Kendal a wink.

35

They got home bedraggled and exhausted. Rosie clutched her party bag like it was a lifeboat. Kendal was completely unsurprised to find Jenny Corrin sitting at the dining table, in the exact spot Khalil had been weeks before. She was considerably more surprised by Rosie's response to her presence.

"Gee Gee!" Rosie ran across the room and grabbed Jenny around the legs.

"She looks just like you at that age, you know," her mother said, as if they were in the middle of a conversation. She hugged Rosie tightly, then released her into the room.

"Tea?" Kendal offered, but Jenny held up a glass that was already half full of scotch. Kendal poured a drink to match and sat facing her.

"You've been running Alex Shapiro?" Kendal asked. No point being indirect with Jenny; she could jump out the window at a moment's notice. Jenny's eyebrows flickered into a frown, and she released the tiniest tut.

"He was a disappointment at every possible stage."

"He saw through Joel Ayre better than I did."

"He was rather vocal about it though, wasn't he. Didn't do himself any favors. Regardless of the who and how, you did the right thing. That cursed project is dead. You managed in an afternoon to finish a job I started years ago. Well done." She held up her glass in a salute, taking just the right amount of credit for Kendal's work. It was elegantly done, and Kendal knew in her bones that there would be no further discussion. She had already thrown a lifetime of unanswered questions into that well of silence.

They took each other in while Rosie bumbled about throwing a tea party at Jenny's feet. They sat and watched her feeding various objects with an invisible cup.

"Do you have any pictures of me as a kid?"

"Of course not." She caught the look that passed over Kendal's face. "I'm sorry, darling, but it wasn't the done thing. It wasn't safe."

"It still isn't."

"No. Quite," Jenny replied mournfully, staring at Rosie. "It's appalling what they can do with a face these days. Perhaps I shouldn't have been so cautious after all. But you do seem to be rather enjoying the anonymity that your upbringing has granted you."

"Do I?"

"Are you not? What would you have liked to do? I let you run off and try civilian living. Tell me, how did you find it?" She tapped a gold ring against her glass and watched her daughter closely, an intensely smug smile playing across her lips.

"You were bored senseless," Jenny went on, ruminating on a past Kendal had no idea she was aware of. "But of course you were. Your childhood was so exciting. I never thought your attempt at a normal life would last. It was a strange kind of rebellion."

"So, what, you've been watching me this whole time?"

"It wasn't difficult."

Kendal balked at this, a reaction she tried and failed to disguise.

"You never exactly went to ground, did you, darling? You went to

Hammersmith. And of course I kept an eye on you. I wouldn't trust Rico Ortez to handle a houseplant."

"Did you not want to meet your granddaughter?"

Jenny shifted in her seat, and Kendal narrowed her eyes. Even after all this time, she could still read her mother like a tabloid.

"You have met her. How?"

"I thought it was odd when you disappeared into that provincial little corner of Europe, so I made sure you had a contact. It was just a matter of recruitment, and in an area like that, you barely have to dangle a carrot. Half of them would do it for the entertainment."

"Mrs. O."

"Maymuna Oko," Jenny confirmed. "Very easily underestimated, especially in a homogenized little city like that. Trained in Congo, if you can call it *training*. She's fiercely protective of children. She's become a good friend, actually. We onboarded her to watch you. I knew you'd like her and I knew you would trust her with Rosie. Although you were very cagey, darling. You must let children off the leash occasionally. It doesn't do to keep them all bundled up and close like that. They become awfully clingy."

Kendal was about to react but could see the smirk resting just under the surface of Jenny's eyes and kept a lid on it.

"Rather clingy than feral and murderous, Mother."

"Psh, murderous. It wasn't my parenting that turned you into a weapon, darling."

"I think therapists the world over might beg to differ."

"You were always a dramatic child."

Kendal resisted the temptation to roll her eyes at this misrepresentation of her childhood. Until she turned ten, she had been practically mute. She didn't believe she had ever once had what normal parents would describe as a meltdown.

"Was I, though?"

"You had rather a penchant for the dark side."

"Not really the same thing, is it."

"It has similar manifestations."

"Don't make things up to suit the story, Mother, you're better than that. Even if you are with the government nowadays."

"Oh, don't be so prosaic. I've simply decided to be on the right side of history."

Kendal snorted. "Whose history?"

Jenny paused. She fixed Kendal with a glare that at another time in her life would have filled her with dread. "Yours," she answered. Kendal held her gaze. It contained multitudes.

"What did your goons do with Khalil?"

"It was very unfortunate to have you tangled up in all that. Mr. Masoumi made the right call to the wrong person many years ago, and I've been trying to unpick the situation ever since. It was quite a surprise to discover that it was you that Mr. Ortez had put in place to watch him. He should have been protected, but instead he was betrayed. For that I owe you both an apology. Suffice to say he is safe for now. In the meantime, what did *your* goons do with Joel Ayre?"

Kendal noticed that her mother had supplied neither answer nor apology. "I don't have goons, Mother."

The doorbell rang, and Jenny smiled. "As if by magic," she muttered. Rosie ran to the door, and Jenny reached out to stop her. She suddenly looked frightened. "What on earth is she doing?" It was as close as her mother ever got to shrill. She was panicked that Rosie wasn't trained. Kendal swallowed her answer and followed Rosie, recognizing Rico's frame behind the mottled glass.

She opened the door and stared at him.

"You didn't do it then?" he said accusingly, walking past Kendal into the house.

"Murder a child's father at her birthday party? Shockingly, not."

"Psssh, you've changed."

Kendal frowned. "Have I, though?"

Rico entered the kitchen and spotted the person sitting there.

"Jesus Christ!"

"I go by Jenny these days."

As if transformed into a gangly teen, Rico tipped forward and awkwardly kissed Jenny on both cheeks.

"Good to see you, JC."

"I'm sure it is," she answered slyly. "Any chance of a coffee, darling? Maybe an Irish?"

"Make that two," Rico added. Kendal couldn't be bothered to argue with them. Their body language was creeping her out . . . were they flirting?! Kendal wanted to puke.

Rosie had taken a seat at Gee Gee's feet and was rummaging through the party bag. There was a box of Ladurée macarons. Evidently Rosie wasn't familiar with them and was pressing them gleefully between her fingers. She licked her thumb and her eyes widened. She looked around the room, saw nobody was interested, and shoved a whole green biscuit in her mouth. At the table, Kendal tried to ignore the palpable chemistry between her mother and Rico.

"I would like to know what happened to Joel Ayre," said Jenny. "My strong suspicion is that he is no longer . . . operational . . . but if that is not the case he would make excellent leverage in a matter very many miles above your pay grade. If you tell me where he is, I may be able to share the location of Khalil Masoumi."

"No deal," Rico said with a glance at Kendal. Ken kept quiet. She wanted that location, but didn't believe for a moment her mother would trade it. Jenny released a long sigh.

"As I thought." With her eyes on her glass she addressed Kendal using her government voice. "Well, here it is. If you want to see him again, I'm afraid this little ordeal of ours is not quite over. I may need to call on your services. I trust you will be amenable to that call?"

From where he was sitting Rico replied for them both, "My door is always open."

Kendal shook her head at his lack of scruples and turned to her mother. "You couldn't just ask to go for coffee, could you, couldn't offer to babysit? It has to be an op. Just another couple of assets that once shared your surname."

Jenny looked at Kendal with a steely gaze. She drained her glass and stood up.

"Well, darling, it's nice to be back in touch. We'll speak soon, shall we?"

"Let's," Kendal replied, staying where she was.

Jenny seemed to magic a box from nowhere.

"For you."

She placed it on the table with a nod at Kendal, then adjusted her scarf to leave.

"Rico," she said.

"Jenny," he replied with a mischievous grin.

"Blurgh," Kendal added.

With the house empty, Kendal set about making Rosie some food and considered the events of the day. She was surprised to find she was pleased to see Jenny. She looked well and despite their checkered past, she was a welcome addition to the Rosie Network, as Ken had started to think of it. In that one shriek of protective panic when Rosie answered the door, Kendal had spotted real love. She'd been a dreadful mother, but maybe grandparent, responsibility once removed, would suit her better. Kendal's phone pinged with a news alert. "Tech Bro Alex Shapiro in Supercar Smash." She didn't read on. Didn't need to. In the past she might have been curious about payouts or trade secrets, but today her only thought was for Lily. How old would she be when she read about this? Would she ever know the truth? Would anyone? It wasn't fair when the shadow world took family away from their children. She wouldn't allow it to happen to them, and she made a silent internal promise to return Rosie's father to her. Kendal reached over and touched the back of Rosie's hand. She was dressed in a brown bear suit and eating a corn on the cob. The summer holidays stretched out ahead of them.

Rosie looked up from her buttery hands. "What?"

"Nothing. I love you."

Rosie nodded sagely and pressed her greasy finger to Ken's nose. "I know."

EPILOGUE

Later, when Rosie was asleep and all was quiet, Kendal checked that the tracker she had placed on Jenny's coat was working. She doubted it would remain undetected for long, but it might give her an initial clue as to where her mother had hidden Khalil. Kendal didn't believe he was in government custody. However much her mother implied she'd become a team player, Kendal knew her better than that. Picking up Khalil in a shopping center was not SIS style. Jenny had gone under the radar. She'd have Khalil somewhere nobody could find him. Which meant the only way to find him was to stay on top of Jenny. Kendal wasn't naïve to the difficult nature of surveilling Jenny Corrin, but by god, if anyone could do it, surely she was top of the list. She allowed herself a small smile. It might even be fun.

She picked up the gift that Jenny had left behind and breathed a sigh of relief when it opened to reveal a children's book. *Myths and Legends*. It had a dust cover with a bright green dragon wrapped around a nest of glistening eggs. Under the dust cover was a plain black book. It was unusual—no other words, no author or barcode.

Kendal opened the book at random and let out a low whistle. Flicking through it, she saw what must have been a life's work. Each chapter was a fresh ID. Her mother had built her a book of personalities that she could drop into at a moment's notice. She sat down and marveled at it. Each ID came with document drop codes. Social media handles. Everything she would ever need to disappear over and over again. Disappear to everyone except Jenny. There were tiny pink tags against about twenty pages, and as she turned to them Kendal realized these were the profiles where there was a daughter Rosie's age. Rosie could become Rachel, Rosalyn, Rebecca. Even on brief inspection Kendal could see how well built they were, how solid and impenetrable. It was an invitation—to get back in The Game, disappear into new identities and leave the house, this life, their reality behind. She wasn't going to do it, but it gave her a strong, longed-for sense of security knowing that it was possible. If they were ever cornered again, they'd have an instant escape. It was the first gift she could remember getting from her mother.

ACKNOWLEDGMENTS

I owe deep and unwavering thanks to Millie Hoskins, who has impeccable taste and timing. I couldn't be more grateful or excited to be working with Catherine Richards and the team at Minotaur, truly an honor and privilege.

I would like to thank Lesley Allen for her diligent and respectful copyediting.

Invisibility is a superpower, but it can also feel like a curse. Thanks to all the mothers who made me feel seen, I hope this book returns the favor.

Thank you to the NW3 collective, who made seven years of pickup more bearable. I'm grateful to Amelia Suchy (the nicest person I've ever met), Mel, Nat, Maria, Netaly, Janie, Danielle, and Anaya for moral support and small talk (the good kind).

Thanks to people around the world who helped at many intervals: my mum Marion, Pam and Derek Jones, Stephanie Sian Smith, Bianca Mollura, Ninna Holm, Annette Rytter Nielsen, and Klaus Holm.

Lucy Hall and Jonah Ahearne let me stay in their house and break the back of this book, and then I stole their green wine. Thank you and sorry.

Thanks always to my best friend and first reader, Claire Wilson; we've been killing Kevins since 1997 and it served me well this season. I am also grateful to Simon Davies, who nodded sagely and bought me martinis at a crucial moment, and Polly Donger, who was there when I was scared of the dark. Many friends joined me on the quest for knowledge that prefaced this process and I might not have pressed on without them. They are too many to name, but they can mostly be found on the Egg thread. Here's to you all.

The research and development for this series was made possible by the generosity of authors and institutions offering insight and expertise across a variety of forums. ALPHA Human Resilience, Amnesty International, UCL Events and UCL Institute of Advanced Studies, the Royal Institution, RSA, Burgh House, Gresham College, the Cold War Museum, the Frontline Club, and the Horse Hospital. Authors Dr. Aaron Bateman, Sherine Tadros, Liza Mundy, Jonna Mendez, Stewart Purvis, Helen Fry and Kate Vigurs, Jason Hanson, Stella Rimington, and Laurent Richard have all made work or given talks that inspired and informed this book.

Rosanna Minchew, the founder of Spyher, provided an invaluable source of fact-checking, inspiration, and firsthand knowledge of the subject matter, and her input was literally exhilarating, thank you.

Finally and most fiercely, the writing of this would not have been possible without inspiration from my daughter, whom I love more than I thought possible, nor without Josh Jones, who provided tireless support and encouragement, and miraculously threw his hat only once.

ABOUT THE AUTHOR

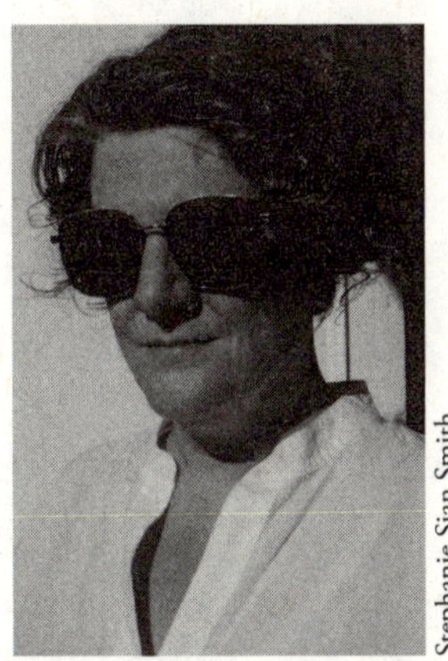

Stephanie Sian Smith

L. M. KEMP lives and works in upstate London (Essex). She writes for a vast variety of creative, cultural, corporate, and clandestine clients: most recently coauthoring personalized books for Wonderbly; writing an abstract reviews column for *Ralph* magazine; and editing lengthy and devastating reports for Greenpeace. For the past two years, her work has been dominated by the research and development of *I, Spy* and a deep dive into the murky world of modern spycraft.